T0057963

PAPER LANTERN

PAPER LANTERN

Love Stories

STUART DYBEK

Farrar, Straus and Giroux

New York

Farrar, Straus and Giroux
18 West 18th Street, New York 10011

Printed in the United States of America
Published in 2014 by Farrar, Straus and Giroux
First paperback edition, 2015

The stories in this book originally appeared, in slightly different form, in the following publications: "Blowing Shades" in *Ontario Review* (1997) and *The Pushcart Prize: Best of the Small Presses* (1999); "The Caller" in *Double-Take* (1995); "Four Deuces" in *A Public Space* (2012); "If I Vanished" in *The New Yorker* (2007); "Oceanic" in *Zoetrope* (2011); "Paper Lantern" in *The New Yorker* (1995), *Best American Short Stories* (1996), *The Year's Best Fantasy and Horror* (1996), and *The Workshop: Seven Decades of the Iowa Writers' Workshop* (1999); "Seiche" in *Granta* (2009); "Tosca" in *Tin House* (2012); and "Waiting" in *Zoetrope* (2009).

The Library of Congress has cataloged the hardcover edition as follows:
Dybek, Stuart, 1942–
    [Short stories. Selections]
    Paper Lantern : Love Stories / Stuart Dybek. — First edition.
        pages   cm
    ISBN 978-0-374-14644-3 (hardcover) — ISBN 978-0-374-71054-5 (ebook)
    I. Title.

PS3554.Y3 A6 2014
813'.54—dc23

                                                            2013034414

Paperback ISBN: 978-0-374-53538-4

Designed by Jonathan D. Lippincott

Farrar, Straus and Giroux books may be purchased for educational, business, or promotional use. For information on bulk purchases, please contact the Macmillan Corporate and Premium Sales Department at 1-800-221-7945, extension 5442, or write to specialmarkets@macmillan.com.

www.fsgbooks.com
www.twitter.com/fsgbooks • www.facebook.com/fsgbooks

What mad pursuit? What struggle to escape?
What pipes and timbrels? What wild ecstasy?
—John Keats, "Ode on a Grecian Urn"

Contents

PAPER
LANTERN

Tosca

Ready!
　Aim!
　On command the firing squad aims at the man backed against a full-length mirror. The mirror once hung in a bedroom, but now it's cracked and propped against a dumpster in an alley. The condemned man has refused the customary last cigarette but accepted as a hood the black slip that was carelessly tossed over a corner of the mirror's frame. The slip still smells faintly of a familiar fragrance.

　Through his rifle sight, each sweating, squinting soldier in the squad can see his own cracked reflection aiming back at him.

　Also in the line of fire is a phantasmal reflection of the surprised woman whose slip now serves as a hood (a hood that hides less from the eyes looking out than from those looking in). She's been caught dressing, or undressing, and presses her hands to her breasts in an attempt to conceal her nakedness.

　The moment between commands seems suspended to the soldiers and to the hooded man. The soldiers could be compared to sprinters poised straining in the blocks, listening for the starter's gun, though, of course, when the shot is finally fired, it's their fingers on the triggers. The hooded man also listens for the shot even though he knows he'll be dead before he hears it. I've never been conscripted to serve in a firing squad or condemned to stand facing death—at least, not any more than we all are—but in high school I once qualified for the state finals in the high hurdles, and I know that between the "Aim" command and the shot there's time for a story.

Were this a film, there'd be time for searching close-ups of each soldier's face as he waits for the irreversible order, time for the close-ups to morph into a montage of images flashing back through the lives of the soldiers, scenes with comrades in bars, brothels, et cetera, until one of the squad—a scholarly looking myopic corporal—finds himself a boy again, humming beside a pond, holding, instead of a rifle, a dip net and a Mason jar.

There's a common myth that a drowning man sees his life pass before his eyes. Each soldier taking aim imagines that beneath the hood the condemned man is flashing through his memory. It's a way in which the senses flee the body, a flight into the only dimension where escape is still possible: time. Rather than a lush dissolve into a Proustian madeleine moment, escape is desperate—the plunge through duration in "An Occurrence at Owl Creek Bridge," or through a time warp as in "The Secret Miracle," Borges's *ficción* in which a playwright in Nazi-occupied Prague faces a firing squad.

In this fiction, set in an anonymous dead-end alley, the reflection of a woman, all the more beautiful for being ghostly, has surfaced from the depths of a bedroom mirror. The soldiers in the firing squad, who can see her, conclude that she is a projection of the hooded man's memory, and that her flickering appearance is a measure of how intensely she is being recalled. Beneath the hood, the man must be recalling a room in summer where her bare body is reflected beside his, her blond-streaked hair cropped short, both of them tan, lean, still young. The mirror is unblemished as if it, too, is young.

"Look," she whispers, "us."

Was it then he told her that their reflection at that moment was what he'd choose to be his last glimpse of life?

Each soldier is asking himself: Given a choice, what would I ask for *my* last glimpse of life to be?

But actually, the hooded man never would have said something so mawkishly melodramatic. As for having the unspoken thought, *Well, so shoot me*, he thinks.

Back from netting tadpoles, the scholarly corporal, sweating behind his rifle again, imagines that rather than recalling random times in bars, brothels, et cetera, the hooded man is revisiting all the rooms in which he undressed the woman in the mirror.

One room faces the L tracks. The yellow windows of a night train stream across the bedroom mirror. After the train is gone, the empty station seems illuminated by the pink-shaded bed lamp left burning as he removes her clothes. Beneath the tracks there's a dark street of jewelry shops, their display windows stripped and grated. Above each shop, behind carbonized panes, the torches of lapidaries working late ignite with the gemstone glows of hydrogen, butane, and acetylene. Her breasts lift as she unclasps a necklace, which spills from her cupped hand into an empty wineglass beside the bed. Pearls, pinkish in the light, brim over like froth. A train is coming from the other direction.

In the attic she calls his tree house, the bed faces the only window, a skylight. The mirror is less a reflection than a view out across whitewashed floorboards to a peeling white chair draped with her clothes and streaked by diffused green light shafting through the leafy canopy. The shade of light changes with the colors of thinning maples. At night, the stars through bare branches make it seem, she says, as if they lie beneath the lens of a great telescope. Naked under a feather tick, they close their eyes on a canopy of constellations light-years away, and open them on a film of first snow. Daylight glints through the tracks of starlings.

In a stone cottage near Lucca, rented from a beekeeper, they hear their first nightingale. They hear it only once, though perhaps it sings while they sleep. At twilight, the rhapsodic push-pull of an accordion floats from the surrounding lemon grove. To follow it seems intrusive, so they never see who's playing, but on a morning hike, they come upon a peeling white chair weathered beneath a lemon tree. When he sits down, she raises her skirt and straddles him. The accordion recital always ends on the same elusive melody. They agree it's from an opera, as they agreed the birdcall had to be a nightingale's, but they can't identify the opera. It's Puccini, he says, which reminds her they have yet to visit Puccini's house in Lucca. Tomorrow, he promises.

Recognize it—the aria playing even now, the clarinet, a nightingale amid twittering sparrows.

Sparrows twitter in the alley from power lines, rain gutters, and the tar-paper garage roofs onto which old ladies in black toss bread crusts, and this entire time the aria has been playing in the background. Not pumped from an accordion, probably it's a classical radio station floating from an open window, or maybe some opera buff—every neighborhood no matter how shabby has one—is playing the same aria over, each time by a different tenor—Pavarotti, Domingo, Caruso—on his antiquated stereo.

The clarinet introduces the aria's melody and the tenor echoes it as if in a duet with the woodwinds. *E lucevan le stelle*, he sings: *And the stars were shining. Ed olezzava la terra: And the scent of earth was fresh . . .*

> *Stridea l'uscio dell'orto,*
> *e un passo sfiorava la rena.*
> *Entrava ella, fragrante,*

mi cadea fra le braccia . . .
The garden gate creaked, and a step brushed the sand.
She entered, fragrant, and fell into my arms . . .

Admittedly, "E lucevan le stelle" is a predictable choice for an execution—so predictable that one might imagine the aria itself is what drew this motley firing squad with their unnecessarily fixed bayonets and uniforms as dusty as the sparrows brawling over bread crusts.

Doesn't the soldiers' appearance, from their unpolished boots to the hair scruffing out from beneath their shakos, verge on the theatrical, as if a costume designer modeled them on Goya's soldiers in *The Disasters of War*? A role in the firing squad doesn't require acting; their costumes act for them. They are anonymous extras, grunts willing to do the dirty work if allowed to be part of the spectacle. Grunts don't sing. In fact, the corporal will be disciplined for his ad-libbed humming by the pond. They march—*trudge* is more accurate—from opera to opera hoping to be rewarded with a chorus, a chance to emote, to leave onstage some lyrical record of their existence beyond the brutal percussion of a final volley. But their role has always been to stand complacently mute. This season alone they've made the rounds from *Carmen* to *Il Trovatore*, and when the classics are exhausted then it's on to something new.

There are always roles for them, and the promise of more to come. In Moscow, a young composer whose grandfather disappeared during Stalin's purges labors over *The Sentence*—an opera he imagines Shostakovich might have written, which opens with Fyodor Dostoyevsky, five days past his twenty-eighth birthday, facing the firing squad of the Tsar. Four thousand three hundred miles away, in Kalamazoo, Michigan, an assistant professor a few years out of Oberlin who has been awarded his first commission, for an opera based on Norman

Mailer's *The Executioner's Song*, has just sung "Froggy Went A-Courtin'" to his three-year-old daughter. She's fallen asleep repeating, *Without my uncle Rat's consent, I would not marry the president*, and now the house is quiet, and he softly plinks on her toy piano the motif that will climax in Gary Gilmore's final aria.

And here in the alley, the firing squad fresh from Granada in 1937, where they gunned down Federico García Lorca in Osvaldo Golijov's opera *Ainadamar*, has followed the nightingale call of "E lucevan le stelle" and stands taking aim at a man hooded in a slip.

If you're not an opera buff, you need to know that "E lucevan le stelle" is from the third act of *Tosca*. Mario Cavaradossi, a painter and revolutionary, has been tortured by Baron Scarpia, the lecherous, tyrannical chief of Rome's secret police, and waits to be shot at dawn. Cavaradossi's final thoughts are of his beloved Tosca. He bribes the jailer to bring him pen and paper so that he can write her a farewell, and then, overcome by memories, stops writing and sings his beautiful aria, a showstopper that brings audiences to applause and shouts of *Bravo!* before the performance can continue. Besides the sheer beauty of its music, the aria is a quintessential operatic moment, a moment both natural and credible—no small feat for opera—in which a written message cannot adequately convey the emotion and the drama soars to its only possible expression: song.

She entered, fragrant, and fell into my arms, oh! sweet kisses, oh! lingering caresses. Trembling, I unveiled her beauty, the hero sings—in Italian, of course. But in American opera houses subtitles have become accepted. *My dream of love has vanished forever, my time is running out, and even as I die hopelessly, I have never loved life more.*

That final phrase about loving life, *Non ho amato mai tanto la vita*, always reminds me of Ren. He was the first of three friends of mine who have said, over the years, that he was living his life like an opera.

We were both nineteen when we met that day Ren stopped to listen to me playing for pocket change before the Wilson L station, and proposed a trade—his Kawasaki 250 with its rebuilt engine for my Leblanc clarinet. Usually I played at L stops with Archie, a blind accordion player, but it was thundering and Archie hadn't showed. I thought Ren was putting me on. When I asked why he'd trade a motorcycle for a clarinet, he answered: Who loves life more, the guy on the Outer Drive riding without a helmet, squinting into the wind, doing seventy in and out of traffic, or the guy with his eyes closed playing "Moonglow"?

Depends how you measure loving life, I said.

Against oblivion, Ren said, then laughed as if amused by his own pretension, a reflex of his that would become familiar. A licorice stick travels light, he explained, and he was planning to leave for Italy, where, if Fellini films could be believed, they definitely loved life more. He'd had a flash of inspiration watching me, a vision of himself tooting "Three Coins in the Fountain" by the Trevi Fountain and hordes of tourists in coin-tossing mode filling his clarinet case with cash. He'd rebuilt the 250cc engine—he could fix anything, he bragged—and even offered a warranty: he'd keep the bike perfectly tuned if I gave him clarinet lessons.

A week later, we were roommates, trading off who got the couch and who got the Murphy bed and sharing the rent on my Rogers Park kitchenette. From the start, his quip about loving life set the tone. The commonplace trivia from our lives became the measure in an existential competition. If I ordered beer and Ren had wine, it was evidence he loved life more. If he played the Stones and I followed with Billie Holiday, it argued my greater love of life.

The university we attended had a center in Rome, and Ren and I planned to room together there in our junior semester abroad. Neither of us had been to Europe. A few weeks before our departure, at a drunken party, Ren introduced me to Iris O'Brien. He introduced her as the Goddess O'Iris, which didn't seem an exaggeration at the time. He assured me there was no "chemistry" between them. Lack of chemistry wasn't my experience with Iris O'Brien. In a state that even in retrospect still feels more like delirium than like a college crush, I decided to cancel my trip so that once Ren left, Iris could move in. I'd never lived with a girlfriend before.

When I told Ren I wasn't going, he said, I suppose you think that giving up Europe for a woman means you win?

Iris isn't part of the game, I said, and when I failed to laugh at my own phony, offended honor, Ren did so for me—uproariously.

Living with Iris O'Brien lasted almost as long as the Kawasaki continued to run, about a month. Although Ren and I hadn't kept in touch, I figured that if he wouldn't return my clarinet, he'd at least fix the bike once he got back. But when the semester ended, he stayed in Europe.

From a mutual friend who had also gone to Rome, I heard Ren had dropped out. He spent his time playing my clarinet at fountains across the city, and fell in love, not with a woman, but with opera. That surprised me, as the love of jazz that Ren and I shared seemed, for some reason, to require us to despise opera. With the money he'd made playing arias on the street, he bought a junked Moto Guzzi, rebuilt it, and took off on an odyssey of visiting opera houses across Italy.

That spring I got an airmail letter without a return address. The note scrawled on the back of a postcard of the Trevi Fountain read: *Leaving for Vienna. Ah! Vienna! Non ho amato mai tanto la vita—Never have I loved life more. Living it like an opera—well, an opera buffa—so, tell the Goddess O'Iris, come bless me.*

It was the last I ever heard from him.

—

I didn't catch the allusion to *Tosca* in Ren's note until years later when I was enrolled in graduate school at NYU. I was seeing a woman named Clair who had ducked out of a downpour into the cab I drove part-time. Nothing serious, we'd agreed, an agreement I kept reminding myself to honor. Clair modeled to pay the bills—underwear her specialty. She'd come to New York from North Dakota in order to break into musical theater and was an ensemble member of Cahoots, a fledgling theater on Bank Street, which billed itself as a fusion between cabaret and performance art. Cahoots was funded in part by an angel, an anonymous financier whom Clair was also sleeping with. Through Clair, I met Emil, the founder and artistic director of Cahoots, and the two of them, flush with complimentary tickets, became my tutors in opera.

Their friendship went back to their student days at Juilliard, where Emil had been regarded as a can't-miss talent until he'd become involved in what Clair called "Fire Island Coke Chic." She'd been Emil's guest at a few of the parties he frequented, including a legendary night when he sang "Somewhere (There's a Place for Us)" with Leonard Bernstein at the piano. Clair worried that Emil's addiction to male dancers was more self-destructive than the drugs.

Emil worked as a singing waiter at Le Figaro Café, a coffeehouse in the Village with marble-top tables and a Medusa-hosed Italian espresso machine that resembled a rocket crossed with a basilica. Each steamed demitasse sounded like a moon launch and the waiters, singing a cappella, were all chronically hoarse. Emil felt even more contempt toward his job than Clair had for modeling. The one night he allowed us to stop in for coffee, Emil sang "Una furtiva lagrima," the famous aria from *The Elixir of Love*. His voice issued with an unforgettable purity that seemed at odds with the man mopping sweat, his Italian punctuated by gestures larger than life. The room, even the espresso machine, fell silent.

In the opera, that aria is sung by Nemorino, a peasant who has spent his last cent on an elixir he hopes will make the wealthy woman he loves love him in return. Nemorino sees a tear on her cheek and takes it as a sign that the magic is working. Watching Emil sing his proverbial heart out at a coffeehouse, Clair, too, looked about to cry. He's singing for us, she said. Until that moment, I hadn't recognized the obvious: she'd been in love with Emil since Juilliard—years of loving the impossible.

Emil's voice rose to the climax and Clair mouthed the aria's last line to me in English, *I could die! Yes, I could die of love*, while Emil held the final *amor* on an inexhaustible breath.

The espresso machine all but levitated on a cushion of steam, and patrons sprang to a standing ovation that ended abruptly when Emil, oblivious to the blood drooling onto his white apron from the left nostril of his coke-crusted nose, flipped them off as if conducting music only he could hear.

After Figaro's became the third job Emil lost that year, Clair decided to risk desperate measures. Emil was broke. His doomed flings with danseurs had left him without an apartment of his own. The actors in Cahoots had grown openly critical of his leadership. Refusing to crash with increasingly disillusioned friends, Emil slept at the theater, whose heat was turned off between performances.

He's out of control, we're watching slo-mo suicide, Clair said, enlisting me in a small group of theater people for an intervention. It was an era in New York when the craze for interventions seemed in direct proportion to the sale of coke. Emil regarded interventions as a form of theater below contempt. To avoid his suspicion, Clair planned for it to take place at the private cast party following the opening of the show Emil had worked obsessively over—a takeoff on *The Elixir of Love*.

In the Donizetti opera, Dr. Dulcamara, a salesman of quack remedies, arrives in a small Basque town and encounters Nemorino, who requests a potion of the kind that Tristan used to win Isolde. Dulcamara sells him an elixir that's nothing more than wine.

In Emil's script, the town is Winesburg, Ohio, an all-American community of secret lusts and repressed passion. The townsfolk sing of their need for a potion to release them from lives of quiet desperation. Emil played the traveling salesman—not Dr. Dulcamara, but Willy Loman. As Willy sings his aria "Placebo," sexually explicit ads for merchandise flash across a screen, attracting the townsfolk. They mob Nemorino, and the bottle of bogus elixir is torn from hand to hand. Its mere touch has them writhing lewdly, unbuttoning their clothes, and when the bottle breaks they try to lap elixir from the stage, pleading for more, threatening to hang Willy Loman by his tie if he doesn't deliver.

Willy finds a wine bottle beside a drunk, comatose and sprawled against a dumpster. As scripted, the bottle is half filled with wine, and Emil is only to simulate urinating into it. But that night, onstage, he drained the bottle, unzipped his trousers, and, in view of the audience, pissed.

"Here's your elixir of love!" he shouted, raising the bottle triumphantly as he stepped back into the town square.

The script has the townsfolk passing the elixir, slugging it down, and falling madly, indiscriminately in love. Willy demands to be paid, and they rough him up instead. The play was to end with the battered salesman suffering a heart attack as an orgy swirls around him. In an aria sung with his dying breath, he wonders if he's spent his moneygrubbing life unwittingly pissing away magic.

Script notwithstanding, opening night was pure improv,

pure pandemonium. When the actors realized Emil had actually given them piss to drink, the beating they gave him in return wasn't simulated, either. Emil fought back until, struck with the bottle, he spit out pieces of tooth, then leaped from the stage, ran down the center aisle, and out of the theater. The audience thought it was the best part of the show.

The cast party went on backstage without Emil. Stunned and dejected, the actors knew it was the end of Cahoots and on that final evening clung to each other's company. Around midnight, Clair pressed me into a corner to say, You don't belong at this wake. We stood kissing, and then she gently pushed me away and whispered, Go. One word, perfectly timed to say what we had avoided saying aloud, but both knew: whatever was between us had run its course. Instead of goodbye, I said what I'd told her after our first night together and had repeated like an incantation each time since: Thank you.

Emil showed up as I was leaving. He still wore his bloodied salesman's tie. His swollen lip could have used stitches, but he managed to swig from a bottle of vodka.

Drunk on your own piss? asked Glen, who'd played Nemorino and had thrown the first punch onstage.

Shhh, no need for more, Clair said. She took Emil's arm as if to guide him. Sit down with us, she told him. Emil shook off her hand. Judas, he said, and Clair recoiled as if stung.

Keeping a choke hold on the bottle, Emil climbed up on a chair.

I've come to say I'm sorry, he announced, and to resign as your artistic director. I guessed you all might still be hanging around, given that without Cahoots none of you has anywhere else to perform.

Clair, blotting her smeared makeup, began to sob quietly, hopelessly, as a child cries. Emil continued as if, like so much else between them, it were a duet. Sweat streaked his forehead as it did when he sang.

Did you think I didn't know about the pathetic little drama you'd planned for me tonight by way of celebration? he asked. So, yes, I'm sorry, sorry to deprive you of the cheesy thrill of your judgmental psycho-dabbling. But then what better than your dabbling as actors to prepare you to dabble in others' lives? Was it so threatening to encounter someone willing to risk it all, working without a net, living an opera as if it's life, which sometimes—tonight, for instance—apparently means being condemned to live life as if it's a fucking opera?

The last friend of mine to say he was living life like an opera was Cole.

He said it during a call to wish me a happy birthday, one of those confiding phone conversations we'd have after being out of touch—not unusual for a friendship that went back decades to when we were in high school. Twenty years earlier, Cole had beat me in the state finals, setting a high school record for the high hurdles. We were workout buddies the summer between high school and college, which was also the summer I worked downtown at a vintage jazz record shop. Cole would stop by to spin records while I closed up. He'd been named for Coleman Hawkins and could play Hawkins's famous tenor solo from "Body and Soul" note for note on the piano. Cole played the organ each Sunday at the Light of Deliverance, one of the oldest African-American churches on the South Side. His grandfather was the minister. I'd close the record shop and we'd jog through downtown to a park with a track beside the lake, and after running, we'd swim while the lights of the Gold Coast replaced a lingering dusk. His grandfather owned a cabin on Deep Lake in northern Michigan, and Cole invited me up to fish before he left for Temple on a track scholarship. It was the first of our many fishing trips over the years to come.

Cole lived in Detroit now, near the neighborhood of the

'67 riots, where he'd helped establish the charter school that he'd written a book about. He'd spent the last four years as a community organizer and was preparing to run for public office. When he'd married Amina, a Liberian professor who had sought political asylum, "Body and Soul" was woven into the recitation of their vows. The wedding party wore dashikis, including me, the only white groomsman.

He called on my birthday—our birthdays were days apart—to invite me up to Deep Lake to fish one last time. His grandfather had died years earlier and the family had decided to sell the cabin. When I asked how things were going, Cole paused, then said, I'm living my life like an opera. I knew he was speaking in code, something so uncharacteristic of him that it caught me by surprise. I waited for him to elaborate. Before the silence got embarrassing, he changed the subject.

We'd always fished after Labor Day when the summer people were gone. By then evenings were cool enough for a jacket. The woods ringing the lake were already rusting, the other cottages shuttered, the silence audible. Outboard engines were prohibited on Deep Lake, although the small trolling motor on the minister's old wooden rowboat was legal. Cole fished walleye as his grandfather had taught: at night— some nights under a spangle of Milky Way, on others in the path of the moon, but also on nights so dark that out on the middle of the lake you could lose your sense of direction.

The night was dark like that. There was no dock light to guide us back, but the tubed stereo that had belonged to his grandfather glowed on the screened porch. Cole's grandfather had had theories about fishing and music: one was that walleyes rose to saxophones. His jazz collection was still there, some of the same albums I'd sold in the record shop when I was eighteen. We chose *Ballads* by Ben Webster. The notes slurred across the water as I rowed out to the deep spot in the middle. Cole lowered the anchor, though it couldn't touch bottom. I cracked the seal on a fifth of Jameson and passed it to Cole; tradition demanded that I arrive with a bottle. We'd had a lot of conversations over the years, waiting for the fish to bite.

I been staying at the cabin since we last talked, Cole said.

What's going on? I asked.

Remember I told you I was living life like an opera? You didn't say boo, but I figured you got my meaning, seeing you'd used the phrase yourself. Never know who's listening in. Cole laughed as if kidding, but, given the surveillance on Martin Luther King, Jr., he worried about wiretaps.

Cole, I said, I *never* used that phrase.

Where do you think I got it? he asked.

Not from me.

Maybe you forgot saying it, he said, maybe you finally forgot who you said it about. Anyway, whoever said it, I'm at a fund-raiser in Ann Arbor, everyone dressed so they can wear running shoes except for a woman I can't help noticing. You know me, it's not like I'm looking—just the opposite—there's always someone on the make if you're looking. She's out of *Vogue*. I hate misogynist rap, man, but plead guilty to thinking: rich bitch—which I regret when she comes up with my book and a serious camera that can't hide something vulnerable about her. *Photojournalist*, her card reads, and could she take one of me signing my book, and I say, sure, if she promises not to steal my soul, and she smiles and asks if she can make a donation to the school, and how could she get involved beyond just giving money, and where's my next talk, and do I have time for a drink? Two weeks later at a conference in D.C. she's there with Wizards tickets. And this time I go—we go to the game. In Boston it's the symphony, in Philly I show her places I lived in college and take her to the Clef, where 'Trane played, and in New York we go to the Met. I'd never been to an opera; we go three nights in a row. Was I happy—happiness isn't even the question. Remember running a race—thirteen-point-seven-nine seconds you've lived for, and when the gun finally fires and you're running, you disappear—like playing music those few times when you're more the music than you? She could make that happen again. One night, I'm home working late, Mina's already asleep, and the phone in my office rings. I'd never given her that unlisted home number. You need to help me, she says, and the line goes dead. Phone rings again. Where are you? I ask. Trapped in a car at the edge, she says. Her calls keep getting dropped, her voice is slurred: Come get me before I'm washed away. I keep asking her, Where are you? Finally she says: Jupiter Beach—I drove to see the hurricane. I say, You're a thousand miles away. The phone goes dead, rings, and Mina asks, Who keeps calling this time of night? She's in her nightgown, leaning in the doorway for I don't know how long. Too long for lies. I answer the phone, but no one's there.

She have a husband? Mina asks. You got to call him now.

The business card from Ann Arbor has private numbers she listed on the back, one with a Florida area code. A man answers, gives his name. I say, You don't know me, but I'm calling about an emergency, your wife's in the storm in a car somewhere on Jupiter Beach.

I know you, he says. I know you only too well. Don't worry, she doesn't tell me names, I don't ask, but I know you.

Mina presses speakerphone.

You teach tango or Mandarin or yoga or murderers to write poetry, film the accounts of torture victims, rescue greyhounds. I know the things you do, the righteous things you say, and I know you couldn't take your eyes off her the first time you saw her, and how that made you realize you'd been living a life in which you'd learned to look away. And like a miracle she's looking back, and you wonder what's the scent of a woman like that, and not long after—everything's happening so fast—you ask, What do you want? and she says, To leave the world behind together, and you think beauty like hers must come with the magic to allow what you couldn't ordinarily do, places you couldn't go, a life you'd dreamed when you were young. But now, just as suddenly, she can destroy you by falling from the ledge she's calling from, or falling asleep forever in the hotel room where she's lost count of the pills. She's talking crazy since she's stopped taking the meds you never noticed, and when she said she loved you, that was craziness, too—you're a symptom of her illness. So you called me, not to save her, but yourself, and it's me who knows where she goes when she gets like this, and I'll go, as I do every time, to save her, calm and comfort her, bring her home, because I love her, I was born to, I'll always love her, and you're only a shadow. I've learned to ignore shadows. She made you feel alive; now you're a ghost. Go. Don't call again.

I told you on the phone, Cole said, that I was living my life like an opera, but he's the one who sang the aria.

FIRE!

A borrowed flat above a plumbing store whose back windows look out on a yard of stockpiled toilets filled with unflushed rain. Four a.m., still a little drunk from a wake at an Irish bar, they smell bread baking. Someone's in the room, she whispers. It's only the mirror, he tells her. She strips off her slip, tosses it over the shadowy reflection, and then follows the scent to the open front windows. A ghost, she says as if sighing. Below a vaporous streetlamp, in the doorway of a darkened bakery, a baker in white, hair and skin dusted with flour, leans smoking.

FIRE!

A bedroom lit by fireflies, one phosphorescent above the bed, another blinking in the mirror as if captured in a jar. The window open on the scent of rain-bearded lilacs. When the shards of a wind chime suspended in a corner tingle, it means a bat swoops through the dark. Flick on the bed lamp and the bat will vanish.

FIRE! DAMN YOU! FIRE!

Whom to identify with at this moment—who is more real—Caruso, whose unmistakable, ghostly, 78-rpm voice carries over the ramparts where sparrows twitter, or Mario Cavaradossi?

Or perhaps with an extra in the firing squad, who—once Tosca flings herself from the parapet—will be free to march off for a beer at the bar around the corner, and why not, he was only following the orders barked out by the captain of the guard, who was just doing what the director demanded, who was in turn under the command of Giacomo Puccini.

Or with the hooded man, his mind lit by a firefly as he tries to recall a room he once attempted to memorize when it became increasingly clear to him that he would soon be banished.

FIRE! I AM GIVING YOU A DIRECT ORDER.

How heavy their extended rifles have become. The barrels teeter and dip, and seem to be growing like Pinocchio's nose, although it's common knowledge that rifles don't lie. Still, just to hold one steady and true requires all the strength and concentration a man can summon.

Turn on the bed lamp the better to illuminate the target. On some nights the silk shade suggests the color of lilacs and on others of areolas. See, the bat has vanished, which doesn't mean it wasn't there.

FIRE! OR YOU'LL ALL BE SHOT!

The lamp rests on a nightstand with a single drawer in which she keeps lotions and elixirs and stashes the dreams she records on blue airmail stationery when they wake her in the night—an unbound nocturnal diary. She blushed when she told him the dream in which she made love with the devil. He liked to do what you like to do to me—what *we* like, she said.

In the cracked mirror each member of the squad sees himself aiming at himself. Only a moment has passed since the "Aim" command, but to the members of the squad it seems they've stood with finger ready on their triggers, peering down their sights, for so long that they've become confused as to who are the originals and who are the reflections. After the ragged discharge, when the smoke has cleared, who will be left standing and who will be shattered into shards?

PLEASE, FIRE!

I can't wait like this any longer.

Non ho amato mai tanto la vita.

Seiche

. . . ai-je enfermé sous ma langue un pays,
gardé comme une hostie.
    —Nadia Tueni, *Liban: Vingt poèmes pour un amour*

A seiche warning was in effect. Both the *Chicago Tribune* and the evening news featured accounts of the killer seiche of June 26, 1954, when a wave ten feet high and twenty-five miles wide rose from a placid Lake Michigan and swept seven fishermen off a breakwater at Montrose Harbor to their deaths. Atmospheric conditions were right for another.

Were the beaches closed? I'm no longer sure. In memory, Lake Shore Drive is empty, barred to traffic, as if awaiting a tsunami. I imagined the seiche like a towering wave from a Hiroshige print, all the more menacing for its froth of moonglow, suspended for a heartbeat before dashing against the night-lit skyline. I didn't want to miss it.

When I considered a vantage point, what came to mind was a single-story utility shed in the shadow of Madonna della Strada, the Art Deco cathedral on the Lake Shore campus of Loyola University. I'd attended Loyola on a track scholarship. Now I was a caseworker for the Cook County Department of Public Aid. My district was Bronzeville, on the South Side, not far from the barrio where I grew up. I was living on the North Side, in Rogers Park, the neighborhood surrounding the university, and on nights when I couldn't sleep I had taken to going back to the campus to run as if I were still training for races. Lately, that was most nights. I'd never had insomnia before and wondered if the job was getting to me.

I'd dug out my old track shoes. A potholed, obsolete cinder track circled the soccer field. I set up the hurdles I found toppled together in the nearly obliterated broad jump pit, and ran imaginary heats until my shirt was pasted to my back by sweat and I gasped for breath. Then, to a ticktock of crickets and lawn sprinklers, I jogged from campus along front yards, hurdling hedges and fences along the darkened residential blocks to the deserted beach at the end of Columbia Avenue. I stripped down to my jockstrap, draped my shoes, shorts, and the T-shirt that would later serve as a towel over a crossbar of the lifeguard chair, and waded out. A moonlit sandbar sloped gradually deeper; underfoot, the sand had assumed the undulations of waves. Waist-deep, I slid into the cool night water and swam from the city without looking back until I was out far enough to imagine I had crossed the boundary of a wake left behind long ago by a priest I once watched swim.

At least, people said he was a priest. I watched his implacable crawl during the summer after my senior year—a confused, solitary time. In the space of the few months before graduation, I had become more involved than I'd realized with an exchange student who had returned suddenly to Beirut to attend the funeral of her grandfather. She had been in the States only since the start of the academic year. Her name was Nisa. We'd met during the winter semester in a poetry class. The first assignment was for each student to memorize and recite a favorite poem. "Howl" was too long, so I chose Eliot's "The Love Song of J. Alfred Prufrock." At a hundred and thirty-one lines, it took five minutes to declaim. When it was Nisa's turn, she rose from her seat with her tangle of black hair pouring down her back and in a clear voice recited:

I want to be where
your bare foot walks,
because maybe before you step,
you'll look at the ground.
I want that blessing.

Then she quickly sat back down. Her recitation had lasted moments. She didn't say who'd written the poem; no one inquired. I'd never heard a poem like that, a poem direct and sensual, and it occurred to me that perhaps she had written it and was too shy to admit it. I didn't ask in class for fear of embarrassing her, but I wanted to hear the poem again, to copy it down, and read more like it. After class, I caught up with her and asked who wrote it.

"Rumi," she said.

"Who?" I asked. Rumi was hardly known in America then, though years later he became a New Age bestseller.

"Jalaluddin Rumi. He wrote in Persian in the thirteenth century. He was a Sufi, an ecstatic."

"Mind if I walk along with you?" I asked.

"*Let us go then, you and I,*" she said in a portentous voice, mimicking my recital of "Prufrock."

We walked to the library, where she helped me find an anthology of Persian poetry. Until reading about Sufi mysticism in the introduction, I hadn't realized that the poem Nisa had recited was a prayer to God, rather than the sensual love poem I'd taken it to be. I decided not to mention my disappointment. Her family was Maronite Christian. Although I had some vague notion that Maronites were connected to the Greek Orthodox Church, I was ignorant as to how they differed from Catholics. I wondered if Nisa's upbringing had been a strict Christian equivalent to that of Muslim women required to wear burkas. When I asked if she was religious, she told me that she made a distinction between living by religious tenets and living her life in a way that allowed for the spiritual. She believed the sacred was everywhere, hidden only because we are not taught to see. She wanted to know what I believed in. I told her that my current saint, if I had one, was Albert Camus, who wrote, "I do not believe in God and I am not an atheist." She asked if I knew that my name, Jack, meant *God is gracious*. Trying to joke, I asked if her name, Nisa, had anything to do with Phoenicia.

"Actually," she said, speaking slowly and clearly, as if to the village idiot, "it means *woman*."

We began meeting at the library after class, discussing poems and novels, and then everything else. By mid-March, on days posing as spring although the tulip trees on campus were still a month from flowering, we'd walk along the lake or wander through neighborhoods, sometimes cutting class. There was a dreamy, timeless ease to those walks, a sense—so brief in a lifetime—when being in college seems like a form of sanctuary. We'd walk for miles and stop along the way at little Mideastern places where the food was cheap, fresh, and fragrant with lemon, parsley, and mint—storefronts I'd have passed by. I'd tease Nisa that her homesickness expressed itself as hunger, and she'd say she wanted me to taste the flavors she grew up with. She could turn the city I was born in into a different city, one that would otherwise have remained invisible.

Her city was in turmoil. We could watch yesterday's street fighting on the evening news. "No matter the time here, I always feel the exact hour at home, like having a clock inside me, and I'm living here and there in both times at once. It has nothing to do with homesickness," she told me, trying to explain. "There's a line in a poem by a Lebanese poet, a woman who actually inscribed a book to my mother. In English, it's something like, *I have hidden under my tongue a land, I keep there like a host*."

Nisa's love of poetry came from her mother, a teacher at a private girls' school in Beirut. Her mother believed that an educated woman was a free woman. That's how she'd raised Nisa, and yet the night before Nisa left for the U.S., her mother warned her to guard her heart. She told Nisa that travel exaggerated emotions, and that foreign travel could both broaden and distort perspective—it could make highs ecstatic, and the depths hopeless. She cautioned Nisa about callow American boys.

"At least she didn't call them decadent," Nisa said.

"Personally, I prefer decadent," I said.

"Then you shall have it. You're my first decadent American boy."

Despite my callow joke about her name, she liked hearing in return that she was my first Phoenician girl.

She had to return to Beirut before the winter semester ended. The day she left, I called a cab and rode with her to O'Hare. We'd never before taken a cab together. On excursions downtown we always rode the Red Line L over the city. Nisa loved the L. Once, during a March blizzard, she made up a fantasy about us boarding an L train with a violet headlight at a snowy, abandoned station and riding the sparking third rail of the Violet Line over roofs and across the dark lake, where we fell asleep to the rhythmic hiss of wheels on water. When we wake it's light and the train stands among date palms at a sun-drenched station in a white city. The doors snap open and she takes my hand. "*Let us go then, you and I*," she says.

The cab smelled of curry. The Pakistani driver was forking his breakfast from a to-go carton as he drove. Nisa and I tried to keep things light, but only managed to seem self-conscious. She became so quiet that I asked if she was all right.

"I'm not afraid of flying," she said, "but airports make me nervous. They remind me of hospitals."

"How's that?" I asked.

"In hospitals people are giving birth while others are dying; it's hello or goodbye, like an airport."

When we checked Departures for her gate, I kidded about not seeing any flights to Phoenicia. "Maybe it can only be reached by galley. I'm afraid you'll have to stay," I said.

Her eyes suddenly teared. "I'm sorry," she said, "I promised myself I wouldn't do this, but I am going to miss you so much. If this is the exaggerated emotion mothers warn daughters about, I'm not leaving it behind."

I put her suitcase down and held her, breathing in the scent of her hair. "You know it's the same for me, right?" I whispered against her ear. "You know where this is going, right? I want to be where your bare foot walks."

"You will," she said.

We promised again to call and write. She didn't have a return ticket, but would be back in maybe four weeks, she said, maybe even in time to take her final exams. Her grandfather had belonged to the Phalange and when the Syrians shelled the Christian neighborhoods, he had refused to move. His insistence that the family remain in Beirut was one reason Nisa had been sent out of the country to school. Now that he was dead, she knew the family would be relocating, perhaps to the Christian stronghold of Rayfoun, or to Brummana, the town of her mother, in the mountains. I'd never been farther from Chicago than New Orleans, and beyond clips on the TV news, I understood little about the conflict and the country to which she was returning, knew next to nothing of its history, language, and culture, nothing of the whitewashed, bullet-riddled, glass-strewn, window-blown, smoldering city she called home.

At the international gate, while travelers hurried by, we stood kissing.

"No cheers?" Nisa asked. "What's wrong with these people? Are they sleepwalkers? Don't they recognize the girl from Phoenicia, who came all this way in a Chicago winter, to have that once-in-a-lifetime kiss, a kiss that would be legendary? If I look back to wave, I'll cry," she said, and then she turned and walked away without looking back. I watched until her black hair disappeared into the crowd.

I took public transportation back. I carried no luggage, but the L ride felt like traveling to a foreign province—the City Where I Missed Her—a place I'd never been before, complete with exaggerated emotion and a distorted perspective.

After a week of silence, I called the numbers she had given me, but the calls never went through. The letters I wrote, nearly every day at first, like pages in a diary, went unanswered. Each day I'd read the paper for news about Beirut. There were so many questions I wished I had asked her. I'd wait for the mail. Everything that summer seemed like waiting. I went to sleep waiting, woke waiting, read waiting, looked for a job waiting, walked beside the lake, as Nisa and I had back in March before walking had become another way of waiting.

The priest swam each morning that summer, far out beyond the whistles of lifeguards. Reflecting light like white marble, his arms milled a steady stroke south toward the hazy skyline of downtown. I assumed he launched his swim from the tiny pebble beach near Madonna della Strada. I don't know how far he swam; I never saw him returning. I wondered if swimming for him was a form of prayer, a daily routine akin to that of the priests murmuring their breviaries as they strolled through the lakeside campus at dusk.

He continued to swim after Labor Day, when the lifeguards left and the beaches officially closed. He swam through early autumn as the temperature fell and leaves rusted and rattled and the windy days stropped the waves to a metallic glint. Fall mornings when the surface of the lake steamed, I'd spot him, always at the same distance from shore, like a man training to swim the Channel. There were overcast days when the sudsy gray chop made him hard to see. I'd test with my hand and imagine immersing my body into water that glacial. I began to wonder if, rather than a prayer, swimming was penance, some form of mortification, like a monk lashing himself in his cell or Raskolnikov embracing suffering at the end of *Crime and Punishment*. What was he swimming from? I tried to imagine his demons, without accusing him of a specific crime—molester, murderer, skimmer of donations on church-sponsored bingo nights. I supposed if there was a sin that had become his secret, then it must have been some betrayal of his office or vocation, a breach of trust that redefined him. By late October there were morning frosts and days you could see your breath, when it was too blustery to walk for long beside the lake. I don't know on what day he either found forgiveness or simply admitted that it was impossible for him to enter the water.

Swimming would never be my prayer, but now, years later, breast-stroking away from Columbia Beach at night, I hoped that, like a kind of meditation, the swim would still my mind.

Instead, my thoughts worked back to my caseload. It was over one hundred cases and I was constantly behind. Ragged unread case files buried my desktop. I thought about the people I'd seen earlier that day, like Serena Dixon, an obese woman who would insist on brewing a pot of coffee so we could "visit like civilized folk." In conversation, she seemed a caring mother, but her four-year-old daughter, Deedee, had just had her third major "accident"—a fall down the stairs that broke her arm—and I'd begun keeping a record of other signs of abuse.

I thought about Mrs. Wise. There was nowhere on the case forms to record the daily courage it took for her to face the daily threats of poverty. She was a grandmother who, despite her own ailments, was raising her mentally impaired fourteen-year-old granddaughter, Alma. Earlier in the year, Alma's headaches had become so severe that she was rushed screaming to the emergency room. They thought it might be meningitis and were prepping Alma for a spinal tap when a festering red bean she'd inhaled into her sinus months before was discovered. The last time I'd visited, Alma looked pregnant. Mrs. Wise claimed it was just baby fat. She slid a steak knife from her sewing bag to cut the thread from the button on a blouse she was mending, ran a raspy, thimbled thumb along its blade, and told me that any man who laid a hand on Alma would get stuck like the pig he was, as would anyone who tried to take her away. She narrowed her eyes and added how from her windows she could see me hanging out at "that whorehouse hotel," pretending I had clients to visit there.

"You ain't fooling nobody, Mr. Cook County," she said. "I seen a lot of your kind, poking your nose in on folks you don't know nothing about, don't care nothing about, never will know nothing about, and one day you ain't here no more, moved on to something better, and there's another fool come to give me his Mr. Cook County card, no damn different than the fool before knocking at the door like he knows something."

I *was* the caseworker for that whorehouse hotel the DuSable—the Mighty Du, as it was known in the hood— eight floors of alcoholics and junkies on disability and prostitutes, mostly young women addicted to crack. There was a soul-food restaurant called Banks located in what had been the old Drexel Bank across the street, and the cops who ate there wondered how I could go into the Mighty Du unarmed. A week ago I'd found a package without a return address in my mailbox in Rogers Park. Inside was a small-caliber gun, its serial number filed off, and a box of bullets. I loaded the clip and instead of going to campus to run, I walked out late at night to the beacon at the end of the pier off Farewell, thinking I might test-fire a shot into the water. But when I got there, I didn't want to ruin the silence. I imagined some stranger lying unable to sleep, who would hear the shot and wonder if there'd been a mugging, and if he should call 911. It had been enough to just once experience the petty power of what it felt like to walk around armed. I unloaded the clip and kept the gun hidden in a locked suitcase under my bed.

I thought of Felice Lavel, a mother on ADC—Aid to Dependent Children—whose daughter, Starla, had been diagnosed with leukemia. Felice was determined to get a college degree. The first time I visited her, I noticed books scattered around her apartment, a few romance novels, but also *I Know Why the Caged Bird Sings*, *The Bluest Eye*, *The Autobiography of Malcolm X*. She wanted to talk about them, and on the next visit I brought her *Go Tell It on the Mountain*, *Invisible Man*, and *Bronzeville Boys and Girls*, the anthology of poems for children by Gwendolyn Brooks, who was still alive then, still living on the South Side. I told Felice the book was for Starla. She thanked me and asked me to bring other books, especially my favorites, so we could discuss them.

"They all don't have to be black," she said.

Her dream was to go to law school. I helped her enroll at Martin Luther King College and got her part-time secretarial work at the office of a lawyer who did pro bono work with welfare recipients, but Felice quit to become a cocktail waitress. She wasn't making enough yet to get off public aid, but she was trying. Visiting her apartment a few days earlier, I'd noticed immediately that the cracked plastic chairs and the wobbly table from a resale shop were gone, replaced by stylish furniture. The windows were open and new silky green drapes billowed into the room. Starla was in the children's wing of County Hospital, but her bedroom was waiting for her, redone in shades of pink and complete with its own TV and a canopy bed presided over by an enormous black-spotted pink leopard.

"Okay, Jack, you're wondering where the money came from," Felice said. "You been straight with me. I ain't going to lie to your face. I'm doing a little tricking on the side. Only connected clients. You're not going to report me and mess up Starla's medical, I know."

I could have said, I wish you hadn't told me; or, Be careful, Felice, prostitution is more dangerous than commercial fishing; or, Have you thought about what will happen to Starla if something happens to you? I said nothing.

"So?" Felice asked.

"So, you're taking too many chances. You just took a chance telling me. You know that saying we talked about? 'Chance favors the prepared mind.' Well, it works in reverse, too, when it comes to bad luck. What if you'd guessed wrong and I said I'm going to report you, like I'm supposed to?"

"Then I'd say, I know you think I'm pretty, Jack. I'd do you pro bono."

I closed the folder in which I was supposed to be making notes for the "Living Arrangements" section of the case report I was required to submit to document the visit. "Good luck, Felice," I said.

"Let me ask you something 'fore you go. If . . . when I get off welfare and you're not my worker anymore, would you ever think to give me a call, you know, keep in touch, talk books, get a drink or something?"

"Maybe," I said, knowing it was the easy-out answer.

"Maybe, huh? Maybe you might do something crazy like have a cup of coffee, huh?"

"Get off welfare and I'll buy lunch to celebrate."

"Thanks, Jack, I'd like that."

One becalmed night when I swam as far as I safely could, still keeping something in reserve for swimming back, I saw, along a streak of moonlight paved like a path on the black surface of water, a body floating farther out. I knew it had to be an optical illusion, only a log, probably, but when fish began to jump around it—I'd never seen fish jumping at night until then—I had the eerie sense they were feeding. I swam along the path of moonlight toward it, but it moved away, farther out, as if swimming, too, inviting me to follow. I was breathing from exertion when I'd spotted it and could hear the sound of my breath echoing over the lake; at least, I thought the sound was mine, but when I held my breath I still heard the resonance of someone breathing. I swam keeping my eyes on whatever it was, sure I was gaining, until as I drew closer it widened the gap between us again. When the thought came to mind that it was the priest, I gave up. It was a ludicrous thought, crazy. Plus I'd never catch him.

Each night I would swim out farther and then, treading water, turn and gaze at the distant Gold Coast, a lustrous veneer behind which the apartheid of slums wasn't even a shadow. If a power outage suddenly plunged the city into darkness, I would be confused as to the direction of shore. The imaginary fear of that happening would get me swimming back.

On the night of the seiche, the campus was deserted; but then, it was deserted most nights. I climbed to the flat roof of the shed, looked out over the oily oscillation of moonlight, and waited, senses cocked, listening for the least change to the rhythmic sloshing from the pebble beach below. It was the beach I had imagined the priest had swum from each morning.

All I knew about a seiche was what I'd read in the paper. It could swell without warning as if the basin of the lake had suddenly tilted, causing water to rush over the shore in biblical proportions. I estimated the shed roof was well above ten feet, but still wondered if I was doing something really stupid. The roof gave me a clear view of Madonna della Strada, whose doorstep began at the lake. Before I learned it meant Our Lady of the Way, I had thought its name translated to Our Lady of the Streets, which sounded to me like a Virgin to whom whores might pray. I'd certainly have been safer watching from the steeple. From my perch on the roof, I could look into the side doorway of the church where, in late March of my senior year, Nisa and I had huddled out of the wind, locally called the Hawk, slashing off the lake. She'd wrapped her long crimson scarf around us. Her dark hair kept blowing into our mouths until I gathered it in an ungloved hand and gripped it as if to steady us as we kissed. We held each kiss and without stopping kissed again. I could feel the warmth of her mouth traveling the length of my body. I slid my hand between the buttons of her coat and brushed her breast and she moaned into my mouth and, with one hand holding her hair and the other cupping her breast, I backed her against the marble portal and pressed against her and she opened her coat so our bodies could touch and pressed back while wind swirled her scarf and our tongues stabbed together. We thought we were alone, hidden in the doorway, but when finally I released her hair and we pulled apart, we were greeted by an enormous cheer. The church doorway faced the dormitory at Mundelein, a Catholic women's college, and the Mundelbundles, as we called the students there, lined their dorm windows cheering and applauding.

I waited for the seiche until three a.m., my body at the ready as if listening for a starter's gun whose report I supposed would sound at first like a reverberation of thunder.

I kept my eyes trained as far as I could see into the formless dark where I imagined that a great moon-glazed wave would rise. Even after I finally gave up and climbed down, I kept looking behind to make sure it wasn't gaining on me as I walked away.

Blowing Shades

Like a boy with a kite.

One he's labored over all afternoon, fashioned from sticks, newspaper, tape, and bakery string. A tail of rags.

Running bareheaded down an empty beach, trailing a tail of footprints through wet sand, shorebirds scattering before him.

How effortlessly the birds mount air, soaring off sideways on gusts of sea breeze, crying out from on high, while the kite stubbornly refuses to rise.

Wind whooshes over foaming water. Despite the drag of the kite he runs harder, faster. If he were a kite, he'd be up there, though it's no longer a day for launching a kite—even a store-bought kite from Japan made of silk the shade of women's underclothes, let alone a kite of sticks and newspaper. Maybe that's why the kite won't rise; it knows flying could tear it to shreds.

Only when the boy acknowledges defeat, slows to a half-hearted jog, and turns at a cross angle to the wind does the kite sail off sideways on a gust, twisting crazily, barely holding together, but climbing, tugging at the ball of string the boy can't unravel fast enough.

He pays it out over the ocean. Stands at the shoreline, squinting up as if it has just occurred to him to read the print on the newspaper the kite is made of, but the words are too far away.

Too late for words. The kite is barely recognizable, a speck above the horizon; and is it merely to see what will happen next, or to set it free, that without warning he lets go?

Or a bird, wingbeats flailing for a hold on air.

Futility strips it of grace. When it falls clumsily to earth, the boy gently gathers it up again.

"Try, please," he whispers, and tosses it back into the air.

Again the bird flaps and falls, weaker for its failed attempt, and the boy gathers it up, gently folds in its wings, and more violently this time tosses it up.

The bird crashes helplessly as if it has forgotten that it ever defied gravity.

"I'm sorry, I didn't mean to hurt you," the boy insists.

How beautiful the bird appears, iridescent like a woman's slip in the gleam of an afternoon in which sun beats drawn shades to bronze.

He traces the curve of its nape. He's never seen a bird like this before, never before been allowed to stroke his fingertips along such smoothness, to touch a life so different from his own, to hold an inhabitant of air, that mysterious sphere about which the boy can only dream. He feels its rapid heartbeat. Its body heat intensifies in his hands, and suddenly he's afraid the heat is blood. But his hands are dry. He doesn't know exactly where he's inflicted the wound.

He's never shot anything with the pellet gun but empty cans and factory windows. True, he's shot at birds—sparrows on wires, starlings in the trees, pigeons on the girders under railroad bridges—but never hit them. He's either a naturally poor shot or his nerve fails at the last instant so that the pellet whizzes harmlessly into the sky or ricochets with a ringing spark off the girders while a flock of pigeons beat from an underpass and swoop away.

He's always missed before, perhaps, because that's what his heart demands. Now he could argue that, though he pulled the trigger, hitting this bird was the merest chance—an accident.

He could argue that, but to whom? Who's here besides the two of them?

Look what he's done.

What difference does the truth make now?

"Like a boy," she said, as if more to herself.

Then she leaned from the bed and released the shade.

Perhaps the pull cord accidentally slipped from her fingers. The shade, gleaming like a sheet of bronze, shot up, and blinding daylight blazed across the bare mattress, slicing the bed in two.

Heat streamed into the room; pigeons launched from the ledge as if a shot had been fired.

She was on her feet, knocking over the chair, kicking through the clothes strewn beside the bed, and pulling on her slip.

A slip she sometimes didn't remove. But today, before they'd exchanged a word, she'd stripped off her clothes, no longer shy about the sag of her breasts. Maybe it was simply too close—still air before a summer storm—to lie beside him in the slip. Nonetheless she'd worn it beneath her sundress. She knew he liked her in it from how he drove her into the mattress kissing her throat like he was crazy for her, her shoulder straps slipping down, a breast popped over the lacy bodice, while the silk rode up her jittering legs so that the V of her dark bush showed like a flash of panties.

"Haven't I been good to you?" she asked, softly. "Haven't we been happy up here in our own little world? You're not being honest with me. I made good on everything I said I was going to do. Something else has come up for you. Who is it?—a girl, no doubt more your age. Or have you found another lonely woman?"

He shook his head: *It's not like that,* he wanted to tell her, to say, as he'd rehearsed it, *I'm getting in over my head with you.*

That would sound stupid now. Looking at her standing against the shade-drawn window at the foot of the bed, her eyes too full of hurt for his to meet, he choked up. The choice was between total silence or rising to hold her. He sat naked on the mattress, paralyzed; she released another shade with a violent yank, clearly on purpose this time, so that it clattered up, and light obliterated the foot of the bed.

"So," she said in that soft voice, unsettling after the racket of the shade, "you thought maybe we'd fuck goodbye."

She let another shade fly as if releasing a kite.

Sparrows on the wire, starlings in the basswood trees that lined the curb and threw the network of their branches across the shades—city-wise birds—beat their wings and flew away. It might have been someone shooting.

"You're not being honest with me. You're dumping me, and I was already so looking forward to seeing you Wednesday," she pleaded gently—too gently—the way he'd answered her once when she asked him why he'd whisper, *No no no,* while she came down on him. *Too sweet,* he'd tried to explain to her then, *so gentle it aches.*

I never wanted it to go this far, he wanted to say, *never wanted to hurt you.*

"What happened? I showed a little feeling and scared you away," she said, answering her own question as she paced, bare feet slapping the floorboards, moving from window to window, tripping the drawn shades the way an executioner might trip the lever on a gallows. "You said I was amazing, that I raised the bar for you. I'm a fool. You really were too young for me."

With the shades up and the fierce light that obliterated the mattress bleaching her skin from bronze to white, it seemed as if she were fading. Before his eyes, their room, secret in the sun-beaten shadows of drawn shades, was revealed for what it was: an unrented apartment with a few sticks of shoddy furniture.

And when she'd reduced it to that, she stood dressing before him one last time, against an open window that looked out on a blur.

"You opened me up, and then just let go. Like a boy—confused, callow, and cruel."

Blocks away the spooked birds resettled on other sills and wires, and on the crabapple trees in a little park.

"My pretty boy," she said, and stepped out, quietly shutting the door.

After a while he rose, pulled the shades on the windows down, lay back on the bed, closed his eyes, spit into his hand. But it was impossible to touch himself with her sweetness.

The braided hoops at the ends of pull cords begin to sway like miniature nooses. A tingle of grit on the panes against which the shades nervously rustle. A whoosh of coolness. The shades lift slightly and float back. Hypnotically. Billowy, translucent, like garments through which summer light outlines the shadow of a woman's body. Until, seized by a sudden gust, they crash like paper cymbals and tread air on the edge of tearing apart. Like trapped birds, they want to fly in this room that once seemed perfectly ordered in its bareness—bed, mirror, chair. Chair on which to drape discarded clothes; mirror in which to watch his hands cupping her breasts.

While on the other side of the door, the girl, who's changed her name from Mary Jane to Marigold, and who has spied all summer, drawn by the forbidden sounds of her mother's love-making, strains to listen. Now that she no longer has to despise and envy her mother, she's free. Free to pity her now for the boyfriends she'll go back to, the guys she brings home rather than hides away with in the unrented flat upstairs, the dorky graybeard, bald under a hat he never removes, six foot two of baby fat singing country western, or Mr. O'Pinions, who thinks he's cool, calls himself Red Crow, commandeers the TV, and leaves the couch smelling musty. Free to concentrate on her own crush on the guy from Frost's Service Station. That's what's stenciled on the back of his paint-spattered coveralls, the white pair he wears partially unbuttoned over a smooth, bare chest. *Rafael* stitched in green over the pocket. "Baby" was what her mother called him, behind the closed door, sometimes sighing it over and over. She's never heard her mother say the real name of the nameless young man with the dark, dreamy eyes, angel eyes, eyes she's seen on holy cards. Saint Francis eyes, or Saint Sebastian nailed down by arrows but gazing up at heaven. Her saint's alone in there. Why won't he come out? she wonders. This time she won't run and hide. Is he weeping, perhaps, like her clueless mother, her mom who still wants to be a girl, or has he merely fallen asleep?

She holds her breath to listen harder, but all she can hear is the thrash of shades blowing in an echoey room.

Waiting

There is really only one city for everyone just as there is one
major love.   —*The Diaries of Dawn Powell: 1931–1965*

I read an essay once—I don't recall who wrote it—about waiting in Hemingway. There's that couple at the station in "Hills
Like White Elephants" waiting for the express from Barcelona,
and the little boy with a fever who is waiting to die in "A Day's
Wait." That situation, waiting to die, is one Hemingway returned to often, as in "The Snows of Kilimanjaro," when
the man with a gangrened leg is recalling his youth in Paris;
nor is he waiting alone—the hyenas and vultures are waiting,
too. In other stories, the men *are* alone. Nick Adams waits
out the night in "A Way You'll Never Be." In "The Gambler,
the Nun, and the Radio," Mr. Frazer listens to a hospital radio
that plays only at night—a clever touch—as he waits out the
pain of his fractured leg. All these characters have, in one way
or another, been wounded.

◆

When the phenomenon known as the Men's Movement was
in fashion, I was invited to give a poetry reading at a "gathering." Chad, the therapist who organized the event, believed
that poetry had therapeutic power. We'd met at a literary festi-

val in Washington, and it was obvious that Chad, who was shopping a book of his poems, also believed in the power of networking. He referred to poetry as the "Po-Biz." The term reminds me that, like any troubadour, Orpheus was part hustler, although he couldn't out-hustle Death. I would have passed on the gathering if Chad hadn't also invited a friend whom I didn't get to see often enough, a Vietnamese poet whose family were boat people. After the fact, I learned that my friend accepted the invitation because Chad told him I'd agreed to come.

On the Friday the conference was scheduled to open, with a sweat lodge, I couldn't get myself to go. I slept restlessly and woke early, feeling guilty enough about reneging to make myself get in my car and start driving. The conference was four hours north of where I was living in Michigan. The Vietnamese poet had flown from Philadelphia to Chicago and then on to a commuter airport in Traverse City the day before. It's beautiful country up there. Sand dunes sculpt the edge of the planet's greatest freshwater sea. I had sometimes rented a cottage there on a lake whose name I kept to myself. I've read that Michigan has more coastline than any state but Alaska. I don't know if that calculation includes the coasts of all the weedy lakes and trout streams you can smell hidden in the woods while speeding north on a highway in summer.

By eleven I'd reached the turnoff on Chad's map and continued down a dirt road. It opened from a papery birch forest into a clearing where a rustic compound stood on the shore of a lake glistening with the rings of feeding fish. I parked and walked by deserted cabins to a log lodge beside the dock. The screen door was ajar, and I went in, past a table stacked with books: *Iron John*, *Fire in the Belly*, *The Myth of Male Power*, *Fatherless America*. Copies of my book, *Welfare*, were for sale along with the others and with the three slim volumes by my friend the Vietnamese poet, who was reading to a circle of maybe seventy men. A couple of the men were perched on wheelchairs; the rest sat Indian-style on the plank floor. Each had a drum the size of a toy beside him. My friend was the only one in the circle wearing a shirt.

No one turned when I slipped in; they were absorbed by the poem. My friend had always been a gently charismatic reader, but he was reciting now with an intensity that reflected that of his audience. After each poem there was a collective exhalation, a moment of respectful silence, and then Chad would invite the men to share personal responses. Several of the poems were elegiac portraits of a once-powerful father who had been reduced by immigrant status and the prejudice of his adopted country to an aged, exhausted man on the periphery of all but his family. The men on the floor shared their stories about fathers and Chad would ask my friend to read another poem.

I stood outside the circle, feeling like an unbeliever at a prayer service. I was scheduled to read after lunch and wondered how I would come up with something appropriate. The few vignettes I'd written about my father, also an immigrant, were at best what Chad might term "conflicted."

My friend read the title poem of his first book, *Friendly Fire*, an indictment of a criminal American foreign policy simply conveyed in thirty lines about the ghost of his godfather, who had been killed by American fire during the war. When he finished, an older man with a bit of a gut, hirsute, with a silver cast to his ponytail and mustache and a faded SEMPER FI tattoo on his chest, raised his hand and asked, "Chad, would this be the right time to share my ghost dance?"

"Could we put that on hold for just a moment, Pete Red Crow?" Chad said. He passed out a shopping bag stuffed with so-called scarlet ribbons that looked like tie-dyed rags. "I want each of you to take as many ribbons as you need and tie them around the places on your body or spirit that have been wounded." To demonstrate, Chad wrapped a ribbon around what I presumed was a tennis elbow. Men in the circle were winding them around their heads like headbands, around their necks like bandannas, around their chests, their drooping bellies, their legs, ankles, and feet. Later, when I described the scene to a woman I was seeing, she asked, "Did anyone tie one to his wiener?"

"Maybe symbolically," I said.

"Where did you tie yours?"

"I didn't take one."

"Where would you have tied it if you had?"

"That information is to be shared only with the brotherhood."

The man who wanted to share his ghost dance banded a ribbon around his forehead and knotted one at each wrist, where they hung like streamers. "Is it a good time yet, Chad?" he asked.

"Thank you for waiting, Pete," Chad said.

Pete rose, bowed to the circle, raised his scarlet-trailing arms in salute to Chad, to the poet, to the sky above the rafters, and, chanting in a tongue that sounded like Hollywood Indian, he began to gyrate and stamp, twisting while his arms milled and waved and the ribbons swirled as if slashed wrists were spouting loops of arterial light. He stopped abruptly, and without a bow folded back into his seated position, buried his face in his hands, and wept.

"It's all right, Pete Red Crow. That came from a release deep within," Chad said. His instinct was right: something needed to be said. Hands shot up from men who had more to share. Chad sensed the mood-shift, and thought that it might be wise to calm things down while he still had control of the group. "It's time to break for lunch," he said. "We'll pick up where we left off when we reassemble. But first let us thank our brother Thanh, a true keeper of the poetic flame, who has graced us with the gifts of purifying fire, solace, and wisdom."

The men heartily applauded, but then a bearded man in a wheelchair festooned with ribbons raised his hand and said, "Chad, I don't think thanks is enough. We need a raising up."

Ever since Chad had introduced the ribbons, my friend had watched the proceedings with an increasingly quizzical expression. He'd let the ribbons pass him by and seemed utterly bewildered by the dance and the weeping that followed. I suspected that he'd agreed to the conference with no idea as to what the Men's Movement was about. As the men in the circle began to drum and then rose and pressed in on him, a sudden fear flashed in his eyes and he shouted, "I have bad knees!" The circle collapsed in on him and he disappeared beneath a scrum of half-naked bodies. I could hear them whispering, "You are my brother, Thanh . . . you have touched my heart . . . you have touched my soul." Then, borne by their uplifted hands, he seemed to levitate above us. Around each knee a red ribbon had been tied into a bow.

◆

Essays on the conspicuous theme of wounds in Hemingway are common, but so far as I know, there's only that one essay about waiting. And once it is pointed out, you see it everywhere. There's the cynical Italian major of "In Another Country," a noted fencer who endures the futile rehabilitation of his mutilated hand. There are stories that are studies in the word *pati*, to suffer—the root in both *patient* and *patience*—like "A Clean, Well-Lighted Place," in which an old waiter prays, *Our nada who art in nada, nada be thy name* . . .

Even as a young writer, Hemingway had a knack for portraying old men, not unlike certain actors who make a career of it—Hal Holbrook doing Twain—though I doubt that even Holbrook could play an aging Papa better than Hemingway played himself. It's fitting that *The Old Man and the Sea* got him the Nobel Prize. That book is about waiting, too, but then what fishing story isn't? *Moby-Dick* is waiting sustained over a thrashing sea of pages. That's the problem with the insight about waiting: you have to ask, Why single out Hemingway? Think of waiting as measured by the interminable winters in Chekhov, or by the ticking of clocks in bureaucratic offices at the dead ends of the maze of cobbled streets in Kafka's Prague. Prague, one of those cities that like London is presided over by a clock.

Limiting the catalogue to just a sample of the writers overlapping Hemingway's time, there's Gatsby's green dock light waiting in darkness and Newland Archer in Wharton's *The Age of Innocence*, longing for another woman during twenty-five years of loveless marriage; *Winesburg, Ohio*, a masterpiece about waiting, an entire community stranded in the stasis of secret lives, yearning for something mysterious and unsayable beneath the cover of night; Joyce's *Dubliners*, with its phantasmal patron saint of waiting, the tubercular Michael Furey of "The Dead"; Katherine Mansfield's heroines waiting for their lives to begin; the passengers on Katherine Anne Porter's *Ship of Fools,* waiting for their baggage-ridden lives to change as they voyage into eternity; Beckett's tramps; Faulkner's devotion to the word *endure*—to suffer patiently, to continue to exist. All these writers, who we think are looking toward us into the present, are actually gazing back.

From that perspective it is as if the forward thrust of narrative, as if the very action of verbs, is illusory, that no matter what the story or how it's told or by whom, the inescapable conclusion is that life—not just life on the page but life at its core—waits. It waits stalled in traffic, doing time at red lights, waits in line for the coffee that signals the beginning of another day, waits for the messages of the day to arrive. Sometimes the wait is imperceptible, but it can also seem interminable— waiting for a phone call from a lover or from the doctor who may pause before delivering what feels more like a sentence than a diagnosis, the kind of call in which the undecided seems suddenly to have been decided long before, as if it's no accident that in the mystical, kabbalistic workings of language, *fate* and *wait* are paired in rhyme.

I don't remember if that essay on waiting mentioned Ketchum, Idaho, on the morning of July 2, 1961. It didn't have to. Whether a public gesture such as Yukio Mishima's seppuku, or a private exit—Virginia Woolf, her pockets filled with stones, sinking into the River Ouse—a writer's suicide becomes the climax of a reality that the reader appends to a lifework of fiction. It has certainly become the final punctuation for Hemingway, an author who traded the typewriter he referred to as his psychoanalyst for a shotgun. Playing analyst, literary critics wrote that his suicide had been lying in wait since 1928 when Hemingway's father, Clarence, a doctor, shot himself at the family home in Oak Park, Illinois, with a Civil War pistol passed down from his father.

In "Indian Camp," an early story, the father, a doctor, while on a fishing trip to Michigan, performs a C-section with a jackknife and tapered gut leaders on an Indian woman who has been in labor for two days. The story is set not all that far from where I rented that cottage up in Michigan, although any trace of Native Americans, Ojibwa probably, is gone. The Indian woman's husband can't endure the suffering and cuts his own throat. Afterward, Nick, the boy who has witnessed both the birth and the suicide, asks his father, "Is dying hard, Daddy?"

"No, I think it's pretty easy, Nick. It all depends."

The story ends: *In the early morning on the lake sitting in*

the stern of the boat with his father rowing, he felt quite sure
he would never die.

◆

The woman, Liesel—she went by Lise—who wanted to know
where on my body I would choose a wound to bind, despised
Hemingway. She despised the popular legends about him and
the values they represented, despised bullfights and braggarts
who spent their considerable disposable income on shooting
animals in Africa, despised what she called the Arrested He-
Man School of American Fiction. When I suggested that
Hemingway deserved his unfashionable reputation, but still,
he had written some genuinely original stories that continued to influence writers even if they didn't acknowledge it,
Lise told me she preferred stories that reached for a transfor-
mative epiphany to those that settled for irony. I don't know
how much of Hemingway's work she'd actually read. She re-
vered Dawn Powell, a writer who like Lise had fled a small
town in central Ohio for the city. I recall a conversation we
had that prompted me to say that Hemingway had referred
to Powell as his favorite living writer, and there was another
time, on the night we met, when I quoted a Hemingway phrase
about how grappa took the enamel off your teeth and left
it on the roof of your mouth, and she laughed. Otherwise
Hemingway wasn't a writer we discussed much, let alone argued about. I wasn't going to defend a guy rich enough for
safari vacations beating his chest for shooting the last of the
lions.

Lise took her literature seriously, although she'd probably
say not seriously enough. She was a self-described ABD—All
But Dissertation—initials she likened to those indicating a
disease, or a social stigma like a welfare mother on ADC. She
was kidding, but before I caught myself, the comparison

between an ADC mother and an ABD from the University of Chicago reminded me of the lack of proportion in those few poems by Sylvia Plath that used Holocaust imagery to convey the pain of a young woman from Smith.

"Actually, ABD *is* a minor epidemic at the U of C," Lise said. "There should be a graveyard in old Stagg Stadium, not under the stands where the atom bomb was hatched, but right out on the playing field where Jay Berwanger dodged tackles, little crosses marking all the dissertations that suffered and died there."

Her unfinished dissertation was titled *One City, One Love: Endless Becoming in the Work of Dawn Powell*. Its three-hundred-plus pages awaited completion behind a closed door in a sewing room she called Limbo in the apartment she rented over a dry cleaner in Hyde Park. To pay the rent, Lise augmented a small trust fund by teaching freshman comp at a couple of community colleges in the Chicago area. One was near Arlington, and sometimes, when I'd drive in from Michigan to see her, we'd meet at the Thoroughbred track there. Our first time at the races we won big—for us, anyway—$687 on a horse we couldn't not bet on named Epiphany. The following night at a French restaurant overlooking an illuminated Lake Shore Drive, we blew our winnings on a four-course meal washed down with a magnum of a champagne from a village fittingly called Bouzy. After the waiter had ceremoniously buried the empty bottle neck-down in the ice bucket, Lise said, "You have to promise we'll run away to Bouzy together." She pronounced it *boozy*.

"Tonight?" I asked, checking my watch.

"Tonight's too late, Jack. It's already tomorrow in France," she said, and then, leaning in to be kissed, knocked over the flute with the last of her wine.

Lise was a self-described "promiscuous kisser," though

that didn't keep her from regarding a kiss as deeply intimate—
especially, she added, if it's my tits being kissed. After a few
drinks, she had a way of releasing from a kiss with her mouth
still open, shaped as if the kiss continued, a facial expression
that her good looks allowed her to get away with, as they allowed her to get away with sounding a little breathless on the
subject of sex. The restaurant was closing, the chefs, sans
toques, leaned in the doorway of the kitchen, drinking red
wine and watching what Lise called our PDAs. We joked that
night about calling it quits as high rollers while we were
ahead, but over the racing season we returned to the track in
Arlington hoping for another score. This time we'd invest in
tickets to Bouzy.

We'd been drinking the night we first met, too, though it
was pitchers of Rolling Rock, not champagne. I'd driven into
Chicago for a reading and book signing by a friend who'd been
a teacher of mine when I was in a graduate program in American studies there. After his reading, a small group, Lise among
them, adjourned to a Hyde Park neighborhood pub. I'd noticed her in the audience at the bookstore. It was bitterly cold,
and I'd taken a chance driving in but thought I could make it
back to Michigan before the predicted lake-effect snow. She was
wearing a furry Russian hat à la *Doctor Zhivago* that accen-
tuated her cheekbones and the green of her eyes. There should
be a word for a flair for looking stylish in hats. For Lise that
included baseball caps, bathing caps, rain hoods, bicycle
helmets, headbands, and probably tiaras and babushkas—
anything that swept her hair up and bared her delicate face.
Tendrils of auburn hair kept straggling out from under the
fur hat and she'd tuck them back with the unconscious self-
consciousness of a girl tugging up her swimsuit.

Later, when we'd tell each other the story of how we
met, the word we'd use was *effortless*. We found ourselves

seated directly across the table from each other in the pub and discussing our mutual friend's new book. Then, looking for things in common, we went on to talking about books that had changed us, movies that had swept us away, music we loved, food, travel, all the while refilling each other's beer steins, until inevitably we reached the subject of our personal lives.

Lise brought it up in the spirit of recounting what changed her, what had swept her away. I hadn't drunk anywhere near enough to tell her about the ill-advised relationship I'd had after I'd quit my job as a city caseworker, with a woman named Felice, who had once been on my caseload. She'd managed to get off welfare by working as a cocktail waitress in a mob bar. Her dream was to go to law school. At the time we met, her daughter, Starla, was in remission from leukemia. When the disease returned, Felice turned to drugs. We'd go together to the children's wing of County Hospital to read to Starla. She loved stories about cats, especially a series about Jenny Linsky, a black cat who wore a red scarf. I bought Starla a red scarf she took to wearing, which was as close as we could get to bringing her the cat that Felice was determined to sneak into the hospital. Starla's death after months of wasting away left Felice inconsolable. It wasn't numbness or escape she was after; she wanted to hurt herself, and I couldn't find a way to help her. Talking about her like that sounded wrong, though—psychologized, abstracted, factual, but also censored, sanitized, and less than honest. I didn't know how to tell what had happened, even to myself, and felt too guilty to try. After Felice disappeared, I had lucked into a teaching job in Michigan on the strength of my newly published first book. A few threatening letters from Felice were forwarded to me—letters threatening herself. They arrived with a Chicago postmark but no return address. I never knew where she was living or with whom, and felt braced for worse to come. That night in the pub with Lise, back in the city from which I felt exiled, was the first time in a long while that it seemed natural to share a drink with a woman. When Lise asked me directly, I simply told her I wasn't seeing anyone.

Lise said that she was involved, off and on, with an older man who was a collector.

"A what?" I asked.

She laughed. "Whenever I say what Rey does, people do a double take."

"Tax collector? Butterfly collector? Juice loan collector?"

"An everything and anything collector. He's got a great eye! That's the name of his business: Great Eye Enterprises. He has this talent for stuff. This stein—he could give you a disquisition on beer steins that would make you have to have a set of them. It's sexy. He's sexy. It's partly smell—I don't think anything indicates sexual attraction more than smell. It's the sense most directly linked with memory. With Rey it was love at first sniff. The first time I met him, I literally started to tremble and had to hide in the Ladies'. Even when we're apart I keep one of his undershirts in my closet for a fix."

"So, is this an off or an on cycle?"

"Sort of in between. He's starting a business in Denver. We talk on the phone at least twice a day. There's so much history between us, and we deserve to be together, but I don't know. I need my doctorate, and though he gets me, he doesn't get that. He's a salesman, not a scholar. He made a half a million dollars last year and wants to support me, but he's getting tired of waiting. He says he needs a woman in his bed every night, which sounds hot, but he's major needy, and in the culture he was raised in I'm not sure 'in his bed' doesn't extend to 'in the kitchen.'"

"So, how long have you two been involved?"

"Seven years."

The people we'd come in with were bundling up to head out into a blizzard that had howled in ahead of schedule. We hugged our mutual friend goodbye, and it was only Lise and me left at the table when the waitress announced last call. We moved to the bar, looking for something to cap off the evening and clean away the aftertaste of beer. I suggested grappa. "Perfect," Lise said. But the bar didn't stock it.

"How about a couple shots of Drano instead?" the bartender offered.

Lise said she had a bottle at her place that she'd brought back from Rome, a trip she'd taken with Buck, a paintings conservator, during an off phase with the collector. She'd bought the grappa because it was flavored with rose petals; it took pounds of petals, thousands of roses, to make a single bottle. In Italy, the relationship with Buck had seemed a romantic adventure, but once back in the States she began to suspect that Buck, despite the macho way he dressed—the Wolverine boots and his prized Stetson Gun Club hat that he had worn during their trip to Europe—was gay and didn't know it. She returned to her ne plus ultra—Rey.

"Once someone has taken you across a line into the best sex of your life, you can't go back. It's not easy for other men to turn my head from Rey," she said. I didn't ask what she meant by "across a line," and I wondered how many other times Rey had been there to collect her yet again.

The sleety horizontal snow had plastered my wipers to the windshield. Given the alcohol, the hour, and the weather, Lise suggested that rather than find a hotel, let alone trying to drive back to Michigan, I sleep on her couch.

The couch was more about decor than comfort, a quality shared by most of her furnishings. Stuff—chiming clocks, threadbare tapestries, knickknacks, ornate mirrors, and murky oil paintings—crowded her small apartment. The room looked as if it might have a musty resale shop smell. I supposed it was decorated in Great Eye. There was a sense of recycled pasts that brought her phrase "so much history between us" to mind.

"Like it?" she asked.

"Very quaint."

"Please, the operative term is *whimsical*. I meant the grappa."

"The operative term is *thank you, I never tasted anything like it*."

"So what do you collect?" she asked.

"What do I collect?"

"Everyone collects something," she said. "First editions, baseball cards, saltshakers . . ."

"Frankly, since moving to Michigan, I've been trying to get rid of shit."

I interpreted the alarmed look she gave me to mean that we were on a subject sacred to her, beyond anything in common between us.

She unrolled an unzipped sleeping bag over the brocade cushions and fluffed a pillow faintly scented by her shampoo against the single fin of the couch. "At least you've dared to remove your shoes, or do you always sleep fully dressed?"

"I forgot to pack my footy pajamas."

"Will you be warm enough without them?"

"If my feet get cold I might need the loan of that fur hat."

"It's been a lovely evening. Thank you. Sweet dreams, Jack," she said, and tucked the flap of the sleeping bag over me.

"No peck good night?"

Amused, she leaned toward me, chastely kissed my forehead, and let me draw her in. Her mouth tasted of rose petals and white lightning. She pulled away, and went about the apartment switching off lights, then, silhouetted against the street glow of the windows, stood as if she might be listening for something. Neither of us spoke—a silence made palpable by ticking gusts of sleet. She was shivering when finally she returned to the couch and slid in beside me under the sleeping bag.

From that first night, I always preferred that room in the

dark. The windows above Dorchester, steamy with radiator heat, appeared tinted by the northern lights—an aura reflected from the blinking neon hangers in the dry cleaner's shop window below. The storm faded to a tape hiss in the background of her breathing as we kissed and she lay back with her mouth open, waiting for another kiss.

"I think we can dispense with the pretense of you sleeping in your clothes," she said.

"In my wildest imaginings I couldn't have anticipated this. Not to be forward, but besides no jammies, I don't have protection."

"Me neither," she said. "Just so you know, I've never done a one-nighter."

"I've been tested since the last time I was with someone."

"You're safe with me," she said, and though I hadn't the slightest idea on what that assurance rested, I couldn't at that moment summon the nerve to ask.

The following evening, when I phoned from Michigan, more than a hundred miles away, I said, "That thing about you never having done a one-nighter, how about keeping your record intact?"

"You'd do that for the sake of my record? I'm glad to hear it because I spent the day thinking about you. Not to be forward, but when are you back in town?"

"How's this weekend?"

"Not good, I'm sorry," she said, without explanation. "The weekend after?"

"I'm in New York then, doing a program at the Donnell Library."

"I love New York. I could meet you there."

All it took were those intervening two weeks of waiting for our initial effortlessness to turn into anxiety about seeing her again. I didn't know what I might be getting into, but I

knew already that despite the lightness of that first night together, her effect on me was powerful.

I arrived in New York on a Thursday and stayed at a
friend's unoccupied pied-à-terre, a fifth-floor walkup on
Waverly Place, around the corner from the Village Vanguard,
where Sonny Rollins was playing. On Friday night, after a
dinner with my library hosts during which I tried to conceal
my distraction, I went alone to the late set at a jammed Vanguard and stood by the bar letting the waves of tenor sax
wash over me. It was a practice run of sorts: I imagined Lise
beside me.

"Still remember me?" she had asked when I'd phoned her
on landing at LaGuardia.

"Everything about you but your face," I'd said. "Still
coming?"

"I can hardly wait. Maybe you're suffering from prosopagnosia?"

"Is there an over-the-counter remedy?"

"For lack of facial recognition? Not to be forward, but a
direct application of moist heat is rumored to be efficacious.
And, Jack, don't be duped by an imposter."

I could recall her green eyes beneath the brooding brow
of a Russian hat, her amber tendrils of hair, the shape and
shade of her lips, but not her face, as if that single snowy
night we'd spent together had left me dazed.

In the crowd at the Vanguard, I felt as if I were waiting
for a stranger, a stranger scheduled to arrive the next morning in a cab from LaGuardia and ring the buzzer. Having
already undone the intricate battery of locks peculiar to New
York, I'd race down the five flights to where she'd be waiting in the cold with her overnight bag. We'd kiss hello, and
then climb back upstairs together. Just like that she entered
my life.

◆   ┏

That winter and spring, I gave readings at a literary festival in D.C. and at universities in Chapel Hill, Berkeley, and Miami, from the book of prose poems and vignettes I'd written while working for the Cook County Department of Public Aid. The book began three years earlier as a record of the stories I'd hear from welfare *recipients*, as they were officially called, which I'd write down at the end of the workday as I rode the L from Bronzeville back to my apartment on the North Side. Working on it had seemed effortless. I'd be lost in a trance of writing on the train, and sometimes my stop would go by before I noticed. It was shortly after meeting Felice that I realized I had the rough draft of a book I had never planned to write. If I cut back expenses, I had enough money saved to get by for five months or so, and I quit my casework job to finish a book that still seemed more like an accident than a gift.

There's a tradition of books that have managed to survive their working titles: *Something That Happened* became *Of Mice and Men, The Inside of His Head* became *Death of a Salesman, Trinalchio in West Egg* became *The Great Gatsby*. My book was in that company, thanks only to its inept working title, *Farewell to Welfare*. I had intended to dedicate it to Felice and Starla, but after Starla's death, the book was published without a dedication. It was my first and, I now thought, possibly my only book, one from which I felt increasingly dissociated. Back when I'd started on it, I had felt there was so much that needed to be recorded in the plain language that people spoke on the street, a language real and by nature subversive, in opposition to the sanitized bureaucratic jargon of the case reports I had to file. But since Starla's death, I hadn't written a word.

At each university that spring, once free of obligation, I'd wait for Lise to arrive. The anticipation was a kind of foreplay.

She'd fly in and we'd spend my honorarium on a weekend in a hotel as if we'd won at the track and the college towns were our Bouzy. In North Carolina it was the Grove Park Inn in the mountains near Asheville, where Scott Fitzgerald stayed when he'd visit Zelda. In D.C. we slept on a rickety antique bed at a place that referred to itself as an inn where, Lise agreed, the operative word was indeed *quaint*. At Berkeley we drove down the coast to the Vision Perch, a bed-and-breakfast in Big Sur.

The school that invited me to Miami had a deal with the Fontainebleau for housing guests. Late in the evening after my reading, I called Lise from the hotel. When she asked about the room, I told her I was stretched out on a bed surrounded by floor-to-ceiling marbled mirrors, and was at risk of being inhabited by a spirit who called himself the Angel Frankie.

"Well, then, should you come down with another attack of prosopagnosia before I get there tomorrow, I'll expect a spirited rendition of 'Strangers in the Night,'" she said. "Maybe I'll show up with something to share in return."

"I'm not kidding about the bed being surrounded by mirrors."

"I'm not kidding, either, Jack," she said.

While I waited for her, I had a Friday to swim in the ocean. The weather when I'd left Michigan was spring in name only. In Miami, the summery light seemed tangible enough to blow about like the rattling palm fronds. I woke too early for breakfast. The surf was audible from the boardwalk and the all-but-deserted beach was open despite the wind. I ignored the single red flag that warned of rip currents, since I planned to swim parallel to the shore once I was beyond the breakers.

I wasn't prepared for how quickly it swept me out. I remembered reading that even strong swimmers, exhausted by fighting a rip, drowned, but that if you resisted the panicky urge to swim against the pull, sooner or later the current released you. This one showed no intention of letting me go. I rode it, testing constantly whether I could swim back toward shore, and feeling flooded by mortality, as if the real danger of drowning were from the undertow within. I had no proverbial flashbacks of scenes from my life, only an eerily calm recognition of the obliteration that lurked at the center of each moment—moments I'd taken for granted. That awareness—however fleeting—was a reminder of the privilege of each breath. Lise would be arriving later that day and I desperately wanted to live, if only to learn what would become of us.

I waded ashore shaky from exertion and far down the beach from where I'd spread my towel. I lay on the warm sand, catching my breath beneath gulls yipping as they Holy Ghosted against the wind. I was ravenously hungry but couldn't move. A squadron of pelicans crash-landed where fish must have been schooling beyond the breakers. On Central time, Lise would be up early, grading papers, still hours from leaving for O'Hare. I couldn't imagine Felice, not without wondering if she was still alive. Those trips to County Hospital with her to visit Starla seemed farther and farther away, a distance Felice could never allow herself to accept. She had written the previous November that she could no longer bear seeing me because I'd once made it seem as if the impossible were possible for her, and she hoped for my sake that, should there be a next time, I'd be better at recognizing the difference between the two, as it was cruel and dangerous not to. She had tucked the letter in a perfumed black nylon stocking and folded it into a paperback copy of *The Great Gatsby*—one of the many books I'd given her. That was her last letter to me.

Lise arrived that evening with her satchel of freshman themes and new strappy green heels. We went to Little Havana for dinner and drank too many mojitos as if, beyond our usual shared celebration, we each had some private cause for getting drunk. It seemed hilarious when I forgot where I'd parked the nondescript rental car; neither of us was sober enough to drive anyway. We caught a cab to the hotel and walked out along the beach to clear our heads. A massive cruise ship sketched in electricity passed slowly beneath a low-slung moon. Lise, her dress hiked for wading in the surf, lost a shoe. I was sure the rip had carried it off and tried drunkenly to describe how, when I'd been swept out that morning, I had wanted to live to see her again. She pressed a finger to my lips. "Baby," she said, "you had a revelation. I had one, too." She told me she'd been waiting for the right time to tell me that a week earlier, while Rey was on a buying trip, they'd decided during a long-distance call to end it.

"Stunned silence?" she asked.

"You caught me by surprise. I hope I didn't pressure you."

"Not to be forward, but that's not quite the desired response."

I woke to dazzling brightness. Lise had drawn the drapes on the morning. She was naked, her small, up-tilted breasts momentarily striped with the shadows of the slats of the blinds she was hoisting. The mirrored walls threw back a likeness of sea and sky, and the room filled with the expanse of the horizon. Our reflections appeared superimposed on light and water.

"Look at them, still young," Lise said. "Don't forget their faces."

◆

By early summer I had lucked into the place up north on a spring-fed lake small enough to swim across, and clean enough for loons. The cottage connected to a dock perched at water's edge in a sunlit clearing at the end of a two-track gravel road that crossed a culvert for a trout stream before emerging from the ferny woods.

The sink pumped silver-tasting well water. The shower

was a head outside; there was no stall. And no Internet—
there wasn't even a phone; cell reception was spotty. A chipped
white enamel table; wooden folding chairs with green canvas
seats; a blue corduroy couch; a bed whose wire headboard
twined like the morning-glory vines that laced the porch screens;
a pine writing desk supporting an Underwood typewriter,
which seemed as archaic as the kerosene lamp that drew luna
moths to the porch. Some nights we'd unroll sleeping bags
there on the porch and fall asleep to the lap of water.

The college that hired me expected publication. I had
applied for a few positions abroad in case my appointment
wasn't renewed, including a Fulbright to Trinidad, but that was
before meeting Lise. In graduate school, I'd published some
freelance features, the best of them about a Michigan vintner
determined to make champagne. The winter day I visited his
winery, our interview was punctuated by the sound of bottles dangerously exploding in the cellar—as they continued
to explode for months to come. I thought now of trying a
feature again that I might sell to a magazine like *Michigan
Out-of-Doors*, anything just to reconnect with language and
get myself writing. I needed a subject that wasn't a city. Weren't
there subjects enough for books on one small Michigan
lake?—fish, frogs, ferns, wildflowers, mushrooms, the sand-
hill cranes that announced themselves on arriving punctually
each noon, the resident loons? How many lakes were named
for loons? I thought of writing about how lakes came to be
named. There had to be stories behind the names. The article
could open with a list that read like a line in a poem: Loon,
Crystal, Mud, Bullfrog, Rainy, Devils, Little Panache, Souvenir, Gogebic (an Indian name meaning "where rising trout
make small rings"). Or I could write about what had become
of the Native Americans who had lived here when Hemingway
was a boy, or about the environmental changes to the rivers

since he had fished them. He'd fished the nearby Black River, but his famous story "Big Two-Hearted River" is set in the Upper Peninsula, and actually it was the Fox, not the Two-Hearted, that he'd fished there. The story wouldn't have been the same had he called it "Fox River."

I'd packed a beer box of books for the cottage, including Dawn Powell's collected stories and her novel *A Time to Be Born*. After supper, Lise would read aloud from Powell's diaries. They were set in the New York City of the 1930s, but even to the trill of night noise from the woods around us, the words sounded as if composed fresh that morning. I'd packed Hemingway's collected stories, too, which I hadn't read since school, in case I needed to refer to them for a feature. The rest were books on ferns, mushrooms, wildflowers, birds, Native American tribes. A subject search revealed a surplus of magazine articles on Hemingway in Michigan, so I went with loons. Their presence on a lake is an indicator of its health. I could taste the clarity of our lake water in the pike I hooked at dusk, fishing from my kayak at the edge of an acre of lily pads, and in the hand-sized bluegills I caught at the end of the dock when they fed at sunrise. I'd fry them with bacon for a breakfast of eggs, potatoes, and ice-cold Heineken that Lise and I would have at the picnic table beside the scorched, lopsided fieldstone grill after our swim across the lake.

We swam early each morning in the company of loons, through smoldering mist that hid the shore. Invisible in mist, the loons glided near, their manic bolts of laughter reverberating through a veiled forest. By the time we were swimming back to our dock, the mist had burned off. The only other cottage on the shore was shuttered, and Lise swam naked. She taught summer school during midweek and would drive up from Hyde Park for long weekends. I'd already be missing her when I watched the dust hanging behind her retreating blue

Honda. On the day she was due back, I'd work at the picnic table, listening through birdsong and the thrum of insects and frogs for tires on gravel.

When she didn't arrive at the start of the Labor Day weekend, I figured she was held up in holiday traffic. We had gone without seeing each other for two weeks while she finished grading at the end of the summer semester. That morning, I'd caught three brook trout in the stream that ran through the culvert, I'd bought homegrown tomatoes, sweet corn, and giant sunflowers from a roadside stand, and I'd started a low fire on the grill so the coals would be ready when she arrived. By the time the third round of coals had burned to ash I was afraid she'd had car trouble on the road or worse. Twice I drove the nine miles to a gas station where there was a pay phone, but got only her voice message. By midnight, I couldn't stand the wait and decided to drive the three and a half hours back to my place to retrieve any message she might have left. I worried we'd pass each other in the dark, that she'd get to an empty cottage. I'd left a note and the key beneath the step where she'd know to look, and watched the headlights coming toward me, wondering if they were hers.

There was no message waiting. I almost set out for her apartment in Hyde Park to make sure she was all right. What stopped me was an inescapable flashback to another panicky drive to Chicago when, shortly after moving to Michigan, I had found a letter from Felice forwarded to my campus mail—a suicide note postmarked from Chicago a week earlier. I had been kayaking on a river that morning, and without stopping to cancel classes or to remove the kayak from the rack on my car, I found myself speeding down I-94 as if, despite the postmark, I could get there in time to stop her. I drove through sun showers; an incongruous rainbow, washed out beside the glistening, flame-wicked September trees, spanned the inter-

state. I went instinctively to Felice's old Bronzeville neighborhood and parked by Banks, a soul-food place we'd frequented,
across from the DuSable Hotel, now boarded up for demoli-
tion. I checked the restaurant's huge windows as if she might be
gazing out drinking a beer, and then walked for blocks, stopping to knock frantically on the doors of welfare recipients
whose caseworker I'd once been, reappearing now as a crazed
white guy with no business except to ask if they knew where
Felice might be. No one did. When I returned to my car, I found
all seventeen feet of my white fiberglass kayak spray-painted
with initialed hearts, obscenities, and gang graffiti. I drove to
the cocktail lounge where Felice had worked as a waitress in net
stockings before they'd fired her and she'd had to go back on
welfare. Finally, I contacted a friend at the police department.
We checked the morgue and hospitals without finding a match.
The next day, when I returned to Michigan, another letter was
waiting that said she was sorry she'd sent me the suicide note
but she couldn't think of anyone else to tell, and she was also
sorry she hadn't been able to go through with it.

Lise finally called around nine in the morning. I'd barely
slept. I'd played our last conversations over in my mind for
some hint of what might have happened. I kept returning to
her mention—only a vague one, but it made her voice change—
of how, after seven years, breaking up with Rey on the telephone didn't seem right; she needed to see him again, she said,
to tie up loose ends and finish things properly. I didn't know
what "loose ends" she was referring to and I didn't ask because
by then I knew her well enough to expect her to be evasive.
Despite her initial frankness, once we started going together
she'd begun to censor her history with Rey. There'd been in
her voice the same uncharacteristically deferential tone I had
noticed when she'd told me that it was hard for other men to
turn her head.

She'd been away, she told me, and had only just received my messages. There'd been a last-minute change in her plans. She wasn't thinking clearly, she was sorry, she hadn't meant to make me worry.

"Want to tell me what's going on?"

"What do you think is going on? You never ask directly, Jack," she said.

"I'm asking now."

"I was pregnant."

"You *were* pregnant? What does that mean? Why wouldn't you tell me?"

"Maybe it caught me by surprise. Maybe I hoped not to pressure you. You can understand not wanting to pressure someone, can't you?"

"No," I said, "I don't understand. Are you all right? Let's start with that."

"Why not with surprise? Why aren't you surprised? When Rey and I began sleeping together I was on the pill, but I went through a time when I had to get off, and he didn't like using protection, so we went without it for years, and since he has a son by another woman I assumed it was me who couldn't conceive. Obviously I was wrong."

"That's not what I'm asking. I'm down to the simple, basic questions."

"You mean, like, Will you stay in Michigan or keep running if you get the chance to hide out on an island somewhere, an ocean away?"

"You know that's not fair. How about more like, Does he think the child was his? Or was it his?"

She said nothing.

"Look," I said, "I'm going to hang up now and drive to your place so we can talk."

"Don't, please, Jack, I won't be here later."

"Where will you be?"

"Basic questions don't necessarily make things simple," she said, ignoring my question. "What if I said I didn't tell you because one morning I watched you from the dock fishing for dinner and suddenly wondered who is that out there on this little hidden lake in his kayak tagged like a viaduct wall in the inner city? What is he doing here, so out of place, trying so hard to fit into a new life he's making up as he goes? And I went inside and opened your book and sat reading it as if for the first time on the bed—all mussed from our lovemaking—and the words were so sad and angry, more than I'd realized, more than the writer realized, and I wept, not just for the words themselves. I was thinking that ever since that first trip together in New York, I've been trying to fit in, too."

"Fit in? Into what? Like we haven't been making it up together as we went along? Lise, what are you trying to do?"

"To give you an answer. Remember that first night in the snowstorm, you came over for a grappa I brought back from Italy?"

"Flavored with rose petals. I remember that night in exact detail. I've remembered it countless times. What does it have to do with now?"

"Just listen, okay? I told you I went with Buck to Italy. Buck always bought art on his trips to Europe, mostly legit, though some he smuggled back into the States. After Rome, we went to a private auction in Amsterdam because he knew I loved Dutch painters—I'd collect them if I could—and among all the paintings and etchings there was this drawing of a hand and its shadow, unsigned, that I couldn't stop looking at. It was as if I'd seen it before. Each time I changed the angle I looked from, the hand changed. At first it was as if it might be from a body that had suffered or was suffering, and then from a body asleep—a hand in a dream—or a hand still stinging that had just delivered a blow or left its handprint on a woman's bottom—it was almost as if I'd felt it. Or a hand waiting to hold an unseen pen, waiting to write a secret message that could change a life, a message I knew was coming before it was written. Buck said it probably was a study for a painting, that its realism suggested the Dutch Caravaggisti—the painters influenced by Caravaggio, who in turn influenced Rembrandt and Vermeer. I asked if it could possibly be Rembrandt, and he said more likely it was someone like Hendrick ter Brugghen. You had to have a dealer's card if you wanted to bid, so Buck did it for me. I paid six hundred euros—more than I could afford, but I had to have it. Buck said I needed to get an expert appraisal. If it turned out to be someone like ter Brugghen it would be worth money. 'And if it's Rembrandt?' I asked him. He just smiled, then kissed me, and that night we—well, let's just say we got intimate in Amsterdam in a way we hadn't before. But when I came home, I never had it appraised, because if it was really worth something, I knew that in all fairness Buck and I were partners, like sharing a winning lotto number, like you and me at the track, and it wasn't until I faced up to that partnership that I had to admit it didn't feel right, not for the long term. Do you understand what I'm trying to say?"

"I never noticed that drawing."

"It's over my desk, in Limbo."

◆

There's that couple at the station waiting for the express from Barcelona. One can guess that the woman is going off alone to have an abortion, but we know little beyond that about either of them. It's hot. The woman wants to try an Anis del Toro, so they order two with water. She says it tastes like licorice. "Everything tastes of licorice. Especially all the things you've waited so long for."

"Oh, cut it out," the man says.

That green light at the end of Daisy Buchanan's dock is the color of hope. At the start of the novel, it seems that hope and waiting might be the same shade. Jay Gatsby, Newland Archer, all those nocturnal citizens of Winesburg, Ohio, hope, dream, yearn, and wait. They wait for love, which is, as such stories go, indistinguishable from waiting for life. Even the sickly Michael Furey in "The Dead," singing in the chill rain, who dies for love, is waiting for life. His ghost still waits. Waiting is what ghosts do. If, in such stories, the wait ends in disillusionment, then at least that defines what it means to have lived. Then there are writers like Beckett or Kafka, for whom the disillusionment is so profound that it transcends the theme of love. The disillusionment isn't merely with mankind but with God, the kind of disillusionment that is by definition beyond understanding. *Our nada who art in nada, nada be thy name . . .*

In Kafka's *The Trial*—where a man, all but anonymous, waits to be judged for an undisclosed crime—the situation is not unlike the wait in Hemingway's "The Killers," a story that was often anthologized before Hemingway fell out of fashion—as if fashion could erase the influence of a style that rearranged the molecular structure of American letters.

"The Killers" is supposedly an inspiration for Edward Hopper's iconic *Nighthawks*, which hangs in the Art Institute of Chicago. There are so many reproductions of it that when you finally see the original, at 33⅛ by 60 inches it seems more modest than one might have expected. Although it's a nocturne, it is paradoxically as much about light as any of the Impressionist paintings a few galleries away. The diner illuminates a dark city corner with a stark light it doesn't seem capable of throwing on its own. There's a counterman and three customers—a man and a woman, who might be lovers, and a thickset man off by himself, who could be a hit man. He could be Death. They sit as if waiting, not for something to begin, but to end.

In "The Killers," two hoods from Chicago, sawed-off shotguns under their black overcoats, wait in a diner for the Swede. The clock in the diner runs twenty minutes fast, a clever detail like that hospital radio that plays only at night. The streetlight flickers on outside the diner's window. The killers order bacon-and-egg sandwiches to eat while they wait, but the Swede doesn't show. He's back at his rooming house, on his bed, face to the wall, when Nick Adams, who works at the diner, goes to warn him. The warning has no effect; the Swede knows his situation is hopeless.

"I can't stand to think about him waiting in the room, and knowing he's going to get it. It's too damn awful," Nick tells his coworker, George, back at the diner.

"Well," George says, "you better not think about it."

I put off going back up north to the cottage until the landlord there—a kindly man who'd told me, when I'd first stopped to buy raw honey from him, that he read Yeats to his bees— asked me to retrieve my things, as he needed to close the place for winter. So on a Saturday in October I drove through the last of the color change, an achingly beautiful time in Michigan, tinged as it is with the knowledge that it will be a long, hard season before the leaves reappear. I packed my kayak and my fishing gear, a duffel bag of clothes, the unfinished piece on loons, and a few of the books from the beer box— the field guides, mostly, which I thought I might want to page through again someday.

Four Deuces

You play the buggies, too?

I noticed you studying that racing form like it's a rich uncle's will. Yeah, I know that look, like it's a chess game and you're Bobby Fischer thinking so many moves ahead it's like he can see the future. Tell you, there was a time I could close my eyes and pick a winner like I was following my finger around a Ouija board. It's probably why Frank that sumnabitch married me. Called me his Lucky Bud—not like the beer, you know, like bosom buddies, like a rosebud. Been years, but back when me and Frank that sumnabitch was first married we lived at Sportsman's in the summer.

Win? You bet your *dupa* we won. Won this goddamn bar.

This place, can you believe it, used to be a shithole called the Verman Lounge? Guy named Adolph Verman owned it. Verman the German, everyone called him. Tell you, I had the birth defect of a name like that, I'd think about calling my place a business something else. But men gotta be the big shot. A primo corner location and Verman was losing money. Frank, to give that sumnabitch his due, saw the potential. He was a dreamer, Frank was. I'd tell him that and he'd go, Rosie, you know the difference between a dreamer and a visionary?

No, Frank, you tell me.

A dreamer's asleep, Rosie. A visionary's so wide awake everyone else seems like zombies. It ain't the place, Rosie, it's the name of the place that's a loser. Picture yourself some working stiff. All day in the foundry you been visualizing a cold brewski, its head of foam sliding down a frosty stein. Are you going to patronize some dump that sounds infested— Verman the German's—rats giving the *heil* Hitler, the bar like a conveyor belt of cooties carrying off your beer, flies so thick you can't see the Sox losing on the TV, and when, God help you, you go to take a leak, crabs in the crapper!

I don't know about visionary, but Frank could be a hoot. Always had a way with words. *Voluptuous.* Who but Frank woulda called me *voluptuous?* Sumnabitch wrote me poems when we first met. He'd scrawl them with my eyebrow pencil on two-dollar bills. I hid them from my mother. What Frank called a poem, she'd call a mortal sin. She'd of had to confess reading them and do penance. Even now, thinking about them, I feel the blood in my face. But I always was a blusher. It's a weakness in a poker-faced world. I had naturally red hair, not like girls today dyeing it weird Technicolors. And the figure that went with it was natural, too. It ain't like Frank that sumnabitch didn't notice. *Bosom* Buddy—real subtle, huh? I saved the poems in a shoe box, three hundred and twelve bucks' worth of two-dollar poems. Mementos, my royal keister! I was trying to figure how to cash them without getting arrested for passing pornographic money. You think those dirty bills are still good for spending or did Frank that sumnabitch ruin them, too?

How you liking that Polish beer?

Personally, I don't think it's worth the half buck extra. Czech beer, that's different, and I hate to admit it cause I'm Polish. Frank that sumnabitch was a bohunk. They take their *pivo* seriously. *Pivo's* a breakfast food for them. The Polacks run on vodka, higher octane, but burns you out faster. You Mexican? You look like a bullfighter with that little ponytail, not that I ever been to a bullfight. I aced Spanish in high school. *Cómo se llama?*

Rafael. That's an angel's name, ain't it? You an angel? Don't worry, you can take the Fifth on that. And I ain't gonna card you neither cause angels never look their age. Here, Rafael, *tak*, try a sip of this. Put your money away, first one's free, kid. You don't mind if I join you. *Tak*. Don't want you having to drink alone. *Na zdrowie!*

Like that, Rafael? Chopin vodka, made from spuds, not goddamn cornflakes. Prettiest bottle on the shelf. Not to say it ain't a rip-off. It was Frank's idea to carry imported *pivo* when all those Poles fled here before the Wall fell. We put up an old Solidarność poster and a picture of the Polish pope next to Mayor Daley. Frank figured immigrants want a little taste of the homeland, so we put in Żywiec on tap, but DPs pledge their allegiance to whatever's cheap. Frank that sumnabitch wasn't visionary on that one.

But he was right about buying this bar, not that we coulda afforded it without luck. *Buena suerte*, right? When we first started going out, Frank that sumnabitch was working at the train yards as a railroad dick, which you can imagine made for some lousy jokes. His job was to keep people from stealing and vandalizing and the bums from riding the rails. Frank was the kinda dork who'd saved his toy trains. Loved railroads, but hated his job. He wasn't the kind of sumnabitch cut out for regular hours or getting bossed. Complained it felt like the freights heading west were leaving him behind. He'd always wanted to be a cowboy. Instead a keeping the hobos off, he said he had the urge to join them.

So, Buffalo Frank Novak, what's stopping you? I'd kid him.

He'd go, That was before I met my voluptuous Rosebud. You know, Rosie, it don't hurt to have a fantasy that if things get desperate there's always an escape route. But that

Verman bar's our real ticket out. All it needs is a coat of paint, a blue neon sign, and a new name. The right name can change everything.

Like magic, huh, Frank?

Presto change-o, Rosebud.

So, what would you call it? I ask him.

Well, if it was a ship, with red sails in the sunset, I'd name it after you, Rosebud, but a tavern—you don't want your name plastered on no bar.

Actually, I wouldn't have minded, you know, the Rose Room or something classy, with lighting to match. An electric rose glowing in a Chopin vodka bottle for a bar sign, maybe a piano playing, or at least Sinatra and the Stones instead of the "Too Fat Polka." But I told him what he wanted to hear: No, Frank, don't go naming some bar, even if it happens to be your dream in life, after me.

He goes, Notice its address? 2200 West 22nd. Four deuces. Could call it Deuces Wild, but that seems to invite bad behavior. But Four Deuces, that's a deceptively lucky hand. A man with a hand like that lays in wait for the kill. Know the odds on a hand like that, Rosebud?

No idea, Frank.

Four hundred and twenty-six to one.

So, we get an asking price from Verman, and now that Frank's fantasy has a name, the Four Deuces, it becomes his obsession. He was the kinda sumnabitch always needed an obsession. It's what got him stealing from the railroad—he was a relatively honest sumnabitch up to then. Perfume, leather coats, rugs, booze, guns . . . He'd fence the goods on Jewtown and we'd play the funny money at Sportsman's. Mr. Visionary would be up to all hours calculating the odds on that racing form. Einstein never figured harder. Frank had a theory there was a hidden pattern to luck, and if you could find it the odds would be on your side.

Don't matter if it's astrology or astrophysics, he'd say, they're both about a pattern in the stars that allows you to predict. That Oriental rug you're standing on is just a design to you and me, Rosebud, but if a swami saw it, he'd know there was a prayer woven in it.

Would the swami know you stole it off a boxcar?

Wouldn't matter. That's why in *Aladdin* the carpet could fly, cause he knew its secret power, Frank would say, and go back to his prognostications.

Mostly he'd get hosed.

One night on Memorial Day weekend, I tell him I wish we were at a movie or the beach or anywhere other than Sportsman's, and he says, Hey, nobody's twisting your arm to be here, and I joke I could do better with my eyes closed, then I close them and point to Devil May Care, a long shot. It pays thirty to one on my two-dollar bet.

Rosebud, try it again, Frank says.

I pick three winners that night, and stop only cause I get dizzy. We take home eight hundred and change for three hours' play. Woulda taken Frank two weeks of dicking around to clear that. You can bet that sumnabitch wanted his lucky Rosebud along after that. You and me, Rosebud, he'd say, Romeo and Juliet, Bonnie and Clyde, Lucy and Ricky, and I was too goddamn dumb to tell the difference between love and superstition.

And Frank was one superstitious sumnabitch. He'd wear the same lucky track clothes and make sure I was dressed the same down to my lucky underwear. You can use your imagination as to what that might be. I knew what turned him on. We'd sit in the same lucky seats along the stretch . . .

Sure, you can buy us a round, Rafael. Vodka's on you, brewski's on the house. Fair? Chopin and Żywiec—a Four Deuces boilermaker. *Tak.* No cheap-ass Beam and Millers for us. *Na zdrowie!*

Smooth, but I wonder am I tasting the vodka or the pretty bottle. You like tequila, Rafael? We stocked tequila when the neighborhood went south of the border. Tequila gets me rowdy. Here, we'll have a little taste challenge, Chopin versus No Way Jose Cuervo. *Tak. Na zdrowie!*

That's firewater, Rafael. Remember I warned you: tequila gets me rowdy.

So, yeah, superstition—we always sat along the stretch. Lester, this half-blind smoke with Parkinson's, on Social Security, would get there early and save our seats. Frank would buy him dinner—beer and a brat—and stake him to a couple two-dollar bets. What Lester wanted though was hot tips, or what Frank that sumnabitch took to calling hot *nips.*

No, I ain't going to explain why, and not cause I'm embarrassed, but cause it's retarded. Use your imagination. Frank could be a hoot, but he was also one of those guys who like never got past high school humor. Anything he could turn into a sexual innuendo he would—not something I admire in a man. Like there was a horse I picked named Whinny Pooh—cute, right?—that Frank insisted on calling Whinny Poohtang. That's funny? Like I'm supposed to go tee-hee at a naughty macho word.

Frank that sumnabitch noticed when I read the racing form we'd lose cause I'd pick the horses by their names. I mean, you see a horse named You Bet Your Dupa, well, you got to bet your *dupa.* Or Lady's a Tramp—I love Sinatra doing that, so you got to play that little filly. Same when they'd parade the horses around the track. I'd play them by color or how their manes were styled. He'd say, Rosebud, don't look at their names, don't look at their manes, female intuition's blind, just close your eyes and pick. But I couldn't not peek. Not just cause I hated to miss seeing, but closing my eyes in a crowd gets me light-headed, like my balance is off. Like seasick. Frank that sumnabitch would cover my eyes with his hands, and then he started blindfolding me. In public, I mean. He wore this lucky tie, a souvenir from the Thoroughbred track at Arlington. It was wide and had a sparkly picture of a horse winning by a nose, the jockey whipping him across the finish line. He'd wind that tie around my eyes so there were no distractions to what he took to calling my deal-with-the-devil psychic powers. I played along. But I knew I was faking. I didn't have no psychic powers, just dumb luck.

Some nights I was on more than others, and overall we were ahead. But instead of getting used to prognosticating, I got dizzy sooner each time, and out of breath. It was giving me anxiety attacks. I'd have to tell myself, *Easy, Rosie.* I'd concentrate on breathing and feel that lazy sunset through my clothes like through a sail, like summer streaming through my body. Voices would sort themselves out of the crowd noise: someone praying to the Virgin in Spanish, fingering rosary beads in his pocket; newlyweds arguing about money—the woman crying in her heart cause Sportsman's was her hubby's idea of a honeymoon; an old man mumbling he's going to kill hisself before his disease gets too humiliating, but not today, no, today he'll stay alive to play the ponies. And some creepy voice beside my ear, whispering just to me, but before I could admit to myself what it's saying, the PA blares, and the voices suck back into the crowd-hum of anticipation. I can smell the horses as their shadows clop by, and Frank opens the racing form, smooths it over my lap, and says in his bedroom voice, "Touch it, Rosebush, touch it like you're touching . . ." Use your imagination, Rafael. My hand would be trembling and my finger would move on its own across the racing form like across a Ouija board. I'd be sweating.

I look flushed? Maybe it's the tequila. But *tak*, one more won't hurt. So it's a little early in the afternoon to be buzzed, so shoot me. What's *na zdrowie* in Spanish? Okay, then, Rafael, *salute!*

So, I'm blindfolded, sweating through my lucky underwear, and it's like I got super-hearing—I can hear the hooves
and creaking wheels, and blood's pounding behind my eyes
like that jockey on Frank's lucky tie is whipping the sparkle
horse across my eyelids as the buggies make the turn home,
and Frank's yelling in his clear tenor voice. It always surprised
me when he'd let it loose. I got no idea even what horse we're
cheering. Some long shot maybe I picked at random. One
thing Frank never could figure was a long shot.

By the middle of summer the special bank account we
opened together for the Four Deuces is up eight grand.

I go, Frank, we got the down payment, let's quit ahead of
the game.

See, I don't wanta be responsible if we lose it and he realizes there never was psychic powers. But he was a greedy sumnabitch. Then, who ain't?

There ever something beyond what you could afford you
hadda have, Rafael? Not just something you wanted, something you couldn't live without. Maybe angels don't have de-
sires like that. You paint, right? Nah, I'm no mind reader—I
noticed the colors spattered on the hair of your arms. You a
painter like houses or like an artist? You do any of them murals of the Virgin along Eighteenth? The Virgin-of-the-El on
Halsted or the Virgin-of-the-Lavanderia on Ashland? My favorite's the wall by Nuevo Ramon, you know, the giant blue taco
Virgin shooting light rays, and hovering beside her's a two-
story-tall bottle of Corona shooting the same rays. I told Frank,
Maybe we need a Virgin-of-the-Four-Deuces. And Frank says,
Way this neighborhood's gone, people see Virgins everywhere—
cracks in the plaster, rusty water stains under a viaduct, and,
Mira! A miracle! And they're kneeling, lighting candles.
What's next? The Virgin-of-the-Porta-Potty?

Frank could be one irreverent sumnabitch, but a hoot.

That me you're sketching on that racing form? Let's see. I

won't be offended. Okay, I'll wait till it's finished. You ever paint nudes? Tell you, I had a figure that made men ask would I pose. I might have, too, if they was artists, you know, classy, instead of some jerkoff with a Polaroid who thought he was Hugh Hefner. The real question in life ain't *What would you do?* It's *What wouldn't you?* Where do you draw the line?

Tak. Salute!

So, that August there's a heat wave killing senior citizens, and on Friday, Frank leaves work like a kid ditching school, changes into his lucky track clothes in the car, and we make Sportsman's early. I'm wondering will the horses run? How can they breathe in a furnace? Right off, Frank that sumnabitch blindfolds me with the sparkle-horse tie and I hit the Daily Double, which we never play. The blindfold's smothering me, I'm like faint, and I hear them voices in the crowd. That creepy voice is right against my ear—I don't believe what it's whispering—use your imagination—and I rip the blindfold off, but there's no one there but Frank and Lester.

You all right? Frank asks.

Who was just here? I ask him, and he looks at me like I'm crazy.

I'm getting heatstroke, I say, and Frank goes, Cool it, Rosebush, I got the next race figured, anyway.

When he comes back from the window, he's got cold brewskies for me and Lester. It was that sumnabitch's way of showing he can win without my dramatics. He bets the whole four bills from the Daily Double on White Owl, a long shot, and loses our wad.

After all his crap about playing names, I can't help blurting, Who'd play a pony named after a cigar?

Frank says, They named him after the bird of prey, not the cigar.

Bird of prey! That sumnabitch and his bullshit vocabulary.

Maybe it was the heat, but every time I thought about "bird of prey" I'd laugh until I was like hysterical. Still breaks me up. Lester bets White Owl with him and there goes all his food stamp money, so neither of them are finding it too funny. I go, Shit, nothing like a healthy laugh to make you feel better, go ahead blindfold me. That cheers Frank up. Hot nips time, Rosebud, he says, hot silver-dollar nips. I can't win without my Rosebud.

Only time I ever heard that sumnabitch actually admit it.

He kisses my neck and whispers, I still get hard just thinking about those pink silver-dollar nips. I want you to go to the Ladies' and take your panties off. I'd like to blindfold you with your panties.

I say, You got some peculiar ideas. But I do it. There was like something about the heat that night making us drunk.

We win the fifth race. Heat wave or no, the stands are full, and the regulars know what's going on. You can't hide a winning streak, let alone a blindfolded woman with 36Ds in a white summer dress and no panty line. There's a rumor the IRS has surveillance going, but instead a flying under the radar, Frank's pounding beers, flaunting our luck, yelling, Yeah, Rosebud baby, we're back in the peanuts and caramels! I'm so sweated my lucky dress looks like a wet T-shirt contest. You can see my—you really don't get it?—hot nips.

Look, Rafael, we're both a little buzzed. You wanta hear it like it happened, I gotta get personal. Frank that sumnabitch noticed—not like you could miss it—that when I'm on a roll my nipples have a mind of their own. When he'd blindfold me, it didn't just feel like I had super-hearing. It felt like everyone at the track had X-ray vision and was looking at my boobs, and big-shot Frank the exhibitionist is getting off on it. I'm in the zone with the voices. One's praying a rosary like the Virgin cares who wins in the sixth, and the newlywed has a crying heart cause she knows she's married a loser, and the

old man's mumbling today's the day to go for broke and if he
bottoms out he's going to step on the third rail, it's like he's betting his life, like all their fates are riding on a bunch of Lasix-
doped nags trotting around a goddamn track in Cicero. I can
feel the sparkle horse crossing my eyelids, and then I hear that
creepy whisper, *Move that shapely ass, bitch*, and I think:
Who are you?

I must of said it aloud cause Frank goes, I didn't say nothing, Rosebush. And at the same time, the creepy voice answers: *Zorro.*

This time, instead a tearing off the blindfold I let myself
listen to what it's been trying to tell me all summer, ever since
we been winning.

You need that shapely ass fanned, slut?

That's what's making for hot nips, not *buena suerte* like
Frank thinks. I can hardly breathe in that heat, and my finger's
sliding across the racing form, pointing to I don't know what,
and everyone's looking at the bitch on a roll with the white
dress riding up her legs.

I pick three straight winners, something I ain't done since
that first night.

Lester's pleading for Frank to loan him money to play, but
Frank ain't listening. We're all in our separate trances. Frank
doesn't take the blindfold off between races so's not to mess
with our luck, and for the first time I'm not dizzy anymore.
I lose count how much we're up. Three, four grand. Frank that
sumnabitch is treasurer anyway. We're in the zone, Rosebush,
he says, you're going to hit the Pick 3.

I go, You always said combo bets are for suckers.

Not today. We started with the Daily Double; we're end-
ing with the Pick 3. Going for broke, Rosebush.

Then he sees my picks for the last three races and chickens
out, just bets a grand cause I pick three horses from the same
stable where they name all their horses Bunny—Pearl Bunny,

Precious Bunny, and Cool Bunny—and Frank thinks blind-folded or not I'm picking cute names again. Plus, what's the odds on three Bunnies coming in first?

Well, I can tell you the odds that night: forty-four to one.

Pearl Bunny and Precious Bunny win their races. By then Frank's hoarse from hollering. His shout's a raspy whisper. He's going berserkers cause Cool Bunny is boxed in eight lengths back. The blindfold slips down. Who knows how long it was off before I realized I could see. I'm so overheated I'm shaking like I got chills. I can smell myself. I smell like the bedroom and I think everyone at the track can smell it.

You mind an older woman talking frankly, Rafael? I get the feeling I can be honest with you, that you ain't someone judges people. Maybe that ain't an angel's job—judging. You just bring the messages. It's all just life on earth, right? I imagine a guy with your looks got some stories hisself. What do those nudes tell you? Probably the same stuff they'd blab about dressed. There's a difference between nude and naked. Nude's like art, but naked's exposing the soul. Hell, who ain't got things they'd strip their clothes off and stand bare-ass in the middle a downtown rather than tell?

Everyone's up cheering. But me, I'm sitting like I already know Cool Bunny will bust to the outside, the driver using the whip like that buggy's hitched to the sparkle horse, like the other horses are in slo-mo, like we're all in slo-mo and it's Cool Bunny in a photo, by a nose, and me sitting there shaky like I caught Parkinson's from Lester, still feeling that whip, each lash with its own fever, and then Frank's kissing me and pounding Lester's back, and we're waiting for the total to flash on the board, and when it does, we ain't just won forty-four grand. No, what we won was the Four Deuces. When Cool Bunny crossed that line, our lives crossed a line, too. We won things we wanted and things we only thought we wanted, and things we couldn't imagine, things we couldn't give back.

If we hadn't of won, that slut, the Widow, never woulda stepped into my life. Oh, I'll tell you about her. We won every moment that followed—like even this moment, Rafael. Think about it. If we hadn't won all those years ago, you wouldn't be in here now. So, the night we won is connected to you, too. We won you and me getting buzzed, sitting at the bar with the afternoon light coming in through the open door, and me setting up two more shooters of Chopin to celebrate our victory. *Tak. Salute!*

So, without waiting to catch his breath, Frank's on to beating the system. He don't wanta pay tax on all that money, and to call attention to all we ain't reported. Still hoarse from cheering, he says, Lester, my man, you're on disability, and black, you cash the ticket, and a couple hundred of it's yours.

Should be more, Frank, should be ten percent, Lester goes, that's the minimum a waiter gets for godsake.

Like I said, Rafael, who ain't greedy? I mean, just twenty minutes earlier Lester's begging for two bucks and a brat.

All right, Frank goes, meet you half fucking way, and before Lester can argue he gives Lester's left hand a shake cause Lester got the palsy in his right. Then he gives Lester the ticket, and turns to me with a fistful of cash.

We can afford a cab, my sweet Bud, he says, my amazing, beautiful Rosebud, it should be a limo. Go home and put on "Wild Horses" and get your voluptuous ass ready to celebrate. And he kisses me so everyone at Sportsman's can see. This is how life should feel every moment, he says, and he makes like he's kissing my ear, and whispers that he gotta keep an eye on Lester, that he don't trust no left-handed handshake, and that he's going to give Lester a ride home to the housing project after Lester gets the money for the ticket.

I get home, peel off the lucky white dress, take a long slow shower, and dab on perfume, Red, which Frank stole off the trains and says makes me smell like a Roman whore—that's a compliment, by the way. I'm like in a trance beyond horny, achy to be touched. Hot as it is I put on the black nylons with what Frank calls the mysterious thigh-high scripture, that he kneels before and makes me raise my skirt so he can read with his lips. I been saving a negligee for a special occasion and I slip it on and check myself out in the full-length mirror, and don't believe what I see. Showing right through the filmy fabric, my behind's marked up. It makes me so dizzy I sit down on the bed. I don't want Frank to see, so I put on a black slip instead. I put out cheese spread, crackers, olives, there's a bottle of vodka in the freezer, and I put martini glasses in to chill, light candles. It feels too hot for candles, though I got all the fans humming, but I want it dark. I put on "Wild Horses." I want it playing when Frank walks in, and I turn out the lights, and wait. And wait. The flames are floating on wax puddles by the time he shows up.

Why's it fucking dark in here? he asks in a raspy whisper.

He's like I never seen him, pacing, cursing, moaning in that hoarse voice. I'm pleading, Frank, calm down, tell me what happened. Where's the money?

Gone, he says, motherfucking gone, and pounds the table, and the busted platter and crackers fly like confetti. Weeks after, I was still finding olives under the furniture. He yowls and grabs his hand, and I go, Oh God! You cut yourself.

God, my ass, Frank rasps. That sadistic bastard sets you up, dangles the score of a lifetime so he can bust your balls. Ever think about that on your way to mass, Rosie? Adam and Eve, Jacob and Isaac, Job, all them set-up suckers. Same story: kiss the Big Guy's ass or else.

I think: *Blasphemy*, which is not a word I walk around thinking. Once a Catholic always, huh? After that night, Frank never got his voice back, even after he quit smoking. It made him a great bartender, like everything he told you was confidential. Women would tell him he sounded sexy, but I knew shouting at Sportsman's he'd lost the sweet tenor voice that made him think he coulda sung opera.

I ain't about to take God's side, but it's all I can do not to mention to Frank that if he'd just paid the tax instead of giving Lester a cut, we'd a been eating Ritz crackers and drinking martinis.

He slides down the wall and sits holding his head, a dish towel around his cut hand, telling me how he followed Lester to the window, just far enough behind so as not to look like they're together, watching that winning ticket like a hawk. When Lester gets handed the money he glances over at Frank and smiles, and right then the IRS grab Lester and cart him away. Lester's yelling, Racial harassment! Jesse Jackson's going to hear about this!

An IRS guy looks right at Frank, so Frank vamooses to the car. He changes into his railroad clothes like it's a disguise, puts on a Sox hat and sunglasses, and rushes back through the crowd filing outta Sportsman's. He waits for Lester to be released, but they got him in some office, and by now the lights are blinking out on the track and in the concession stands, and the betting windows are grated, and Frank has to leave. He sits in the car waiting for Lester, not sure what exit to watch. An hour goes by, no Lester. Frank figures they musta took him away, that Lester probably snitched it wasn't his ticket. Oh, goddamn motherfucker, Frank goes, like he's having a coronary.

I say, Frank, they'll let Lester go and he'll come through with the money. And Frank inquires if I was born fucking yesterday.

You believe it? The sumnabitch who hadda beat the system, the big shot dumb enough to give our ticket to a mooch, is asking when was *I* born.

It's human fucking nature, Frank says, the longer that crip has my money, the more it'll seem to him like it's his. He coulda figured out where I'd be waiting. He snuck out some other exit. I'll have to kill him to get it and I would, but I don't know what fucking slum he lives in, or what his phone number is if he even has a phone, I don't know nothing about him. I don't even know his last fucking name.

I'd know it if I saw it, I say, and get out the white pages.

What the fuck you doing? There's millions of names in there and you're going to find one fucking Lester?

I sit on a kitchen chair with the phone book on my lap, and Frank gets up off the floor to turn on the lights.

Leave them off, I tell him. Blindfold me.

Oh, Jesus motherfucker, Frank whispers.

He ain't wearing the sparkle tie. His lucky clothes are still in the car. So he wraps the bloody dish towel over my eyes. You can do this, Rosebush, I know you can, he says like praying.

I got the phone book flipped open at random. Tell me like at the track, I say, and he takes my hand and in his hoarse voice says, Touch the names like you're touching yourself.

More, I say. Dirty. Like those poems you wrote me.

Like you're fingering that beautiful slick flame in the shadow between your creamy thighs. Like you know I'm watching you do it.

Dirtier. Tell me something you never told me.

Take those voluptuous tits out. I love it when your nipples perk up so everyone at the track sees they want to be sucked, but only I get to suck them.

They're *our* tits. I gave them to you. You like them?

I like squeezing your nipples while I fuck your voluptuous tits. You like that?

Pinch them hard. Yeah, harder.

Tell me how you want it, you slut. Tell me the dirtiest thought you ever had.

Tell me you wanta whip my voluptuous ass.

What? he says.

Tell me, you sumnabitch. Like I'm your sparkle horse.

I wanta whip your voluptuous ass.

You gotta really want to.

Phone book's on the floor, I'm over the chair, his buckle makes this *tink* as his belt slides from the loops.

Mark me, I say.

When the knot on the dishrag comes undone, he stops. We're both breathing like we been racing up flights of stairs.

You okay, Rosebush?

I slide up my slip so he can see the marks.

He kneels and traces them with a fingertip, slides his finger lower. You're dripping, he whispers, and wipes my wetness on the marks like salve, then kisses them. Never kissed me like that before, so gentle. The wicks are flickering out, making smacking sounds like his lips. I don't tell him it ain't his marks he's kissing.

Some crazy night, huh, Rosebud?

Ain't over yet, I say.

I'm shaky like electric's running through me, and pick up the phone book from where it fell open on the floor, lay it on my lap, close my eyes, and run my finger along the page. To Lionel James. I look up the James column for Lester. There's Leo and Leonard and Leroy, but no Lester. There's L James, and Frank says, Let's try him.

It's a *her*, I say, but Frank calls anyway, lets it ring and ring this tingly ring, then asks, Lester there?

I can hear L James shouting through the receiver. Frank hands me the phone like it's burning his hand: "Middle of the fucking night, you dumbassed shitkicking motherfuck." A woke-up girl baby's crying behind her.

It's hopeless, Rosebush, Frank says, and starts to cry, too, his face pressed against my legs, the fans whirring at different *voooms*, me turning pages in the phone book. He's got his head cradled in his arms like he's mercifully asleep when I tell him, Frank, he's one of them guys with two first names. It's right here, James Lester living on Martin Luther King Drive.

Could be him! I don't fucking believe it! Only Lester lives in a housing project. Frank gets up off the floor, grabs the phone, and starts dialing the number.

Better wait till morning, I tell him.

No fucking way. Maybe it ain't him. The phone rings and rings like before, but this time it's a man's voice finally answers.

Lester, Frank says, what happened to you, my man?

Frank's looking at me, smiling this nasty smile the whole time he's carrying on his cheery, bullshit side of the conversation: Those racist bastards, Lester, and you with Parkinson's . . . You got the money? Good man . . . Yeah, you earned extra for your trouble . . . We'll discuss it . . . Don't worry, of course we'll renegotiate. I'm coming down . . . Where you living? They got it wrong in the phone book. No, *now*, Lester . . . We got to celebrate. You wait up for me. I'm bringing a cold six-pack and an everything pizza.

He moved to the Lawless Gardens project, Frank says. They named that right.

Let it wait till morning, Frank.

Can't, Rosebush. Too much could happen between now and then. I got to get it before he brags to some friend who'll immediately be figuring how to screw him out of it. Don't worry, Rosebud, we're still on a roll.

Don't give him more percentage than the tax woulda been. He didn't do nothing to win that money, Frank. Suppose he's already told someone and they're setting you up. It ain't worth risking your life out there at this hour.

You let me worry about that, Rosebush. I wasn't born fucking yesterday.

He loads the gun he stole off a freight shipment. Hand-guns were the most prized thing people at the railroad yard stole. You could always sell them, but this one's a six-shooter, a cowboy pistol, and when he brought it home, Frank said it was to keep under the bar at the Four Deuces. Of course we didn't own the Four Deuces yet, but Frank was planning for the future.

A night to remember, huh, Rosebush? Frank says, and he's out the door.

I got a bad feeling about this. I fall into bed thinking I won't sleep mercifully, too many thoughts, and lay there watching lightning, knowing I should turn off the window fan because a downpour's coming to break the heat, but I can't move and don't hear the rain or thunder or nothing until that *tink* a Frank's belt wakes me. He's undressing. The window fan's off.

What happened? I ask.

Got the money, Frank says, and now I gotta get some sleep. Never been more tired, Rosebush.

How much you have to end up giving him, Frank?

So very very fucking tired, Rosie. And he falls into bed half dressed and he's out, rasping in his sleep like having nightmares, like not just his voice but his breath got hoarse at Sportsman's. I cover him with the bedspread and watch him while it gets light, wondering what he's dreaming.

When he wakes up it's afternoon and we go together to see Verman, and put money down and shake on the deal for the bar. Then me and Frank have a drink, sitting right where you are, Rafael, and Frank says, Look around, Rosebud, it's all ours now. We clink glasses and I see the two of us, Frank that sumnabitch and me, staring back smiling from the foggy mirror behind the bar, framed by dusty Christmas lights.

Never went to the track again. Frank was convinced the IRS was waiting for him there.

The cowboy six-shooter? No, I don't keep a loaded gun under the bar. I asked Frank about it once after we bought the Deuces, during an epidemic of robberies in the neighborhood, and he says he couldn't apply for a permit for no stolen piece, so he sold it, and don't mention it again. That was the first time I wondered if Frank had some hiding place, you know, a strongbox or a safe, where he stashed the stuff he stole—the gun, the perfume and jewelry he'd give me on birthdays as if he'd bought them. He always had some deal going. He did the books for the bar, and there was all kinds of unreported income he hid from the IRS.

The Deuces was doing all right. We were our own bosses like Frank predicted. And our own flunkies, like he didn't—bars are work. He put in a kitchen and I cooked—potato soup, goulash, kielbasa, chili—like that, and we'd get a lunch crowd from the train yards and factories along Rockwell.

I'll tell you when that gun came back to mind—five years later, after my miscarriage. I carried that baby nearly to term, working the kitchen the whole time. Was going to be Frank, Jr., if it was a boy, but I told Frank, I knew she was a girl. Frank wanted to name her Bunny after our good luck, and I said, No way, *Playboy* ruined that name, but how about Harriet?

That's good, Rosebud, Frank says, laughing, Harriet, very clever, I love it.

So that was the name we put on the gravestone.

There a special Angel of Death who comes just for the little ones? God should at least make it less scary for them—send something gentle like a butterfly, so beautiful you don't think it's taking you away forever. As they were lowering the casket in the ground I made them stop and spilled water from the flowers on it to baptize her.

Guess I went a little crazy after that. Nearly died myself of sepsis and when I said I wished I had, they put me on meds and I couldn't get outta bed. Frank closed the kitchen and worked the bar alone. I spent a year in a stupor, and woke up fat and faded, with gray in my hair, and one afternoon I put on a dress, the only one that still fit, and went downstairs and started cooking again.

Maybe I had an intuition, because my first Saturday night back in the kitchen, the Widow comes in. For all I know she'd been coming for nightcaps the whole time I was upstairs zonked. She sat where you're sitting—silky black dress, black nylons, dark movie-star glasses, like maybe her eyes were puffy from tears a grief. Believe that and I got a bridge to sell you. Heels, dyed hair braided with a black ribbon, manicured nails same red as her lips. Perfume you could smell through the cigar smoke. Frank waits on her and she orders Chopin neat, tells Frank he got a sexy voice, asks, Do you sing? And when he answers, Not lately, she sashays to the jukebox and plays "Strangers in the Night," and gets him to sing along with her on the *do-be-do-be-do* part. See, I'm why there's Sinatra to play. I swear if she'd of played "Wild Horses," I'd of come outta the kitchen and unplugged the jukebox. Soon as the music starts, Frank that sumnabitch turns off the ball game on the TV, something we never do, but none of the regulars complained. They were all like bewitched, *do-be-do-be-do-*ing. With the jukebox playing, I couldn't hear from the kitchen whatever else she and Frank was talking about, but I see him buy her the next round on the house. She takes a cigarette from a silver case and Frank lights her and takes one hisself when she offers. They touch glasses and none too ladylike she belts it down, exhales like blowing a kiss, and leaves a ten-spot tip. Never seen her in the Deuces again even though she lived just across the alley.

Our new neighbor, Frank tells me. Nice of her to come in and introduce herself. She's Polish. Moved here from Springfield after her politician husband passed away. Said his real estate company owned half the block, including Pani Bozak's old house. Must of left her well off.

If she got money, why in the hell'd she move here? I ask. Why's she living in a house that sat all boarded up? I thought that place was condemned. Did you tell her how Pani Bozak was found dead with her eyes pecked out?

Frank goes, That's just superstition, dumbass like the kids around here who used to torment that old *ba-ba* for being a witch. Fixing that place up will be good for property values. She said after living downstate she was homesick for where people speak Polish and still remember what Solidarność meant.

Solidarność! Yo, Frank, try Viva Zapata! You said yourself Twenty-second looks like Tijuana. You never noticed how a native-born Pole thinks American Polacks are ignorant? Maybe she needed a neighborhood where she can look down on people, and by the way, when'd you start smoking again?

Just being friendly, Frank says. Friendly's good business.

And who comes into a neighborhood dump like the Deuces dressed like it's the goddamn Copacabana?

Ain't no dump, Rosie, Frank says.

I have to tell you, Frank, it's got to looking uncared-for.

I done the best I could on my own, Rosie, while you was upstairs.

There's a two-bedroom flat upstairs. One of the bedrooms, Frank's so-called office, was going to be for Harriet. Frank had it piled with magazines and paperbacks—*Forbes, Bartender, Wild West, Railway Collector*, his *Best Loved Poems of the American People*, old opera LPs he wouldn't pitch. He was a pack rat. He called it being a collector. Boxes of greasy, old-smelling junk—flares, padlocks, warning flags, signs, bells, timetables, engineer caps, kerosene lanterns. Toward the end of his career as a railroad dick he went on a spree. If it wasn't nailed down Frank collected it. Hell, if it was nailed down the sumnabitch stole the nails—spikes, wooden ties, switches. Claimed there were people who'd pay for railroad memorabilia. So he moves his junk out onto the enclosed back porch along with his desk, file cabinet, La-Z-Boy, and a kerosene space heater from Sears, which I never trusted— every winter in the neighborhood there's fires from those things and carbon monoxide. Frank insisted they burn odorless, but I can smell it. We fixed up Harriet's room real nice. He never moved back.

I never liked that porch. When we first moved in I tried to have morning glories, but the light back there's no good. Not to mention the pigeons—generations homing from before Verman probably, their crap crusted like concrete. I hate that smell of shit and feathers when it rains. Horny bull pigeons pacing the sills, puffed up, making that nonstop spooky *ooh-ooh* like a backyard of ghosts. I asked, Frank, ain't there some way to get ridda them?

He bought a sumnabitching pack a M-80s, and blew off a couple, which scared the flock across the alley to Pani Bozak's, where they could shit up her yard, not like it mattered cause she kept illegal chickens, and a one-legged rooster that woke up the neighborhood. Next day the pigeons are back on our side.

I go, Frank, how about a BB gun or rat poison?

What you need's an owl, Frank says. Pigeons are terrified of owls. That's what they do to scare them off the skyscrapers downtown—set a plastic owl out like a scarecrow and it keeps them away for good.

You're talking a bird a prey, not the cigar, right, Frank?

Real funny, Rosie, he says.

But the sumnabitch never bothered bringing home an owl, so I avoided the porch. It was Frank's new office for "doing the books," an activity that looked a lot like reading Wild West paperbacks, listening to the ball game, drinking beer, taking naps, and scribbling in the spiral notebook he kept in his back pocket. When we were young, he wrote his poems and his predictions about the races in those notebooks. I hadn't seen him writing in them since we stopped going to Sportsman's.

I asked him, What you always scribbling lately?

Just words, he says.

What kinda words?

Words I see going by on trains.

Like what? *Get Fucked, Blow Me*?

Yeah, Rosie, like *Get Fucked*.

One Saturday I hear the opera station mixed up with the creepy pigeons. Usually Frank played it quiet cause opera annoys me. But it's blaring. I walk to the porch and he's standing by the windows looking out, waving his arms like he's Pavarotti. Jumped like I'd caught him in the act. I look out the window to see what he's singing at. Across the alley, where there used to be Pani Bozak's chickens pecking at a dirt yard, there's the Widow's laundry hanging on a pulley clothesline from her back window. What sun shines back there's shining through her flimsy black panties. It's like Frederick's of Hollywood: lacy slips, camisoles, D-cup bras, nylons—not pantyhose—silk nylons like she was wearing when she sashayed into the Deuces, like women used to wear with garter belts. You see underclothes like that and know why they're called *unmentionables*. Everything's black but her bedsheets, silk sheets that must of cost a fortune. With every breeze, her panties wave on the line like pennants over a used car lot.

I go, Enjoying the view?

I was just wondering the color of those sheets, Frank says, all innocent.

Sumnabitch is right—in the sun those sheets ain't white

or silver, pink or peach. They're pearly. I never laid eyes on such beautiful sheets. Obviously she wants the world to see what she lays her rich ass down on. I go, If she's so goddamn rich, why don't she let the Chinese do her laundry?

Probably wants it smelling fresh, Frank says.

That yard smells like chickens and cat piss, I say. And how come she still got the back door boarded up? That place still looks condemned. So much for property values.

Frank just shrugs. Then the sumnabitch asks, Ever wonder what it must feel like to sleep on sheets like that?

Words can be a slap in the face, but that was a sucker punch. Knocked the breath out of me. I suddenly knew, plain as the nose on a face, something was going on. That the weaselly sumnabitch was in so deep he couldn't hide it. He hadda play the opera loud, hadda be writing poems again in those notebooks, hadda be sneaking out at night, hadda ask, You ever think what sleeping on those sheets is like, cause that's all *he* can think about. Maybe it's his way a telling me he already has.

Maybe the sumnabitch thinks after over a year I still ain't awake. Well, that woke me up. I don't say nothing. But my mind's racing about how when I'm laying sick upstairs, he'd taken to going out at night after closing the bar, like walking the dog, except we ain't got a dog.

Frank, where you going? I'd ask.

Just for a walk to clear my head, Rosie. I don't get enough exercise. You go back to sleep.

You taking a shower before going for a walk?

I stink from the bar, he says. That cigar smoke gives me migraines. You know they're finding smoke's a BOH.

B O Wha?

Bartender occupational hazard. Like black lung for miners.

When he'd come back, God knows what time, I'd smell

cigarettes on him and figured the sumnabitch was going out cause he was smoking again on the sly.

It's late, Frank. Where'd you walk to?

Over to the yards to see the trains rumble by. You know I like watching the trains. I miss their smell. Tonight I saw a boxcar go by with RAGE on it, and the next car said RAGE, too, and the next car said AGAINST, and the next THE DYING . . . then OF THE . . . and the last car said LIGHT.

People sure write some weird shit on trains.

If you just read stuff on one car, yeah, but put all the cars together and there's patterns, like messages. The sound of trains keeps some people up. Me, it cures insomnia.

Since when you got insomnia?

Insomnia's a BOH—having a screwed-up clock. Midnight for normal people's noon to bartenders. Go back to sleep, Rosie. Be glad you can.

Go to sleep, Rosie. Oh, yeah. I don't say nothing, cause trying to talk would be like choking. And what if I'm wrong? It's just possible the sumnabitch is so goddamn oblivious it never occurred to him not to ask the woman he's married to whether she ever wondered what it would be like sleeping on some slut's sheets.

Oblivious or not, the sumnabitch don't know I'm on to him, and that means it's me holding the four deuces, a hand he don't see coming from that single deuce showing on the table. I got the luxury of waiting to pounce, watching him dig hisself deeper. It calms me down when I realize it. Gives me patience.

That slut's laundry hangs for days. Who lets their laundry hang through the middle of the night? When Frank ain't tending bar, he's on the back porch communing with it. I start noticing changes on the clothesline—a different pair of panties, a half-slip that wasn't there before. Maybe it's like a message that *szmata*'s sending, reminding him a the clothes he stripped off her stitch by stitch on the sheets they rolled around on and left stained and sweaty.

But then I think, *What if I'm wrong?*

One year all I done is sleep and now I'm up all hours watching to catch her at her window, reeling in the unmentionables, reeling out new ones. At night, I haul the garbage out and stand looking over the fence into her back windows. The plywood's off, but she got those Old Country lace curtains that look transparent, but there's no seeing in. I can make out candles burning, and I remember how me and Frank would light candles when we got romantic. He had an old record player and would play the Stones cause he knew it got me in the mood, and later when he thought I was asleep, he'd smoke a cigarette and play his opera at a whisper.

See, ever since we lost the baby, me and Frank weren't really living as husband and wife. Maybe something changed even before, when I got pregnant. I don't know exactly when it started. Things happen in slivers too tiny to notice until they suddenly add up and you're amazed you been living in their shadow. That night we won the Deuces changed us. One minute Frank that sumnabitch was crying like a baby in the dark, and the next he's asking me to tell my dirtiest secret. And when I did, I told him, Frank, you gotta really want to do it. Well, he got into it, all right. I think he kept waiting for me to draw the boundary, you know? I think the sumnabitch was wondering if there was a boundary in his little Rosebud. Best sex of my life. But we had a keep upping the ante. For him it was how outrageous could we get. Me, I was listening for that voice that whispered dirty to me at the track, only I never heard it that clear again even when I'd whisper it to myself.

We'd given up on trying to have kids, then I got pregnant and it felt like we got lucky again. Only, when I lost the baby, there was no miracle bailing us out. I went numb. When I finally got outta bed and tried to go back to my life, Frank had become like a stranger. He'd growed a mustache and was wearing fancy Buffalo Frank Novak cowboy boots that made him taller. He'd never had a case of BOH—you know, drinking up the profits—but he was drinking now. He'd put a cot on the back porch, and slept out there when he was loaded, which was more and more often. He'd complain in this wheezy-ass voice, The bedroom's too stuffy, Rosie, it's giving me asthma.

No more Rosebud. I was Rosie now, and he didn't look at me when we talked. I didn't know how to get the sumnabitch to look at me. I wanted him to look at me like he looked at that *szmata*'s laundry.

One night there's a thunderstorm. I think, *Her laundry's getting soaked*, and suddenly I wanta see those pearly sheets splattered with mud. But in the lightning flashes, the clothesline's empty.

It stays empty till the next Saturday, then there's those beautiful sheets billowing in the breeze. I can't stop imagining them splattered with mud. I wake in the middle of the night, not sure if I'm up or dreaming. Something wakes me that makes it seem real—alley cats yowling in heat. I open the window to shoo them off, and watch the toms spraying piss on her sheets. I realize I've been lying in bed listening to a song I haven't heard in years: *Shirts and shorts the kids outgrew, your favorite dress now far from new* . . . And I know it's the loony beggar woman we used to call Raggedy Sal. When I was a little girl, she pulled a coaster wagon through the alleys, and people would give her used clothes she'd sew and wash and sell. I look out the window and she's stripped the laundry off the Widow's line and replaced it with rags. A couple drunks are arguing like winos do. They killed all Pani Bozak's chickens with straight razors and now they're having a tuga-war, wrestling like ghosts tangled in the sheets until one slashes the other's throat. He looks up and sees me, and nods. He knows his secret's safe. I wake and think, I been dreaming. Pani Bozak don't live there anymore—there wasn't dead chickens or no murder. I get up to check. The moon's coated the alley, but otherwise everything's usual, until I notice a stained sheet on the line, and the longer I stare, the more the stain looks like a mural of the Virgin spray-painted in blood.

By morning, Raggedy Sal, the winos, the Virgin's all gone, but now that I saw them, it's like they're waiting for night to return.

I start laying out hard corn on the back porch sills to attract more pigeons. That cooing's worse than cats. Cats are a goddamn opera, but pigeons are nonstop gossiping about sex. I dish out corn until our yard's mobbed. Then, Saturday night, after the Deuces closes and Frank's supposedly out watching trains, and the pigeons got their heads under their wings, I light a M-80. KA-BOOM! Wakes up the neighborhood. The pigeons flap around the dark and settle over Pani Bozak's. Next morning that fancy laundry's streaked with a downpour of pigeon shit.

The clothesline's empty all week. It's September, leaves scuffling down the alley from some backyard tree. I figure that's the end of laundry day, but goddamn if the next Saturday it ain't all on the line again. The *szmata* must change her push-up bra and panties twice a day. The pigeons are back on our side. I think, *You dumbass slut, you didn't get the message the first time, you will now*. That night when Frank's closing up late, I make like I'm sleeping till I hear him leave, and then triple KA-BOOM!

When I wake it's getting light. Frank's passed out on his cot, dressed except for his missing cowboy boots. His white socks are filthy. He don't snore, he wheezes through his mustache, stinking of liquor and smoke like he's smoldering, and some powdery smell. I used to love his smell, would bring his T-shirts to my face and inhale before I threw them in the machine. Maybe them meds did something to my nose. I look out the porch windows at her shit-bombed laundry.

Her wash is hanging perfectly clean.

Ain't a pigeon to be seen, not on her side or back on ours. I think, *Maybe I blasted the pigeons right outta the neighborhood.* Then I see the owl.

It's perched on her attic windowsill. In the shadow of the roof peak it looks like a mallard decoy—painted feathers, plastic beak, gold no-mercy eyes—a bird with shoulders, standing at attention, guarding the laundry. The Widow sure as hell didn't set out no owl. Only way for it to get on that sill is Frank that sumnabitch put it there. Meaning he was in her house—you know, being a good neighbor and all, protecting the *szmata*'s unmentionables from his crazy wife blasting off M-80s. The M-80s *he* brought home when I asked him to get rid of the pigeons so I could sleep at night and not have the rain ruined by their shit. He told me, Rosie, you need an owl, but the sumnabitch never cared enough to bring an owl home. He could haul home tons a greasy junk smelling of tetanus—goddamn spikes and lanterns, flares, signal flags, but not one sumnabitching plastic owl.

When I stand over him on the cot, it feels like I stood up too fast. I can see the vein beating in his neck under stubble and smell his wheezy-ass breath. I go, Where's your boots, you sumnabitch? You sumnabitching awake? You left your boots under her bed, didn't you, and snuck home drunk in your socks. It would be so easy to slit that vein. Bet that'd wake you up.

You ever wanted somebody dead, Rafael? People who get through life never wishing for that, they're the lucky ones.

I go in the kitchen and pick up the butcher knife, just to imagine doing it, but wishing him dead ain't the same as having the nerve to ruin my life over it. What I imagine is life without him, starting fresh, selling the Deuces, cashing his insurance, feeling flush, maybe buying beautiful sheets and whatever else I wanted from the bank account we worked like dogs for. Then I realize Frank does the books and I don't have a clue how much we got or where the money goes. Being Frank, he's no doubt got all kinda schemes for hiding it from the IRS. Plus he's gone BOH, smoking and drinking, so maybe he's gambling again, too. I need to find out where he keeps things stashed. I think, *Rosie, don't be stupid, you still got a killer hand he don't know you're holding.*

It wasn't wanting to shoot him so much as needing to know about all he hid that made me remember the gun. I never believed he sold it, cause he's a pack rat—excuse me, a collector—and collectors don't sell stuff without bragging how much they got for it. I figure, find the gun and I'll find God knows what all he's stashed. Which brings to mind the dirty magazines and videos and sex toys he called our props that he used to keep in his dresser drawer. I go through his drawers. None of it's there, but I know he wouldn't pitch that stuff. It's been a long time since I thought about the two of us at the height, me on my knees saying, I adore you. I remembered the night we first crossed that line when I told my dirtiest secret, and I remembered after, Frank loading the gun, leaving for Lawless Gardens, like the sex and gun were two sides of the same coin.

What happened? I asked when he came back.

Got the money and now I gotta get some sleep.

How much you have to end up giving him, Frank?

Frank never told me what happened at Lester's, and I never asked again. Why? Why do you think? Cause I wanted us to believe we were blessed with luck. But I remembered him saying he'd stole the gun to keep under the bar, so why get rid of it? Back then, I didn't wanta know. Now knowing was like picking up the fourth deuce in the hand I was playing.

I get the white pages out and look for James Lester. There'd been a lotta phone books since that night I picked his name out of a city of millions. There's no James Lester listed, but hell, he's probably dead by now. I call Information: no such listing. I need to find out when Lester died, and how, cause suddenly I'm convinced Frank that sumnabitch killed him. It was the owl convinced me beyond a reasonable doubt.

They don't keep old phone books at the branch library, but they tell me the Main does. I can hardly stand the wait till Saturday when we don't serve lunch.

You're going where? Frank asks. The library? That's a first.

The wiseass don't have a clue why.

I take the L downtown and the librarian shows me where they keep the phone books, and after she's gone, I open the white pages to the page where I found James Lester that August night nine years ago. It's like I don't expect him to be there, like I made it up, like it happened to somebody else, and maybe it did, maybe I was somebody else, but there he is listed on Martin Luther King Drive. Just seeing his name makes me shaky.

I page back and there's Lionel James and Leo and Leonard and Leroy and L James with her colicky baby. It's like they're the ones in the present, and me, I'm sitting at a library table looking back from a future that don't seem quite real. Maybe that's the only way you can time-travel—when you ain't living in real time yourself anymore. The night we won the Deuces was real. Me and Frank were the real me and Frank. I have to get up and go to the Ladies' cause I'm losing it. I lock myself in a stall and sob into a roll a toilet paper.

A woman in the next stall asks, You all right, hon?

Hunky-dory, I say, and wait for her to leave, then go back and check the next year's phone book and sure enough, Lester's gone. Vanished. I know that in itself don't prove nothing in a court a law. When I page back to the James column, Leo's gone from there, too, which don't mean he's murdered. I look through the phone books for the next eight years. Lester stays gone. If I'd seen a new number, I'd have called him. Eight years later, L James is the only one of the bunch still there, living the whole time on Forty-seventh. Her little baby's a schoolgirl by now.

There's pay phones by the ladies' john, and I don't know why, but L James's number sticks in my mind. I could tell it to you now. I dial it just to hear the tingly ring, not thinking she'll answer. When she does, instead of hanging up, I say, Hello, Lorraine?

I expect her to go, *Ain't no Lorraine here. You got the wrong number.*

She goes, Who this?

Someone from the future, I say, who wants to wish you and that sweet little girl of yours the best of luck.

She's gasping, Oh! Oh! Oh! like she can't breathe. Oh, you sickass cracker bitch, wasn't killing her enough, how can anyone be so fucking cruel? she says, and the line goes dead.

I all but run outta the library, like they're coming to arrest me, like everyone knows what I'm there to find, and what I just done.

Back then, everything was getting switched to computers. I wanted the library to check their computer for newspaper or police reports. If someone's murdered—even an old sick black man in the projects—there has to be a police report, right? I didn't know how to find it on the computer, and I was worried about the librarian wondering why I'm asking her to look up Lester. I rush out, figuring I'll come back for more evidence later. But I was already sure what Frank did. That was the real reason why the sumnabitch never went back to Sportsman's.

It goes from fall, when you start to see your breath in the morning, to Indian summer, and the *szmata*'s laundry is back on the line. I think, *This is the last time I'll see those beautiful sheets*, like it's laundry not the falling leaves that's the last look of summer. It'll be May before you can hang out wash again. What'll life be then? I think of Frank singing at the window the first time she hung her wash and that question that woke me up. *Ever wonder what it must feel like to sleep on sheets like that?*

Frank, I wouldn't even know where to buy them for you.

The owl on the attic windowsill stares across the alley like we're under surveillance. I could swear once he blinked at me. The pigeons are gone, maybe to some bell tower—St. Paul's down the block, or St. Pius on Ashland. Think they feel homeless? A pigeon's instinct is to return, right? Do they send a dove like Noah did to check if it's safe yet? In dreams I hear the owl going, Oh! Oh! Oh! like Lorraine James. Since I got off them meds, it takes a couple drinks to self-medicate myself to sleep. More than a couple some nights.

Night sweats, trouble sleeping—I'm too young to be going through the Change, and what do I have to feel guilty about? Maybe that's why Frank goes out at night, maybe he really has insomnia from feeling guilty, maybe what he done haunts his dreams. But that gives the sumnabitch credit for a conscience. A man with a conscience wouldn't a brought her an owl. It's like I've become his goddamn missing conscience.

One Saturday I feel the time's right to go back to the library. It's windy, paper flying. I'm not dressed warm enough and stop in church. Not St. Paul's. The priest there's a drunk—

drinks at the Deuces on money he skims off bingo. I go to St. Pius. I heard they got this young kumbaya priest there who got tortured in Latin America for trying to liberate the poor. People say his scars from torture bleed on Good Friday. Supposedly it's always crowded when he gives Communion, but today he's hearing confession and hardly anyone's there—a couple old ladies in black mantillas like mourners, one praying like moaning. What sins could an old lady commit to deserve a penance like that? I've got nothing but a Kleenex I bobby-pin to cover my head.

Been a long time since I was in church. I was a daily communicant till high school. Wasn't I stopped believing, just that I grew boobs. I always prayed to the Black Madonna. Sometimes I could swear she'd wink at me, which is why I didn't take the owl blinking too seriously. The Virgin's not like *black*. Her face got sooty when the infidels burned the churches. But her icon wouldn't burn, and the miracle drove the infidels outta Poland—or something like that. She's Queen of Poland, like the Virgin of Guadalupe is of Mexico. You know, Mexicans and Poles got a lot in common—the Virgin, drinking, lame polka music, a weakness for the color gold. When the parish went Latino, St. Pius traded in the Black Madonna for the Virgin of Guadalupe. I light a candle to her anyway. I'm worried I forgot how to confess, but as soon as the priest slides open his curtain, the words say themselves.

Bless me Father for I have sinned. My last confession was . . . a long time ago.

Welcome home, my child, the priest—his name's Father Julio—says in this gentle voice with a smile in it.

My child makes me think, *I'm probably older than him.* He's wearing aftershave. I'm not fond of aftershave on a man, but this scent I want to breathe in. I've smelled it somewhere before.

I'm not sure where to begin, I say.

He asks, What brought you back today?

I think my husband killed someone.

What?

I think my husband killed a black man.

You aren't sure? Why do you think that? Did he tell you?

The sumnabitch ain't about to tell me. He's shtupping the widow next door. Did I need him to tell me that?

Father Julio doesn't say anything. I listen to his breathing. Finally, he asks, Do you have a troubled marriage? The smile's gone from his voice.

You think I made up he killed someone? I can prove it. Only, if I do, does that make me an accomplice? What's a worse sin: not wanting to know, or knowing and not doing anything about it?

To be human, he says, is to have feelings that can be confused and troubling, feelings that make us ashamed or guilty, but feelings aren't sins. Which doesn't mean it isn't good sometimes to tell them. You can tell me anything you need to say.

I already told you, my husband killed someone.

But you're not sure, and even if he did, you can't confess for him. He has to ask for forgiveness himself.

Would you forgive him?

When the Lord forgave all sins, he made an exception for none. Let's talk about you. You're going through a crisis. What will bring you inner peace?

So you're saying if I knelt here and said I killed someone, like slit his throat while he was passed out, you'd forgive me.

It's God who forgives. I can only help you find his voice in your heart.

But you give penance. I heard the old lady before me crying her eyes out over hers. What would my penance be?

I think you are already doing penance. You haven't told me yet for what. It's not more penance you want.

What do I want?

The Bible tells us, *He who forgives an offense seeks love*. That includes forgiving yourself. In Luke, Jesus says of Mary Magdalene: *Her many sins are forgiven for she loved much*.

Love? What do you mean by love, Father Julio? You ever loved anyone besides Jesus? You ever been married? You ever lost a child?

You're grieving, he says. I'm sorry, I didn't realize . . . wait, please, don't go . . .

But I'm gone. Confession's not how I remembered. The priest never wore aftershave that made me want to taste it. I can hear bullshit about love across the bar most any night at the Deuces.

Someone opened the church doors like they're getting ready for a funeral, and the wind off Ashland's blowing out the candle racks. All the people who dropped a coin, lit a vigil light, and made a wish—it's up in smoke. The old lady kneeling before the Virgin beats her fist against her chest, repeating, *Lo siento, lo siento*, like she speaks in echoes. I walk back to the Deuces trying to think of the name of that aftershave.

Why you wearing a Kleenex? Frank asks when I come in. He's behind the bar with a clipboard, doing inventory. How's the horseradish holding out? We need more kraut?

I'm through cooking, I tell him.

You know, I was thinking, he says like he didn't hear me, you were right, Rosie. This place could use a face-lift. Something to perk up business.

I said, I'm through cooking, Frank.

No problemo, Rosie, given the menu's down to hot

dogs and kraut. I can handle dogs and kraut. You rest. You tried to come back too fast. I'll get the place fixed up nice, you'll see.

Rest? While the sumnabitch is playing the martyr working the bar and kitchen both, I'm upstairs like Sherlock Holmes. The gun he stole was brand-new—you can smell once they been fired, right? I buy a heavy-duty cop flashlight and search the closets top to bottom, frisk every hanging coat, dig through every dresser drawer, check under the beds, even in Harriet's room. I leave his porch office for last. I can feel that owl watching through the drizzle from across the alley. I go through the file cabinets, desk drawers, the mess on Frank's desk—catalogues, bills he ain't paid, receipts he ain't filed, overdue notices from bill collectors, threats from the bank he ain't mentioned. Makes me wonder where he's stashed our money and how he's spending it. He'd be the kinda sumnabitch with a off-shore bank account. There gotta be a record cause the sumnabitch saves every receipt—probably hid somewhere's a receipt for the goddamn owl. I go through the grungy boxes of railroad junk. There's nowhere I ain't looked but a little metal toolbox he keeps locked. It's too small for the props and porn and feels too light for a gun. When I give it a shake to hear if there's rattling, it pops open, and notebooks fall out. Not bankbooks, little spiral notebooks he scribbles his great thoughts in. They're full of drawings of trains, each page's a boxcar with words on it like a long line of graffiti going by: DON'T . . . GO . . . MR. MOJO . . . B&O . . . BEAUTY . . . & . . . OBLIVION . . . HESHEMEHOPELESS . . . I especially remember that one. Maybe it's like a code, otherwise why hide such senseless crap? Two days of searching with nothing to show for it but HESHEMEHOPELESS. You know, that could be the name for a horse—Heshemehopeless, a long shot.

At least now I know his stash ain't upstairs. He wouldn't

risk keeping it in the bar. There's the basement, which I avoid
as a rule, but the next night he's out, I go down there with the
flashlight—the basement light's burned out—and a sponge
mop. The mop's not much of a weapon, but better than
nothing cause I got ratophobia, and the one time I was down
there I saw the dried-out carcass of a huge rat with his snout
crushed in a trap.

It's more a cellar—musty, stacked with cases of empties
and wooden beer barrels stamped with names of local brew-
eries that went under before I was born—Atlas Prager, Yusay
Pilsen, Edelweiss. Piles of cobwebbed junk Verman left behind: three-legged barstools, spittoons, a cracked GO-GO SOX
pinball machine, bushels of coal from before the furnace was
converted. Finding anything down there's HESHEMEHOPELESS,
you know, but I figure Frank would keep it all in a suitcase so
that's what I'm looking for, shining the light, poking with the
mop, when the basement door opens.

I'm fucking armed, Frank says from the top of the stairs
in his raspy voice. Who's fucking down there?

Don't f-ing shoot, I say.

Jesus! Rosie, what you doing down there?

We're aiming our flashlights at each other. He's wearing
his Buffalo Frank Novak fringed jacket, too light for this time
of year, and holding the Little League bat he keeps under the
bar like a blackjack.

I thought you had a gun, I say.

Jesus, you scared me. I thought you were some thieving
crackhead. If I had a gun I might have put a cap in your dope-
fiend ass. What you doing down there? Mopping up? What
you looking for?

Whatta you think I'll find?

Frank flicks his flashlight off.

Maybe where they buried Jimmy Hoffa, he says. Or

Verman's rodent droppings collection. Or hey, how about the last remaining bottle of Edelweiss bock in the universe! Want some help looking?

My flashlight blinks out. I'm standing in the dark, pounding the batteries against my palm, but the piece of shit won't stay on. Frank flicks his on again, shines it in my face, up and down my body, then along the stairs.

Careful, he says, these steep old stairs are killers.

I climb up slow. He's at the bar, still holding the bat, staring at me funny. So, Rosie, he goes, I got a question.

What's that, Frank?

You remember hearing the Edelweiss beer song when you were a kid?

Before my time, I say, and suddenly I'm exhausted.

Before mine, too, Frank says, but somehow I remember hearing it. Bet you remember the Oscar Meyer wiener jingle: *Acquire the desire to buy Oscar Meyer* . . . How much you think the guy inspired to rhyme *Meyer* and *desire* made off that? Frank asks, and pours hisself a shot.

Don't drink up all the profits, I tell him, and start upstairs to bed.

He goes, *Na zdrowie!*

It's flannel nightgown weather. I get the feather tick from the closet. Funny how many winters I took that feather tick down and don't remember. But I remember that night, how even with the mothball smell of the feather tick, I could still smell the musty basement in my hair. But I was too tired to run a bath. I lay there thinking I shoulda found something, if not the gun or stolen goods or the porn, *something*—bankbooks, insurance policies . . . He's socked it all away somewhere—a safety deposit box, a storage locker . . .

The *clonk* of trousers full of keys and coins hitting the floor wakes me. The mattress sags, and reeking of whiskey and kerosene, Frank that sumnabitch slides in on what was his side before he started sleeping on the porch.

Ah! he goes, the homey scent of mothballs when a chill's in the air. How about sharing some covers?

I'm turned away from him and make like I'm asleep.

I remembered the song, he says, then in his hoarse voice sings: *Drink Edelweiss, it tastes so nice, it tastes so nice, drink Edelweiss.* Catchy, huh?

I don't say anything.

Hey, he goes, it can't all be "Wild Horses." You notice how in one song, *Edelweiss* gets rhymed with *nice*, and in the other, *Oscar Meyer* rhymes with *desire*. Think it's just coincidence that the beer that's *nice* goes bankrupt, but the wiener that people *desire* makes a fortune?

I lie still, and outta nowhere the name of the scent the priest wears comes to me—sandalwood.

No comment? Frank asks. Sorry to bore you. All right, then what would you guess is the number of times people the wide world over did it to that song?—"Wild Horses," not "Drink Edelweiss." When's the last time we listened to it?

The whole time he's talking, he's pressing closer against my back, running his hands over my hips, down my legs, over my boobs.

Of all the songs ever written, which one do you think people fucked to the most? he whispers. And don't try telling me it's M-I-C-K-E-Y M-O-U-S-E.

I can feel him hard through my flannel nightgown.

Take those titties out. Still like it rough? he asks, and I remember he'd clamp plastic clothespins on them. He tugs up my nightgown, rakes his fingernails across my ass, then slaps it so I cry out.

That wake you up?

The handprint's burning. There's more coming, but he's holding back, which makes my body tremble waiting for what's next, and I already know once it starts I won't care about the gun or HESHEMEHOPELESS or the four deuces I'm holding.

Did you forget you have to tell me what you want? he asks.

And suddenly it comes to me where our props are, and maybe everything else, too. He took them over to her house.

I seen the owl, Frank, I say.

Huh?

I seen the owl.

Was he with the pussycat? Frank asks, but he stops touching me. Last I heard, he says, they'd gone to sea in a beautiful pea-green boat. They took some honey and plenty of money.

Get up and check, Frank. That owl's looking in at us from across the alley right now. I know who put it there.

What are you talking about, Rosie? Go back to sleep.

I know you're asking *her* her secrets.

He rolls away and sits up on the edge of the bed, and pulls on his trousers. I slide my nightgown back over myself.

You're sick, Rosie. You need to see a doctor. Your head's not right.

How about I know you killed Lester? You ain't fooling no one, Frank.

That shuts him up. The way he's breathing reminds me of Father Julio.

I know you did it, Frank.

How would you know that, Rosie?

You forgetting my powers, Frank?

Your *powers*, if you ever had any, and that's debatable, been long gone, Frank says.

I wouldn't bet on it. Whatta you think the police will make of my powers when I tell them to check their files for James Lester and to match the night he was shot with the records of who won big that night at Sportsman's? Think maybe they'll ask, *Where would an old black man on disability get a thousand dollars to play a Pick 3?* Whatta you think they'll figure when they find out a few days later we bought the Four Deuces? Maybe the IRS would be interested in what you didn't pay in income tax that year.

I hope you haven't told this crazy shit to anyone, Rosie, and not just cause your signature's on our tax returns, but cause people have been committed to the loony bin for less.

I confessed it to the priest.

What priest? Wrobel?

Wrobel's a drunken lech. He should be confessing to me. I told it to the young priest at St. Pius, the one with the stigmata. I told him if anything ever happened to me, you did it, Frank, and he should tell the police.

You really think I could ever hurt you, Rosie?

Whatever would give me a loony bin notion like that, Frank?

It's hard for me to live like this, Rosie. It's been hard for a long time. I want you to know, despite my failures, I tried to hang in there.

It's hard for me, too, Frank. It's kind of like that's what we have to share.

A day later, he's gone.

He'd been drinking all that day. And that night, after he closed the bar, he went out and didn't come home. Drunk, hungover, sick—in all the time we'd owned the Deuces, Frank never wasn't there to open the bar.

That morning, pounding wakes me, a delivery probably. Let them bang. When it's quiet, I go downstairs and unlock the dead bolt, but the bar door won't open. I go out the back, past our rustmobile Mustang still parked with the hood up in the backyard where Frank was supposedly putting on new belts. The open engine's full of dead leaves. I walk around to

Twenty-second, and there's a boxcar padlock on our tavern door and a hand-printed sign taped in our window. THANKS FOR YOUR PATRONAGE CLOSED FOR RENOVATION.

The back porch smells like winter, not kerosene. I can see my breath. The space heater's off. First time ever his desktop's clean, all the papers stuffed in the wastebasket. No note. Only thing on the desk's a checkbook with a fresh block a checks. I look if there's a balance. He's wrote in $22,000—half what we won on Cool Bunny. Money I won. The sumnabitch musta figured he earned half for killing Lester.

Sumnabitch! I've taken to talking to myself, and only when I hear the echoes through the empty rooms and wonder who's screaming do I realize it's me. Maybe I been screaming like that inside a long time. It's like my own voice has become one of those desperate voices I'd hear at Sportsman's. They probably thought they were whispering, too, under the noise of the PA and the crowd and the horses, but I heard.

I check his closet. His old, worn boots and leather jacket's gone and his duffel bag. He ain't gonna get far on that.

Okay, I say, as if wherever he is the sumnabitch can hear me. I see your f-ing game: I upped the stakes, and now you're raising me back, calling my bluff, trying to outpsych who you can't outplay. I'm holding all the cards and you can't stand it. Well, I'll be goddamned if you're gonna scare me into thinking that without you all we worked for goes up in smoke. The Deuces is my place now, sumnabitch, whatever it takes to run it will be worth it just for the look on your face when you come slinking back and see you weren't needed.

Sign says we're rehabbing. Okay, make a to-do list: (1) CALL WORKMEN . . . Like who? Illegals maybe. Frank always said they work hard for cheap.

(2) REUPHOLSTER THE BARSTOOLS, NEW JUKE-BOX, NEW MUSIC, NEW LIGHTS, TAKE DOWN THOSE

DEPRESSING XMAS DECORATIONS THAT BEEN UP ALL YEAR ROUND SINCE HARRIET . . . or maybe not . . . the holidays aren't that far away . . . come back to that later . . .

(3) INVENTORY: LIQUOR, CIGARETS, HOT DOGS, MUSTARD, BUNS, CHIPS, KRAUT, BEER NUTS . . . come back to that later . . .

(4) GET A LAWYER . . . not Urbowskus, Frank's crooked drinking buddy—find your own lawyer, someone with your interests at heart who you can trust . . .

(5) WHERE YOU GONNA FIND THAT PERSON?

There's so much to list. It don't ever cross my mind to put down *CALL MISSING PERSONS.*

Whenever the phone rings I think it's Frank that sumnabitch, but it's bill collectors, salesmen, attempted deliveries, so I stop answering. The mail's all bills, so I let it pile on his desk like he did. It starts looking like he's still around. People pound on the door, so mostly I stay upstairs, cause everyone's waiting to ask questions about where the sumnabitch is. I start a list for that: *(1) Gone to Mayo for his asthma. (2) In Canada, searching for his birth mother. (3) Don't tell no one, but he's in the Cayman Islands, keeping our accounts secret from the IRS while I hold down the fort* . . .

It starts to snow. Telling you about it now, with dust floating in the sunlight and the door open on a summer afternoon, it seems impossible that's the same doorway buried in drifts. I lived in a haze of frosted windows, like being trapped inside a burned-out lightbulb, the whole world muffled. No more deliveries pounding, so little traffic I could hear the planes overhead like they were taking off down Twenty-second, and I'd wonder where that sumnabitch went—maybe he's in a loud shirt playing the ponies at Hialeah, while I'm here wearing my fur coat like a bathrobe and I'm still chilled to the bone. It's a fox fur the sumnabitch helped hisself to off a boxcar because the color matched my hair. He'd wanta go out walking, me in red heels, bareheaded, buck-naked under that coat.

I'd start self-medicating earlier and earlier. I could sleep the day away like I was hibernating, but not the night. One night there's wino laughter. I go to the porch windows. Lacy flakes floating from outer space. Roofs, wires, fences, pavement, everything outlined in snow and moonlight. Our Mustang's a gaping hood and a white engine. The winos have made a snowman in the alley. He's wearing a trash-can cover like a coolie hat. His eyes and grinning teeth are beer caps. He got a beer can snout, a wine bottle hard-on, and a pair a grapefruit-sized white balls. Snow balls. I guess that's why they're laughing. Beyond him, over Pani Bozak's fence, the owl's standing guard over that beautiful laundry frozen on the pulley line. Who but a crazy witch hangs wash to dry in a blizzard? In the Dark Ages, they'd a come for her with torches and a stake.

Gusts hiss off the roofs; the sheets are back, waving in the moonlight! The winos have vanished down the alley, leaving the laughter behind like it's the snowman laughing. Whoever's laughing is laughing like they know that the whole time Frank's been gone, with deliveries pounding, the phone ringing, mail piling up, and me waiting for that sumnabitch to come back, just so I could tell him he ain't wanted, that whole time, he's been just across the alley shacked up with the *szmata* behind the boarded-up door. I been concocting bullshit about where he's gone, while everyone in the neighborhood, down to the winos, knows I'm a goddamn fool. And now, to top it off, he's letting me in on it, upping the ante, like he and the *szmata* are flying their flag of fucking right under my nose. *Ever wonder what it must feel like to sleep on sheets like that?*

Jesus, how I wanted that gun then. How I wished for another chance, like I had that night he came home in his filthy socks, to cut his sumnabitching throat.

I put on my galoshes and slog through the backyard out into the alley in my nightgown and fur coat, with a butcher knife like I'm auditioning for *Psycho*. When I hack the grin off the snowman's face, his head goes poof!

I stand in Pani Bozak's yard staring at the halos on the candles through the *szmata*'s curtains like they're hypnotic. Her back door's boarded up, so I go around to Twenty-first Street. The plywood's off her front door, but the windows are still boarded like the house is abandoned. There's a boot-high spiked iron fence with a rusted open gate, and six steps up to the door, which is unlocked. It opens on a dark entryway. The inside door is locked. I put my ear to it, but can't hear nothing. When I step back outside, I notice that below her nameless mailbox stuffed with junk advertisements there's a latch you can put a padlock on same as at the Deuces.

That night's the first, since that sumnabitch left, I sleep. I wake like an animal curled in my own fur. It's Saturday. Nobody in the neighborhood has shoveled, but there's a twisty, trampled path just wide enough for one, that goes for blocks like it's leading to St. Pius. After a big snow, you can see that people don't walk a straight line.

The church is empty except for the blind organist practicing hymns. Her muzzled dog is staring down from the choir loft. This time I got a scarf to cover my head. No one's praying to the Virgin. I don't even know if Father Julio's there, but as soon as I kneel down in the confessional, I smell his aftershave. I been waiting to smell it again for weeks. If Jesus had a smell it would be sandalwood.

Bless me Father for I have sinned. My last confession was maybe a month ago.

You've been in my prayers ever since, my child, he says. I prayed you'd return, and the Lord sent you. I'm sorry I failed you. The Lord will never fail you, but his servants lack his perfection. Thank you for another chance. Tell me what you've come out in the cold for. I promise anything you say here is protected by the Seal of Confession.

I can tell you anything?

Nothing's too secret.

Can I ask a question?

I'll answer if I can.

Is the aftershave you wear sandalwood?

I don't wear aftershave. What else have you come back to say?

When I was a little girl, Father Julio, I remember the nun telling about a saint who was poor and lived in a hovel, but he had the sweetest smell. Did you ever hear that story?

Probably she was telling about Saint Francis.

Was he the one who had Christ's wounds? Was it the wounds that smelled so sweet?

There is that legend.

Do they hurt?

Is this what you came in the cold to talk about?

Is it a secret? One that's safe to share in here?

The pain Christ suffered, he suffered out of great love for all the children of God. He suffered to give us eternal life.

And when others have the wounds, what are they suffering for?

The last time you were here you were having problems with your husband.

It's not a problem anymore. I took care of it. It's why I came to see you again.

I'm listening.

To beg forgiveness. To do penance.

Christ died that we might be forgiven. Never forget that

he is a God of compassion, not of vengeance and punishment. Can you tell me what you are seeking forgiveness for?

Remember me telling you the sumnabitch was shtupping
the widow across the alley?

Yes.

So, I will tell you *my* secret. Late last night, while they
were sleeping naked, I cut their throats. They woke choking
on blood while I set fire to her house. Maybe you heard all the
sirens from over on Twenty-second?

I hear his breathing again through the cloth partition and
this time feel his breath, a wave of sweetness. He's crying.

Father Julio, is it like the way there's secrets you can't share
even in confession, there's also certain sins you can't forgive?

He's still crying when I leave.

The organist is practicing the Ave Maria and her dog has
his muzzle raised, softly howling to match some pipe in the
organ. I don't bother to light a vigil candle.

I follow the path back to the Deuces. Not one person comes
the other way. I sit drinking vodka like I'm my only customer
at the bar, and wait for it to get dark. When it's late, I dig out
a padlock from Frank's railroad junk, and a funnel, and a fuel
can I fill with kerosene for his space heater. I shove a couple
railroad flares into my coat pockets and step out the back.

Last night's footprints are drifted over. There's tire treads
from a garbage truck probably where the snowman stood.
Over Pani Bozak's fence, the *szmata*'s laundry is still hanging
in the floating snow.

I walk to Twenty-first, through her gate, up the stairs, and
take the junk mail from her box, step inside, and close her
front door quietly behind me. There's no light. I wouldn't
flick it on if there was. I listen at the inside door, and then,
all but blind in the dark, crush the advertisements and pour
kerosene over them and over the floorboards, careful not to
splash it on my coat. You'd never get that smell outta fur. But I

haven't eaten all day, maybe all week, and in that dark enclosed space the fumes jab right up into my brain and leave me so dizzy that before I can light the crushed papers and clamp the padlock on the door, I gotta step out and suck cold air. Finally, the dry heaves pass. I'm shaking.

I walk back into the alley and stand knee-deep in Pani Bozak's drifted little yard, beside those sheets, breathing in the outer-space sky. The sheets are mother-of-pearl in the moonlight and I can see my shadow on them. I don't feel dizzy anymore. I haven't taken off my fox fur since it got so cold, and I feel alert like an animal, one with steamy breath that comes out at night to hunt when everyone's sleeping. An animal with night senses. Everything's clear, the snow satiny like the sheets. I can hear each falling flake fitting into place as it touches down on the surface of all the flakes that fell before. Whoever invented lace curtains must have spent a lot of nights watching snow. *Ever wonder what it must feel like to sleep on sheets like that?* I can see the candle flames nodding yes and no. I lift each sheet up from the bottom, like I'm holding the train of a bridal gown, and pour slow, so the kerosene soaks in. When I used to worry about a house fire, Frank that sumnabitch would tell me you could touch a match to a teaspoon of kerosene and it wouldn't ignite. Well, that's not the case if you touch it with a lit railroad flare. Flames lap from a stinking cloud of smudge, the sheets flame up, and there's a screech from under the eaves.

The owl opens its wings and dives like how it must swoop down on pigeons—so sudden I topple backward like in slow motion, dropping the fuel can and swiping with the flare to fend it off from raking out my eyes, and as it veers off, I stare into its ghost face, into its huge gold no-mercy pupils. I lay there in the snow, looking up. The owl, screeching like it has a stammer, circles twice above the burning laundry, then flaps away over the white roofs.

That's a very flattering likeness of me, Rafael.

You not only got the boobs right, but the nipples. I see when I told you, use your imagination, you took me at my word, or can angels see through a woman's clothes? Don't think I'm so vain to miss that you took off a few years, and more than a few pounds. Made me voluptuous again if only for an afternoon.

You got a God-given gift, like maybe I had once. You know someone's got a gift if they wanna give it. What good's a gift if not to give? Bet if Sinatra hadn't been discovered, he'd a kept singing for nothing. Not everyone gets rich as him or Jagger. I mean there's painters at carnivals who for five bucks in five minutes can do a portrait that makes you look like your inner movie star. I knew right off you weren't no housepainter, Rafael. And no mural painter, either, at least not the murals around here, the spray-paint Virgins even the gangbangers don't dare deface. I got a feeling the kinda Virgin you'd paint would be the kind that Frank that sumnabitch woulda liked slapped up on the Deuces—an apparition in red heels two stories tall and naked, in a fur coat open to the world, a giant bottle of Chopin vodka ascending beside her. That woulda got our tavern some free publicity all right, until they burned it to the ground.

That picture deserves one more on the house. Chopin versus Señor Cuervo, round three. *Tak*. Thank you, Rafael. *Na zdrowie!*

The Widow? She don't live there, no one does. It's boarded up, front and rear. Condemned. I heard she moved to Miami, but who knows.

Frank that sumnabitch?

Weeks after he left—day before New Year's Eve—I get a call from the police in Libby, Montana. A freight train got derailed by a avalanche. Knocked eighteen boxcars off the track and buried them under rock and ice, and when they finally dug out the train, they found Frank in a mangled boxcar. He was frozen stiff so they don't think the crash killed him. They think he got locked in, that he coulda been in there for weeks, maybe since the night he disappeared, just before the weather turned bitter and snow blew in. Maybe he was drunk and climbed in the boxcar to get outta the cold and lay there smelling that train smell he loved, and when he woke up, the boxcar was sealed, and nobody could hear him screaming *help* in his hoarse voice. Maybe hobos knocked him over the head. I asked the cop, What was that boxcar carrying?

How's that, ma'am? he asks.

You know, what was in there—guns, fur coats, cases of liquor?

Can't answer that, ma'am, the cop says. Mind if I ask why it matters?

Could he have been stealing and got locked in? I ask.

The cop goes, No need to worry, ma'am. He says the only stealing far as they're concerned was done *to* my husband—his watch gone, wedding ring, his jacket. Somebody'd picked him clean and the only way they ID'd him was his wallet hid in his cowboy boots. Those boots probably didn't look like they'd fit whoever robbed his body.

I ask what it said on the side of the boxcar they found Frank in, and the cop says he don't rightly know anything about that neither and he's really sorry he can't give me more information, cause he knows from his own times of loss how the little details about a loved one's last hours take on sacred meaning.

I go, Yeah, well, the reason I wanted to know was that whatever that boxcar said, they could put on his tombstone. And the cop says, You telling me you don't want us shipping the body back to you, ma'am? And I go, Hey, he always wanted to be a cowboy, so why don't you do the sumnabitch a last favor and bury him out there on the lone prairie?

For his epitaph, I went with *Cool Bunny by a Nose.*

Tak. Salute! I warned you, tequila gets me rowdy. Tell you what, Rafael, I got a gift for you. Do me a favor and close the door. We don't want someone getting the wrong idea if they walk in. And play "Wild Horses" on the jukebox—A7.

You can feel them for luck, Rafael. *Buena suerte.* Hot nips, just like you drew them. Let's see that racing form. I'm gonna close my eyes and run my finger along the races, and where I point, you play that horse. I don't care if it's a loser at fifty to one. You put everything you got on it, tonight.

The Caller

Let us love, since our heart is made for nothing else.
　　　　　—Saint Thérèse of Lisieux, *The Story of a Soul*

The phone is ringing in the crummy downstairs flat where Rafael lives, ringing and ringing, but Rafael isn't home. It rang this morning at five and on and off all day through the hot afternoon. Now it's after midnight, still sweltering as if the satin nickel moon is throwing heat, and this time the ringing doesn't sound as if it's going to stop. Someone really wants to talk to Rafael, someone who obviously hasn't heard he's disappeared.

That's the word on the street: Rafael's gone—as thoroughly as people disappeared in Argentina, removed as efficiently as if he's been ethnically cleansed, or maybe one of the death squads from Central America went out of their way one night to stop by the southwest side of Chicago and pay Rafael a visit.

He's joined the disappeared, but in the barrio incongruously called Pilsen, a hood famed for its graffiti art, there won't be mothers with the mournful Madonna look, bringing down the government by holding blowups of Rafael's picture—the self-portrait with respirator and nighthawk wings—pasted to placards that read MISSING. At St. Paul's on Hoyne Avenue, or St. Procopius on Alport, or St. Ann's on

Leavitt, where Rafael was baptized, there won't be radical padres risking martyrdom by protesting from their pulpits that Rafael must not be forgotten.

A stooped, veiled figure lights a candle for a soul. It's Sister Two Teresas, who chose her name in honor of both the Little Flower of Lisieux and Saint Teresa of Ávila. Her life has been lived by the words of Saint Teresa of Ávila: *Accustom yourself continually to make many acts of love, for they enkindle and melt the soul.* She once oversaw the altar boys when St. Ann's still had a grade school and now, in her dotage, arranges the altar flowers. She can't remember yesterday, and yet recalls how twenty-three years ago Lance Corporal Milo Porter, the most devout boy she'd ever coached, stood in his dress blues as if they were a surplice, cradling the son he'd named after an angel, while Father Stanislaus dribbled the water of eternal life over the wailing infant's head. And she remembers how two years later when Lance Corporal Porter, missing in action, couldn't attend his own requiem mass, she wept and prayed: *Oh, how everything that is suffered with love is healed again.*

In the years after the requiem, first Rafael's mother deserted—paid off by the alderman whose bastard she was carrying, or so the rumor went—then one by one the extended family scattered into oblivion, until only Rafael was left in the care of Tia Marijane, his "beatnik aunt," an exotic dancer half blinded by lasers, who spent her days painting watercolors of the cosmos and her nights praying the rosary to the opera station. Rafael liked to say he was raised by the spray-painted streets of Pilsen in the way that kids in fairy tales are raised by wolves. And now he's MIA like the father he never knew. Those superpatriots Sly Stallone and Chuck Norris won't be dispatched to liberate him. He'll be lucky to make the Eleventh District's list of missing persons. It runs in the family to disappear.

The vigil candle at St. Ann's will melt into smoke, though at this moment, after midnight, its tiny flame has the locked church to itself and in the darkness emits a numinous green light that has the stained-glass windows facing the L tracks on Leavitt glowing from the inside out. If a soul flitted mothlike, lost in a once-familiar neighborhood, the light might attract it. An empty L, lit by a similar glow, rattles by like massive links on the chain of a ghost. Blocks away the ring of a phone echoes in a musty airshaft, and all along the street graffitied pay phones, most of them out of order and all of them obsolete and scheduled to be torn out, begin ringing. And then the steeple bells of three churches toll.

When a phone rings long enough it acquires a voice of its own. You hear it despite the pillow squashed over your ears or the boom box turned up until the guy next door starts hammering the wall. With your eyes closed each ring is a spray of color—karma-violet, clandestine-red, revolving-dome light blue—the auras of a voice that's as beyond words as the night cries of urban animals—nighthawks wheeling above mercury-vapor lights, chained watchdogs that won't stop barking, a rat tossing in the trap that's managed only to break its back.

Come on, man, fucking pick up.

The call seemed merely impatient at first, like Rafael's gangbanger homey Milton who suspects that Rafael is skimming on their petty dope deals. They'd agreed on 50/50, Rafael supplying the supposedly aphrodisiac, hallucinogenic gummies called liana smuggled from a research study at the U of C, and Milton doing the pushing. *I'd rather huff fumes like a punk than drop that shit, man,* Milton said after he tried liana. *Crazy fucking colors, closing your eyes just makes it worse, jungle cats jumping out of doorways, ese, you call that a love potion?* He thought he'd mess with Rafael's head in return by leaving a warning that the Devil's Disciples were looking to express their displeasure with the recent apparitions of bare-assed girlfriends—phantom reflections on the cracked windshields of junkers and the soaped plate glass of deserted storefronts—that Rafael, masked like a surgeon, had spray-painted along Eighteenth, a street otherwise made sacred by its murals of the Virgin of Guadalupe. *Yo, van Gogh of the Krylon can, when you gonna get that piece-of-shit answering machine fixed? I got a message might save your sorry ass. Why you can't paint nothing but chicas? Do you always have to paint with your dick?*

By late afternoon desperation has crept into the jangle of the Good Humor Man's bells and into the gut of the plain-looking woman who's been feeding a pay phone that rings and rings, then chucks back her loose change as if ejecting a cartridge. Cindy, the "older woman"—she's thirty-two—who cleans condos on the Gold Coast, is calling from the Blue Island Laundromat, where, between the boil of washing machines and cyclone of dryers, it's hot enough to faint. Rafael has immortalized the cracked walls in his flat with a portrait of her dressed in glass platform heels and a transparent gown that makes the wall phosphorescent in the dark as if painted with a spray distilled from a hatch of fireflies. Actually, it's Cindy's body showing through the gown that's luminous.

Where'd you come up with that beautiful gown for me, babe?

It's a web, he told her, spider silk stronger than steel. Once, I found a field of it.

He'd been tripping one Friday night, on his way to Motown in a hot-wired Buick to see the murals Diego Rivera had painted for Henry Ford. Radio playing whatever was hymning in the CD changer, and not a coin in his pocket, Rafael blew through tollgates and kept going until lost somewhere in

Michigan, the Buick rolled to a stop, out of gas along a deserted road. Rafael stood wasted, knee-deep in mist, taking a leak, and suddenly, like a lens focusing, he could see how every weed and wildflower beyond the barbed-wire fence was connected as far as the horizon. Dawn shimmered through dew-beaded webs as if a goddess had tossed her gown over the gone-to-seed field. The spiders must have spun a new gown each night. He imagined all the silk that had been spun since the origin of spiders, unspooling into a single thread with the tensile strength to connect the cosmos. The murals in Motown could wait; he needed to hitch back to Pilsen while that thread still connected his mind.

If she could just talk to Rafael, Cindy would stop touching her tongue to her front teeth. She's calling to tell him that her hotheaded, jealous old man, Darrell, is on to them. Jade, the stepdaughter who never accepted her, snitched to Darrell that when she got home early from school because of cramps, she caught Cindy passed out, and Rafael, high in the shower, flashed his thing before slamming the door. Cindy wants to say she knows that flashing part's a lie, right? Ever since Cindy dropped some weight and started to fix herself up and feel alive again, Jade's been competing with her. Her stepdaughter's got a dirty mouth and each morning is a battle to keep her from going to school dressed like a slut. Darrell called them both whores, smacked them around, and punched Cindy in the stomach so she still can't breathe. So Jade has run away from home and Cindy's calling from the *lavanderia* on Blue Island because she's got nowhere else to go. Her front teeth are chipped and her lip split where it collided with his wedding band. She hasn't worked up the courage to look in the mirror, and oh, babe, Darrell slammed the clip into his army .45 and is looking for you.

And if it's not Cindy then maybe it's that walking hunger

strike Brianna, calling because someone's spreading evil rumors, saying that she caught needle disease, and she hopes it
hasn't soured their relationship because it isn't true. Okay,
there was that one time he told her she owed him a twenty for
the Zithromax he had to take, and maybe she *has* been looking a little faded lately, sleeping all day, but that's because
she's been depressed that things between them haven't been
going well, and when he disappears as if he never wants to
talk to her again it makes her terminally anxious. She wonders if he isn't answering because he knows it's her calling.
Sometimes she's convinced that Rafael's got telepathy, a way
of getting inside your mind that feels intimate until he uses
your own thoughts against you. *Oh, baby, don't make me
keep calling and calling when all I need to ask is a single question: Am I still the little* maja *posing on your bedroom wall,
Sleeping Beauty drifting on the crystal ship of your mattress
down the wavy, black river of her unloosed hair? I been growing it out for you. It grows twice as fast when I'm asleep.*

There's a lull after supper when what's left of the day filters
through the dusty blinds. Each slat is a ray—runway-blue,
mescalito-violet, replicant-red. Above a horizon of tracks
where L trains hurtle past looking as if they've been tagged
while moving, the sky reverberates around a sinking fireball.
The phone can no longer hide its utter lack of control. It re-
peats itself, a soprano practicing scales, in the airshaft, roust-
ing pigeons, like the voice of that biker, face half hidden by
the visor on the black helmet, who cruised the hood photo-
graphing murals. Stomper boots, black leather jeans, jacket
scarred by zippers, KA-BAR knife slung from a tread belt—
the full macho, but he didn't move like a guy. Then, on a night
of record-breaking heat, the biker rumbles up wearing a tank
top that reads SERA OUTLAW and shows off her underarm hair

and nipples punctuating white cotton as she bumps the custom red Harley with its vanity plate over the curb and parks it on the sidewalk. Her arms look pumped. A chartreuse luna moth has alighted on one shoulder blade. On the other, there's a symbol that could be a ram's horns or a rune from an ancient alphabet, welted up raw so that you wonder if she hit high C when she was branded. She pays the kids hanging out in front a buck each to watch her bike. Until then, she was the *he* they'd nicknamed Mr. *Mariposa*. Seeing her in the tank top, with her green moth tat, she's rechristened Madame Moth.

Not like she cares. She saunters to the corner, buys a snow cone from the old vendor who doesn't scoop crushed ice, but shaves it off a block kept cold beneath a canvas as it was done in the country where he was a child. Yellowjackets swarm his bottles of tropical flavors. Madame Moth orders electric-blue syrup that tastes like no flavor in nature. Beneath the black visor, her lips at the melting edge of the paper cone turn frostbite-blue. Not pausing to drop her change into the sombrero of the blind accordion man pumping conjunto, she strolls back as if the only reason she's come to the barrio is for a snow cone and, without raising the visor, vanishes through the doorway and up the stairs into the building's ripe, unlit corridors.

It's not long—time enough to finish the cone, maybe for a toke or two, or to snort a line or huff fumes or chew one of those spooky gummies Rafael deals—before the airshaft echoes a chant that has renounced words, but not meaning. The city is full of people who can't understand one another's language but get the meaning—like listening to opera when all you have to go on is the pure emotion of the voice. Her voice sounds naked, and though the kids outside mock it, they know they're listening to a sin.

If in the stifling heat Rafael put on his respirator and painted only her streak of voice, he wouldn't have to worry about finding the space on his walls to fit in a life-sized portrait of Sera Outlaw from the burbs, slumming on a pricey Harley, in her defiantly arrested *Wild One* getup. The portraits of the women from the hood who have staked out a place on the walls feel it's already overcrowded. They don't need Sera Outsider playing let's pretend. Maybe there's a patch of peeling plaster beneath the sink in the cramped john with its roaches and running toilet where Rafael could squeeze in a still life: the black helmet draped with a Victoria's Secret cinnabar thong, weighting down the tank top, leather trou, knife, belt, stompers, piled on the buckled linoleum.

The women see themselves reflected on Madame Moth's visor. They can't see her face. They wonder how they look to her, if she's able to see beyond her own reflection. The women's eyes don't blink, never close, don't sleep—even Sleeping Beauty's eyes are painted open. Night is when they're most awake. They watch over the dreaming artist tossing on a sweat-stained mattress surrounded by melted candle stubs. Their lips are parted as if they're about to moan, pray, or whisper a lullaby, but he's left them mute, a limitation they were unaware of until now as they silently listen to the yearning voice amplified by the airshaft. To paint her voice, Rafael would need to feather the spray into the icy impression of her lips; he'd need a hue that matched the unnatural taste of the blue nectar that's soaked into the tongue she licks along his body.

Sera Outlaw has her own ideas of what he'll paint. She's discussed the fantasies that haunt her at obsessive length with her shrink, Dr. Fallon, for whom talk is decidedly *not* cheap. "You need to work through them. Life is risk: experiment," he's counseled her. "When you'll instinctively recognize the right one, it will shake you to the core." If her fantasies could be perfectly realized outside the secret cell of her mind, then perhaps she could separate from them.

Pose me as a queen blindfolded at the wild border of a realm I once ruled, bind me to a signpost to be abused by passing wanderers who care only for their own pleasure; paint me as the desecrated, living statue of a goddess, a deity from a shattered urn in a temple defiled by barbarians—brutish-looking men have always turned me on. Paint me as Saint Teresa in Ecstasy, or as Joan of Arc, stripped of armor and, threatened with punishment, flaring colors as if the mattress she's staked to is a stained-glass window in the cathedral at Rouen.

"Where?"

"France."

"There's not enough wall space. I'll have to make up a big canvas."

"No, I want it to be a mural locked away in this room. I'll need a key to visit it. You can whitewash the walls, paint over the others. You did them free, right? I'll pay."

The voiceless women on the walls have begun to scream.

"It'll be your first commission. Paint the walls the white of a bride's veil. Obliterate the skanks, then call me. It'll be a new start for both of us. I'll be your masterpiece."

She returns during Fiesta del Sol, a time in August when Pilsen is baubled in lights. Blue Island Avenue closes from Eighteenth to Twenty-first Streets—three congested blocks of carnival rides whirling to mechanical mariachi music. A Ferris wheel, tall enough to reflect its luster along a shadowy church spire, rotates hypnotically. A ring has been erected in which masked *luchadores* wrestle in the way that life and death are locked in daily combat. There are galleries for games of chance, booths where fortunes are told, concession stands, and food stalls. A spicy haze from grilling chorizos smolders in the beam of an enormous searchlight battered by moths. For five tickets you can pan the beam along the undercarriage of clouds or off the skyline of downtown. When firecrackers start popping like a drive-by, no one dives for cover.

Blocks away, inside St. Ann's, a vigil candle strobes as it sputters in melted wax and the bullet-pocked stained-glass windows flicker.

Stumbling back to his flat, buzzed on a cocktail of liana and mescal, Rafael notices the red Harley parked on the sidewalk. He looks up and down the empty street. Everyone not asleep, including the snow-cone vendor and the accordion man, must be at the fiesta. Rafael climbs the dark stairs yodeling out *gritos* in a soulful *yi-yi-yi!* Ordinarily, he's quiet, tight-lipped. Perhaps he has confused his flirting with a fortune-teller for feeling intimations of the future. When the fortune-teller asked to read his palm, Rafael told her he was sorry, but he didn't have the five tickets that seeing the future cost. She caught his wrist and pulled him close. "For you, a free sample," she said. Smiling at his handsome face, she turned his palm over and traced its lines, before jerking her finger back as if she'd been shocked. Or as if she had seen too many cheesy movies where a phony gypsy fakes the same theatrical response— which is what Rafael told her.

"If you don't believe in telling the future, do you believe in telling the past? The past is just as secret and mysterious," she said. "But I can read what's hidden in your eyes."

"I'm listening," he said.

"You are hiding twelve tickets. If your first fortune didn't please you, you'd of had enough tickets left to buy a completely new one. Only a fool thinks he can deceive a Roma."

Rafael laughed, reached in his pocket, and dropped a handful of tickets on the counter before her.

"Too late," she told him. "Once you miss your chance you can give all you got, but won't catch fate's attention again."

"I guess it's good night, then," he said.

"Don't go without this," she said, and handed him the key to his flat. "You just tried to give it away along with your tickets. You're drunk, angel."

"So are you," he said, and leaned into the booth to kiss her.

"I told you, it's too late," she said. "Even a kiss that will be my first thought in the morning won't matter."

In the dark hallway, at the door of his flat, Rafael searches his jeans for the key. He knows the fortune-teller returned it. He can summon the cinnamon taste of her mouth. She must have been eating churros. The key is in his shirt pocket where he never puts it.

"Somebody had a fun fiesta," Sera Outlaw says. "How come you didn't invite me? We could've held hands on the Ferris wheel. I've been waiting for you to call, I can't say patiently. Any idea what that feels like—waiting when you really want something, when you can't stop thinking about it, and the more you obsess, the more you need it?"

He unlocks the door and she follows him into the dark flat and strikes a match to light the twist of a joint. The eyes on the walls reflect the flame of the match. Cindy's transparent gown glimmers. "They're still all here," she says. "Did you even get the fucking whitewash?"

"Been busy." He accepts the joint, sucks the smoke, and holds it in.

"Don't turn on the light," she says. "Creeps me out when roaches run for cover." She strikes matches until all the candle stubs ringed around the mattress are flickering.

Down the street, L trains traveling from opposite directions, jammed with fiesta revelers, arrive with a simultaneous screech at the muraled Leavitt station. The station's stairs and their risers are a mosaic waterfall. After the trains racket off, regular street noise passes for quiet.

"Your bitches don't like me," she says, "and I don't appreciate the way they're glaring at my tits. You're their master, make them disappear."

"I'm no one's master—including my own."

"Don't get vanilla on me, Rafael. How old are you? Twenty-one? I told you I'll pay. What's holding things up? You fall in love with your own creations, your own fantasies? They demand allegiance, don't they? Hard to let go. It's lonely without them adoring you, waiting when you come home at night. Look at the cummy stains on this mattress!"

She inhales as if sighing and lazily passes him the joint, and then, before he can react, draws her knife and flings it into Sleeping Beauty.

"Whoa!" he says, exhaling smoke.

"No scream? Blood should be gushing down the wall, puddling the floor. You got to get your red paint out if you want to see that. So, okay, no more passivity, we're going to have a little private fiesta of wall-cleaning."

She springs up, yanks the knife from Sleeping Beauty's heart, and jams it into the painting's face, then wheels into a practiced kickboxing move, and the heel of her stomper boot caves in one of Sleeping Beauty's plaster breasts. She's balletic in her fury. Rafael finishes the joint, while watching from the mattress what looks like a cardio routine run amok. She jabs, whirls, slashes, kicks, and plunges the knife, working herself into a breathless tantrum of destruction. Good thing whoever lives next door is probably at the fiesta.

On Blue Island, the Ferris wheel is stuck. Couples lean over the sides of their gondolas shouting, "Yo, get us down!" A carny worker shouts up, "Remain seated, please! Do not try climbing out!" "Yo, we going to have to fucking spend the night up here or what?" "No need to panic. The fire department is on the way!" It's a still, sultry night, and the gondola at the very top—nearly the height of the steeple—has started to stir in the rhythmic way that lovers can get a parked car rocking. It catches the attention of a few people in the crowd. They're pointing up.

Tonight, Sera Outlaw is a warrior—Joan of Arc, stripped of armor and waiting to suffer further indignities. Twisted coat hangers secure her ankles and bind her arms over her head. On the mattress beside her, Rafael sits baking one end of a straightened wire hanger over a candle. Along with the scent of weed and melted wax, and the musty updraft of the airshaft, the flat has acquired an acrid, metallic smell.

"What do you think you're doing with that?" she asks. "Get your paints."

"Too bad I'm out of marshmallows."

"That's a guy crack. I took you for someone who could get into the drama. You think the saints didn't know submission's how you get the attention we crave from God?"

"I'm setting the mood," he says. "You told me when they threatened her, she like got off in Technicolor."

"I don't play with fire—at least not that way."

"Somebody did," he says, and gently lowers his lips to the brand on her shoulder.

"That was an initiation. I'm an Aries. Untie me, I mean fucking now."

Instead, he blindfolds her with her white tank top. He fastens his mouth over hers, and then touches the tip of the clothes hanger to the luna moth. It's not the end that he's heated, but she screams with a force that makes him swallow as if she's filled his mouth with electric-blue syrup. Her teeth clench on his lower lip and he hollers back.

On Blue Island, a kid who's spent his last five tickets on the searchlight instead of buying a taco has trained the beacon

on the gondola at the top of the stalled Ferris wheel. The dazzling beam doesn't inhibit the couple who's up there. They've
ducked down and must be lying together flat on the bench
seat, and can't be seen from the ground. Still, the spotlight
has made them stars—daring acrobats without a net, determined to put on a show. The gondola rocks recklessly, desperately, as their grand performance builds to a climax against
the night sky. The crowd below cheers, even as sirens wail and
the fire trucks run red lights down Eighteenth toward the fiesta. The firemen will be here any moment with their axes,
bullhorns, and ladders. No one in the crowd is leaving until a
ladder rises as it would to a blazing tenement window and, to
riotous applause, the couple climb out and begin their de-
scent back to the ordinary world.

Rafael presses her white tank top to his bloody mouth. "I
was just messing with you," he says. "You bit through my lip,
you goddamn flake. Look what you did to my walls."

"Untie me, you crazy dick. Do you know who you're fucking with? I'm like totally connected. You have any idea who
my uncle is?"

"You're the one came to me to get painted. You don't have
to pay. I work better free."

He slips on his respirator, conscious of his swollen lip,
and, careful of her bound legs kicking at his balls, fits her vi-
sored helmet over her coral Mohawk while she spits nonstop
curses. He starts with her bare feet: sprays them alchemy-
gold. The black stompers standing beside the mattress get a
coat of rubber-ducky yellow. Candy-cane stripes twirl up her
legs and polka dots float from navel to the Cousteau-blue ruff
inspired by her tongue. On the back of her helmet he paints a
cherry-red honker and a white-lipped, watermelon-slice smile
from which a blue tongue sticks out at the world. When she's
on the bike, a clown will appear to be looking backward.

Raphael takes the precaution of dislodging the knife from where she's rammed it into one of Cindy's eyes after the spiderweb gown resisted her attempts to hack it to shreds.

"Even though you're about as convincing a badass as Michael Jackson, something tells me it would be a mistake to return your blade just now," he says. "Sorry I don't have something to swap for it like a rubber horn to honk on your Harley."

"I'll be back for it with a nine-mil to honk up your ass, and not by myself, either. You just used up all your lives in one fucking evening."

On Blue Island, the aerial ladder truck has successfully completed its rescue of all the couples on the Ferris wheel. By the time the ladder cranked to the top of the wheel, the highest gondola was hanging motionless, becalmed on the still night air. The crowd stared up, waiting for the disheveled, daredevil lovers to emerge. They would become fiesta legends, a Romeo and Juliet crisscrossed by beacons, their suspended, pearlescent boat sailing past the suffering Christs on all the steeples in the city, afloat on dark matter with novas exploding like flak, and the infinite blackness decaled with skyrockets and gold-glitter comets. Actually, when a fireman reached their gondola, they were gone. Where, who can say? Maybe the rocking gondola had been an optical illusion—a gentle sway in an indiscernible breeze—as seen from below. A few measly skyrockets pop and parachute down on Pilsen, a signal that the fiesta is over for tonight. Bulbs blink off in the shuttered stalls. With the mechanical mariachi music silenced, it's possible to hear the accordion. The snow-cone vendor pushes his cart along Eighteenth dragging a trail of melted ice.

Alchemy-gold footprints trail down the stairs and out the doorway. Her motorcycle is parked illegally on the sidewalk where she left it. Some joker returning from the fiesta in a party mood has tied a pink heart-shaped balloon to its handlebars. The streets resound with the pipes-and-tambourine laughter of blitzed revelers heading toward the L station. The searchlight, shooting from Blue Island, sweeps along the apartment buildings. A painted woman sits on her motorcycle, staring up as the beam crosses Rafael's dark third-story window. He stands half naked, looking out, the bluish beam smoldering with the smoke of his cigarette, each slat in the blinds a slash along his body.

"You motherfucker," she yells at the window, in a voice nothing like that soprano in the airshaft, "I'm coming back packing, when you least expect it. You're going to beg. You're already a dead man, asshole." She revs her bike as if the snarling engine knows words she can't find and guns along the sidewalk, sending revelers jumping out of the way and shouting at the goofy face looking back at them, *"Pendeja loca!"*

The whine of the engine grows increasingly distant but refuses to disappear, as if someone were riding in furious, self-destructive circles at the edge of consciousness, a 500cc Buell Blast boring into sleep, invading dreams, and morphing into the ringing of a phone.

Squash a sweaty pillow over your ears, but the reverberations continue. The call is no longer pleading. When it's hopeless to plead, there's rage. When it was hopeless to rage, Rafael stood staring at the mattress he no longer could lie on. The silhouette of her body was visible, shaped by the pointillist spray around it, like the impression of a body chalked on a sidewalk by police. He lugged the mattress to the bathtub, squirted it with lighter fluid, watched the flames ignite and wither. When the bathroom filled with smoke, he turned on the water taps, and sat beside the airshaft window.

He wasn't going to sleep anyway, so why not stuff some clothes in the backpack with his paints and, from the can of bandages, take the skinny tube of dope-deal dollars and,

checking that the street is empty, walk off? The extension
lamp of a mechanic working on the Ferris wheel to the wheeze
of an accordion illuminates the street behind. The street
ahead is unlit as if there were a power outage. It must be that
the strobing vigil light in St. Ann's has guttered out. Still,
within the darkened sanctuary, the resident saints and angels
continue their supplications. *One must not think that a person who is suffering is not praying. Oh, how everything that is
suffered with love is healed again.*

Wait alone on the L platform for an empty night train, the
kind of train that clatters through sleep, a train boarded by
nightmares and dreams masked like *luchadores,* indistinguishable from one another in their babushkas, fedoras, respi-
rators, and dark glasses. When it reaches the end of the line it
won't stop. It goes by I'm Sorry Street, by Forgive Me Avenue,
by Fucked Up Again Boulevard. By the time it passes What
Have I Done, it's traveling too fast. Maybe this once it will
hurtle by fate and you'll be free. And then what? Rafael might
have boarded that train, if he could have thought of where to
get off.

Listen, the telephone, driven mad with rejection, doesn't
even want to be answered any longer. It is like an alarm that,
rather than a warning, wishes to be the thing it's warning
against—a break-in or a fire burning out of control. The caller's
ring is like an ambulance siren that wants to be the accident
itself—a head-on collision or a hit-and-run, a mugging, a
drive-by.

The women on the wall with their hacked faces and staved-
in bodies hear it ring but don't answer. Maybe they are calling
themselves. Cindy locked for the night in the laundromat, too
weak with internal bleeding to speak, or her lost daughter, Jade,
calling Rafael's number in the hope that her stepmother
might answer, or Brianna, OD'd on pills, calling to say *adiós*
through the plastic bag she's pulled over her head, or Rafael's

old *tia*, who holds the receiver to the radio so for once in his life he can hear Pavarotti hit that high C in *Turandot*, or his mother calling to say that his half brother, Gabriel, was stillborn, or his father calling from Hanoi; nuns, priests, teachers, cops, parole officers, social workers, the Devil's Disciples, Darrell, all in a snaky line waiting before a gutted pay phone for their turn.

Now that it's gone on long enough to assume a life of its own, the call never wants to stop. It's too late for talk now anyway, and if someone, anyone, answered, suddenly picked up the receiver and said hello, there'd be no answer in return.

"Hello? Hello . . . who is this? Who the fuck are you? What fucking business do you have calling and calling at this hour? Don't you get it: nobody's fucking home."

Not even the breath of an obscene breather. Only silence.

"After all that fucking ringing, say something . . . anything . . . please, talk to me."

Oceanic

It was probably fair to say, as beachgoers did, that the Lifeguard had returned to duty too soon. Though the shark attack occurred long ago, his wounds had yet to heal. Was it to compensate for his reduced physical stature that his guard tower rose higher than such structures normally did? Its ointment-white paint peeled like a sunburn. Sunbathers avoided the shadow it cast across the sand, not to mention the furrowed trail of rusted blood between the chair and the water. After the beaches closed on Labor Day, and the crew of lifeguards turned in their emergency-orange tank tops and went back to school or to less glamorous jobs, he remained behind with the ghost crabs and shorebirds. The prints of terns and sandpipers mottled the sand around the high throne where he sat, silhouetted against an Indian-summer sky, like a king deserted by his subjects, his realm of sand and water reflected across his mirror lenses, a silent silver whistle clenched between his teeth.

Local legend had it that he was awaiting the return of the dolphin that had saved him, in order to express his thanks. He'd been in shock from loss of blood when the dolphin ferried him ashore, and in his confused state the Lifeguard thought a mermaid had rescued him. Yet some rejected that story as apocryphal. They quoted eyewitness accounts that it wasn't a dolphin but a child's blow-up rubber frog—the toy the Lifeguard had swum out to save and then washed back up in.

It was a story in flux. In another version the Lifeguard's vigil had nothing to do with a dolphin, let alone a rubber frog, but with a drowned girl he'd revived with the kiss of life. The experience was for him a kind of conversion—Saul on the road to Damascus. At that impressionable age when boys entering manhood assess their futures, the Lifeguard became convinced he possessed a gift for saving lives. No matter the cost, he'd found his destiny.

On midnights lit by the palpations of driftwood fires, when ghost stories were passed around a circle along with charred marshmallows, reefers, and jug wine, his tale was whispered like a secret. After the Lifeguard pulled the drowned girl from the water, his frantic attempt at mouth-to-mouth resuscitation failed to stir her. At last, exhausted and defeated, he stood dizzily and stared at her lying at his feet. Her eyes were closed as if she were asleep, her lips parted as if uttering a silent *Oh* lodged in her throat like a bite of poisoned apple. Her bikini top had come undone, exposing a breast whose nipple, plum with cold, should have been puckered but looked erect. She was so lovely that he dropped back to his knees, gathered her wet, sun-streaked hair in a fist, and brought her lips to his, this time in disregard for prescribed CPR technique. Their teeth collided, he jabbed his tongue into her cold mouth, traveled the unevenness of her gumline, pausing to examine a chipped canine, and the ridges behind her teeth, then flicked his tongue across the pores of hers, and felt her respond. The Lifeguard had never believed the rumors—if he'd heard them at all—about a flat-chested, nondescript girl in a hot-pink bikini who became seductively beautiful only after drowning. She drowned herself at beaches up and down the coast so that lifeguards might resuscitate her, and in the process she swallowed their souls. Even if he had heard the rumors, the kiss would have obliterated caution. It flowed between them, composed of breath, time, and briny spit, and seemed to surge into a life force that was breathless, timeless, and oceanic. He didn't realize until too late that the climactic urge to surrender to it was his soul being sucked from his body.

"So she was a swallower," someone at the fire would say, a tired joke that served as an excuse for stoned laughter.

But it was no joke to the lifeguards who'd braved riptides and undertow to save her, those athletic boys earning money for college, whom she left hollow, directionless, and arrested by a narcissism fixed on adolescent reflections: worn snapshots from which they grinned back still young and golden, with movie-star sunglasses perched on their white-slathered noses, whistles dangling like holy medals. Unable to love another woman, unable to live alone, they'd gaze at those demigods they were for one brief moment of summer, and weep.

The Lifeguard didn't weep; he watched and waited. When the girl came to drown once more, he'd save her again, and from her cold mouth suck back his soul. Night enlarged an already enormous sea. A seabird cried out. As if in answer, a voice could be heard over the surf, singing. Come dawn, the Lifeguard was still there, his hair bleached silver as if he'd spent too much time beneath the moon.

2

Duane Shelly, my roommate the year I spent in military school, claimed he was a reincarnated Romantic poet. He relived his previous legendary life in dreams from which he hated to wake, and so he'd oversleep and miss his morning classes. It was the kind of affectation that had persuaded his father to send him to military school. A coterie of girls at our sister school found him intriguing, and I was allowed to tag along as Lord Byron if I agreed to limp. Shelly, who hated to be called Duane, provided us with good weed and fake IDs for the bars, and it took only a few drinks before he'd begin to declaim: "O haloed Bud sign, O toke of mystery! O night's black lipstick! O life that is a fake ID!"

The timidity of my own Romantic rebellion disappointed him.

"All you need for a barbaric yawp, Byron, is the circular vowel that this vulgar century we're forced to inhabit has appropriated for the Big O," Shelly confided. "It's the secret of Romantic transformation: O sullen soulless homework! O sperm-crusty plaid boxers! O morning woody saluting attention, sir!"

Shelly returned to mind on a weekday when Mariel and I played hooky from our sullen soulless jobs in order to sneak in a last trip to the beach, and I found myself yawping: "O final flame of Indian summer before the frost!"

"I hope that term hasn't become offensive," Mariel said. "Do you think Native Americans call it Indian summer, too?"

"Stop worrying and give the old poetic O a whirl," I told her, not that she struck me as the type who would have gone in for black lipstick, or for a poseur like Duane. But then, despite all our time together, I knew next to nothing about what she'd been like in high school, or, for that matter, about the kind of boys she'd found attractive. Early on, Mariel told me she wasn't one to dwell on the past. She thought the boomers still lining up for Dead concerts were pathetic. She said nostalgia, like most things self-indulgent, was ultimately boring.

"O hidden heart of fading summer," she said, being a sport and playing along in a way meant to be ironic. Yet I caught a note of such wistfulness in her voice that I had to suppress an impulse to ask: *Are you talking about us?*

And if she had answered yes, I would have had to admit

that I, too, felt that something had faded between us, and I missed Mariel and Bryan, that crazy-about-each-other-couple-living-for-the-moment we'd once been. I wanted to be them again.

O haloed trips to the beach when we first met! It was thrill enough then simply to watch Mariel strip down to her swimsuit as if she couldn't wait to shed her clothes. She'd kick off her sandals and unbutton her blouse while simultaneously shimmying from unzipped jeans, and then adjust her swimsuit like a teenage girl, tugging it over a buttock and hitching up her top as if concerned with modesty even though the choice to wear a revealing pink bikini was hers. She'd stretch out facedown on a beach towel, untie her bikini straps, and have me slather her with lotions scented with coconut and almond. Her sun-streaked hair seemed a perfect complement to her gleaming skin. I told her once, "A lot of people would pay to have hair your color."

"And I'm one of them," she said.

I'd laughed. We were still all but strangers then, having met earlier that spring, and I remember wondering if she was the kind of woman whose self-deprecating humor sprang not only from a distrust of vanity but also from a refusal to play along with the manipulative flattery of men. It turned out that she was gracious when told she was beautiful, although the fact that she *was* beautiful may have made the compliment acceptable. She prided herself on being a realist, someone who, as she liked to say, "tells it straight or not at all." I hadn't realized yet that the emphasis fell on *not at all*.

I drove a vintage VW Bug at the time, pumpkin-orange with the engine in the rear and a convertible top that folded down by hand. Mariel liked my choice of car—"the ultimate beachmobile," she observed—even though it was April, rainy and chill and therefore cruel given the Bug's dysfunctional heater and leaky top. Once summer kicked in, that car lived up to her name for it. We'd pack a cooler with a picnic lunch—cold pizza and a bottle of wine—and drive to one beach or another, each weekend farther south along the coast. We were on a quest to find a beach with a riding stable nearby. Mariel, who moonlighted as an instructor at a school for dressage, had heard about a place where you could rent horses to ride through the surf, though we never found it. I'd never seen her ride, but horses were the measure in the sweetest, most haunting thing she ever told me: "The way I know I'll always love horses, I know I'll always love you."

After the battery dropped through the rusted-out floor, I sold the beachmobile to a collector. I drive a Ford Taurus wagon now.

It was a day for hooky. The twisting shore road climbed through the color change, its macadam pasted with leaves. We sped along windward stretches where the rainbow haze of spindrift made it seem as if we'd just missed a sun shower. This time we were heading north, where the coast was wilder and deserted, as if making a getaway. And maybe we had escaped, if only for the drive, from Mariel and Bryan—a couple we referred to in the third person. "I liked those two people," Mariel would say in a rare nod to the past, and I'd agree. Despite their unfair competition with the present, I liked them, too.

On a stretch of beach selected at random, I set down the cooler, slipped off my backpack, and Mariel plunged the stake of her beach umbrella into the sand. Then she kicked off her sandals, undid her blouse, and eased off her jeans. She was wearing a black one-piece I hadn't seen before. We hadn't been to a beach in a very long time. The suit emphasized the swell of her breasts and the width of her shoulders. In an evening dress, those shoulders were arresting. She had a rider's posture and a swimmer's build.

"That's an athletic-looking suit," I said.

"I'm afraid my bikini days are over."

"Nonsense, you're trim as ever."

"Forever young?" she asked. "Do you think, to remain so, one has to become her own child?"

"You're still a beautiful woman, is what I think."

"Thanks, Bry. I know you mean it. We've grown older and it's sweet of you not to notice, but I don't want to be someone who doesn't realize when it's time to dress appropriately."

The beach was deserted, and the water, despite the sun flaring off its surface, was already too cold for swimming. We sloshed barefoot, stopping to skip stones and to collect shells, though they were wave-worn beyond recognition. It was like wading along a coast of broken china. We were about to turn back when Mariel noticed hoofprints in the sand. They emerged suddenly from the water and continued at a gallop down the beach in the direction we'd been heading.

"Let's follow them," she said.

I was sorry I'd left my watch and the car keys behind, in one of my shoes. We walked, glancing back to see if our encampment was safe: our towels, the cooler with its iced bottle of champagne, the blue ukulele on which I could pick out "Blue Moon" but no longer remembered how to tune, and the umbrella she called her Italian umbrella.

That faded beach umbrella obviously meant something to her. I recalled a day toward the end of one of our first summers together—they seemed a single, seamless summer now—when we'd accidentally left it behind. We had camped on the windward shore of a peninsula that wasn't on the highway map and, after drinking a bottle of wine, lay kissing beneath the umbrella, beside the surf as if—Mariel joked—we were auditioning for parts in the love scene in *From Here to Eternity*. We'd fooled around at beaches before—Mariel called it mashing—but that particular afternoon we kissed in a trance. I stretched out against her and she began to tremble until she was in the throes of an abandoned shuddering. It felt like we were connected only by the pressure of our lips, even when she locked her legs around me and clung, intent upon taking me along to wherever she was rushing. Her breath seemed to echo through my body, through a labyrinthine network of self I didn't know existed until I heard her moaning lost in it.

Afterward, we lay drowsily staring at the underside of the umbrella, Mariel squeezing my hand with each aftershock. The sounds of gulls and surf arrived as if from a great distance.

"That was oceanic," she whispered.

"Have you ever come kissing before?" It wasn't the kind of question I normally asked, but I felt shaken, changed. It had never happened to me with anyone.

"Sometimes in dreams," she said. "Sometimes I wake coming."

"With whom?"

"I don't know."

"You don't remember who once you wake?"

"It's always a stranger."

We repacked the beachmobile in a daze and must have driven off leaving the folded umbrella leaning against a tree I'd parked beneath for shade.

That night, Mariel called to say she'd just realized her Italian umbrella was missing. I felt I'd left something behind, as well, though I couldn't say what. Truth be told, the umbrella was ratty—lopsided, rust-stained, mildewed—an anomaly, given her otherwise tastefully chosen beach gear. When I offered to buy her a new one, she was insulted that I'd think it was a matter of money. Her sense of loss over an umbrella seemed at odds with her avowed disregard for the past. It was well after dark when she called, and the beach we'd happened upon was an hour and a half away down an unlit back road. I wasn't sure I could locate it again even in daylight. Although

I didn't hold much hope for finding the umbrella, I offered to go back with her the next morning.

In the middle of the night, unable to sleep, Mariel unhitched the horse trailer from her pickup and drove back alone. The entrance to the beach was unmarked and she wasn't sure she'd found the right turnoff. Her headlights followed a sandy two-track to a crest of hissing pines. On the other side, a dune descended to the water. She could hear the scuff of combers. She dug a balky flashlight from the glove compartment and stepped out but she couldn't identify the tree we'd parked beneath. She searched around each tree as her flashlight flickered and died. While she pounded the battery chamber against her palm, marbled clouds parted above, revealing a moon of luminescent blue.

Oh, look at the moon! she told herself.

The vision was worth the drive. Then, across the beach, near the water's edge, she saw the silhouette of an umbrella. She distinctly remembered uprooting her umbrella as we'd gathered our things from the sand, and my asking her, "How could I not love you?" to which she'd replied, "A rhetorical question?"

Wind in her face, she skidded down the dune, and jogged past the embers of a driftwood fire reflecting off shards of wine jugs, expecting the silhouette to be revealed as an optical illusion, a mirage of moon glow. A snatch of song stopped her in her tracks. *You saw me standing alone*: over the surf, a voice carried the melody of "Blue Moon" before a gust blew it away. Shadows thrusting beneath the umbrella seemed to possess the substance of bodies. *It's just kids, lovers*, she thought. At the same instant, she realized how alone she was—no one even knew she was there. The wind thrashed the water and drove the sky. A fuming collision of clouds snuffed the moon just as a draft lifted the umbrella off the sand, whisking the shadows beneath it into darkness. Mariel had the urge to flee back to her pickup before she was erased, but she'd come too far to give up.

She chased the umbrella as it wheeled along the shore and was sucked into the surf. She waded in, grabbing for the canvas canopy, but the backwash ripped it away, knocking her off balance. She floundered to her feet, lunged for the umbrella, and was knocked down again. Choking, she fought to surface against an undertow of raking hands. She was clubbed across the mouth but managed to seize the bobbing pole of the umbrella and, in a momentary trough between waves, drag it ashore.

She knelt on the beach gasping for breath, already shivering, suddenly aware the waves had shredded her blouse. The umbrella, waterlogged and caked with sand, was as ungainly in the wind as the sail of a dismasted boat. Its ribs were bent, but she was able to fold it partially and lug it up the dune. She'd lost the flashlight and was terrified she'd lost her truck keys, too, but they were wadded in wet Kleenex in the pocket of her jeans.

By cab light, she dabbed the Kleenex over her bloodied breasts looking for where she'd been cut until she realized the blood was drooling from her split lip. It felt to her tongue as if she'd chipped a canine. She loaded the umbrella into the truck bed and, careful not to spin the tires in the sand, got the hell out of there.

The next day, when she told me the story, I chastised her for going alone. "You should have called me," I said.

"I wasn't going to wake you at two a.m. If I hadn't gone then, I'd have lost it."

When I asked what it was about the umbrella that made it so important, she answered that what had drawn her to me was that I seemed to understand instinctively that a person is defined by the present—and by the possibility of change that living in the present affords. The past, as far as she was concerned, was another word for stasis; the only means of changing the past was to lie about it. She'd thought I agreed that it wasn't necessary for people to know every little boring, neurotic detail about each other. The way she said it implied that maybe her assumptions about me had been wrong.

I didn't reply, but her rebuke bothered me, and not just because it was unfair—from the time we'd met I'd been anything but overly inquisitive. What I found disturbing was that the more defensive she became, the less she seemed to realize how sketchy her past actually was.

I had presumed that part of the attraction between us was that we were both loners. As loners do, we'd made a private world together. What did I care, at least at first, about her past? The relationships I'd had until then never lasted long enough for history and its supposed predictive power to matter. It seemed enough that Mariel was beautiful to me. If that was a questionably romantic basis for a relationship, then I was willing to admit, at least in retrospect, to having chosen—in that unconscious way one chooses without being aware that one has—a life of sensation over a life of meaning. Maybe the real choice I made was to accept the consequences. Perhaps beauty was different in Keats's time, but I never expected that beauty, at least physical beauty, would equate with truth.

The lost umbrella, a small thing in itself, was a turning point. Until her strange behavior about it, I hadn't admitted to myself that Mariel was in hiding, perhaps simply hiding how disconnected she was. Isn't that, after all, the secret we most keep both from the world and from ourselves—not what we know, but the extent of our ignorance? True or not, the thought consoled me. The incident with the umbrella confirmed what she had already intimated: the kind of men Mariel was attracted to were the kind who didn't ask questions. That had narrowed the field to someone like me.

She didn't begrudge me a past. I'd told her my well-rehearsed repertoire of stories about growing up as an alienated army brat, the pacifist son of an alcoholic drill-sergeant father whose reassignments from military base to military base—not to mention all the schools from which I'd been expelled along the way—ensured I was from nowhere. She'd listen politely, but did not reciprocate. After a while I stopped recounting my past, as if I didn't have one either. But rather than accept ours as a relationship in the present tense, I secretly began to imagine for her a past preferable to my own, with the beach umbrella at its epicenter.

3

With no more origin than a wildflower, the umbrella sprouted, gaily striped, from the pebble beach of a nameless cove where she went to sunbathe nude. That was the summer when, after graduating from art school, she'd taken her first trip abroad. If not for the umbrella, the cove wouldn't have been visible from the water. It couldn't be accessed by land. She had discovered it one morning when, following a pod of dolphins, she pedaled her rented pedalo beyond its usual range. Stretched in the umbrella's shade was a young man with golden hair and bronze skin, wearing green swim goggles. There was no beached boat, no indication of how he'd arrived, and she had the curious thought he might be the lifeguard there until she noticed his trident spear.

Each successive morning she returned to find him waiting.

Each evening she retired to an affordable pensione that had formerly been a convent for an order of nuns who'd taken the vow of silence. The converted cells were clean and spare: desk, chair, a narrow bed lit by a vigil candle. Above the washstand, where one might expect a mirror, a crucifix hung on the whitewashed wall. There, behind the bolted door, instead of keeping a journal she sketched from memory studies of the shapes that her body had composed that day in concert with the young man's.

Those figure drawings were the only subject in the leather-bound sketchbook she had bought in Florence. If she colored in the shadow of the umbrella in charcoal, then she drew their bodies in pastels. If the umbrella was sketched so that its stripes swirled like a psychedelic color wheel, then their bodies were inky shadows shaded with graphite. No matter how kinetic the image, the tension between light and shadow suspended it upon the stillness of the deckled page. Still, as the pages turned, the swish of ocean, the foam soaking into pebbles, the scuttle of crabs, the hum of swallows swooping along the cliff walls, the punctuated language of dolphins cruising just offshore, became audible. In school, she had been taught to control the medium. What she learned in the shade of the umbrella and then transcribed in her cell was surrender. Her drawings were not about release, they *were* release—an immersion into an ungovernable invention that swept her beyond anything she might have conceived in school, let alone anything she might have dared to reveal.

On the night she drew on the last page in the sketchbook, she fell asleep and dreamed that she continued to draw, first on the bedsheet, and then across the white walls. Aroused by the scenes she'd depicted, she opened her eyes to find the drawings from her dreams frescoed across her room. That morning, before leaving for the cove, she took the crucifix down from the wall now illuminated as if to make the cell a temple to Venus, and hid it beneath her mattress. She packed her suitcase and set it beside the door. She sealed the sketchbook in waterproof wrappings with candle wax and brought it to give to the young man.

But as she pedaled up and over swells, the marker of the umbrella was nowhere to be seen and the location of the secret cove had disappeared with it. Crystalline reflections of water marbled the outcroppings of cliffs, fish leaped around her, and when she gazed along the light shafting into the clear indigo, it appeared as if the pedalo were suspended on a glittering shoal of sardines. Dolphins shot through the fish in a frenzy of feeding, and then she saw the flash of the young man's body. The tint of water gave his golden hair and skin a verdigris cast. Staring up at her, trident in hand, he ascended with a surge of such streamlined force that for a moment she wondered if he'd forgotten she was bound to air and might be rising to carry her under. His lips brushed the underside of her reflection, and he arched down without breaking the surface, which was now mirror-slick with the oil of the sardines. She realized then that during those timeless earlier days the pod had circled, waiting, calling the dolphin-rider back. Pursued by plunging gulls and cavorting dolphins, the school of fish moved out to sea. She didn't follow.

The folded umbrella bobbed amid the flotsam along the salt-bleached, guano-stained dolomite cliffs. She lifted it dripping from the water, and in return released her sketchbook to the sea. "Someone will find you," she whispered as it floated into that blue expanse of water between the parentheses of horizon and cliffs. She knew that when she returned to the pensione, her suitcase would be waiting outside the gate and the gate would be locked.

4

After her parents were numbered among the victims of a rogue wave that took the cruise ship *Guarda La Luna* to the bottom of the Bermuda Triangle, she was placed in the care of her only living relative, an aunt whom she'd never met—had never so much as heard of—her mother's identical twin.

At least, that was the account she was given of how she came to awaken in this drafty, listing house that creaked in time to the creaking of the frozen cove. Supposedly, upon hearing that her parents were lost at sea, she fainted and fell, striking her temple on the runner of a rocking chair. When she regained consciousness, she had amnesia. The doctors had assured her aunt that in such cases memory usually returns, though they couldn't say when.

The Girl tried to visualize a room with a rocking chair, perhaps because she could summon up its creaking with each gust off the cove—or had loss struck so suddenly that she became acutely aware of the teetering of a once-stable world? But the detail of the rocking chair failed to promote any recall of the house where she'd been born and raised.

"Your mother, bless her soul, shawled in a vermilion afghan, nursed you on that rocker. Even after you were weaned, my dear, whenever you were upset or afraid, your mother would swaddle you in that afghan and rock you to sleep," her aunt told her. "If she could, she'd rock you now."

The Girl stared out the bay windows at the cove, unsure as to whether her amnesia might be gradually lifting, or if she were merely growing familiar with the absence of all she'd forgotten. She could hear an ocean hidden beneath the ice, one that maintained its intimate connection with the moon. Its tides still rose and fell, its waves washed in and out. The rhythms entranced her. Within the trance, the past signaled at her peripheral vision, too elusive to be seen directly. Remembering was like trying to call back a dream whose fragmented imagery and troubling emotion had bled into her waking hours. Its protean transformations defied the logic of language and the linearity of a story.

"Imagine a white sea visible from a deserted house whose windowpanes flash as if the house were wearing spectacles. How myopic that house must be to need so many pairs! It has no idea of who could be looking out and yet each window has a different view."

"My dear, you must be careful not to confuse amnesia with all that's missing, all that's mysterious in life," Auntie replied. She wore a vermilion kimono that kept falling open to expose her breasts; silver bracelets jangled up her forearms when she drank, revealing scarred wrists. Before a window streaming light and dander, she sipped what she called her afternoon zombie from a cut-glass tumbler shaded by a tooth-pick parasol. "I'd guess any number of quote 'normal' folks feel to some degree a disassociation similar to what you're de-scribing, my dear, not to mention all the garden-variety mys-tics, seers, and poets. I wouldn't be in a hurry to re-create the past. Once it returns, you might find yourself grateful for your respite from it."

The Girl didn't disagree. She became convinced that find-ing herself wasn't an exercise in recalling her prior life—that was futile, anyway. Rather she needed to dream it. When after her fall she'd regained consciousness, but as a stranger to her-self, she had been told her name. Instead of accepting it on faith, she was determined to wait until she remembered it un-aided before she accepted it. Until then she would continue to regard herself in the third person as "the Girl."

Auntie always addressed her as "my dear."

"My dear, come summer when the lifeguards return, the sea air will do you good, but it's too dangerous to set foot outside now. The ice appears firm, which only makes it more treacherous."

"My dear, this house is your home now. Feel free to treat it as your own, but I must ask you not to venture up the stairs. The upper floor is in disrepair, and the attic a den of rabid bats. I lack the funds to rehab. Besides, there's nothing up there of interest."

"My dear, if you are going to sit all day staring out, at least put on a sweater. This old house is drafty. Here, this belonged to your mother when she was a girl, or perhaps it was mine, we shared everything. Our parents couldn't tell us apart. Even we couldn't tell each other apart except that one of us was right-handed and the other left. Now, isn't that more comfy?"

The corridor warped with dampness on the forbidden second floor was lined with locked, empty rooms. Auntie complained that when winter turned bitter enough to freeze the cove, the sprawling house became too expensive to heat and she'd had to take in roomers, but they'd repeatedly defaulted on the rent, leaving her no choice but to lock them out and keep their personal belongings as collateral. Others—a lifeguard, a scissor-sharpener, a hurdy-gurdy man, and a ventriloquist among them—simply disappeared, leaving the tools of their trades behind. Tragic outcome aside, Auntie said, the Girl's parents had had the right idea of escaping to the Tropics. Auntie herself could only fantasize about such a trip, as what scant funds she had were tied up in this ramshackle place.

"At least, my dear, once the settlement comes in you won't have to scrape by as I have. We—*you*—should have collected something already but for the crooked lawyers' claim that the cruise line is exempt from liability in the case of a rogue wave. It's a game to lawyers to dicker over the price of grief. But the day of reckoning will come."

Until it did, Auntie kept her own reckoning. While Auntie slept through the late afternoons, with the zombie tumbler tumbled over beside her canopy bed, the Girl would sneak into the study and open the black ledger. In ink the shade of grenadine, beneath columns labeled MY DEAR! a running account in Auntie's smeary left-handed scrawl detailed each steaming cup of cocoa, each bobbing marshmallow, each animal cracker—enumerated by name: giraffe, monkey, kangaroo—each bonbon, macaroon, and petit four. There was a separate column for SOAP—a fresh bar every morning: lavender, verbena, coconut, chamomile, rosemary. Auntie had overlooked the sliver of brown floor soap pried from the bottom of a bucket. BUBBLE-BATH shared a column with SHAMPOO. RIBBONS included bows, barrettes, combs, tiaras. There were columns for SILK & SATIN, UNDIES, DOLLS & TEDDY BEARS—and a figure beside each item for what Auntie was owed. Each page concluded with an updated tabulation plus the usurious interest on the ever-larger reimbursement Auntie expected when the settlement came in.

The Girl stood at the end of the corridor of locked doors, before the full-length mirror framed in black like a sympathy card. Through a fog of dust a girl in a moth-eaten sweater who lived on prunes, stale oyster crackers, and a faint snowfall of Kraft's Parmesan stared blankly back, her hair unwashed for weeks, bangs trimmed with a serrated bread knife that likely had been used to butcher liver. As usual, the Girl's own gaunt twin seemed in no mood to commune. Somewhere a toilet flushed. The water in the old house gasped out gritty with rust and too cold to bathe in.

The first time the Girl heard the mewing she became alarmed that, unbeknownst to Auntie, one of the roomers had abandoned a kitten. Then it was a puppy whining, and then a chattering that caused her to wonder if the hurdy-gurdy man had left without his monkey. She proceeded door by door along the corridor, and heard a parakeet repeating what presumably was his name: "Fine Feather, Fine Feather." The puppy's whines intensified into the sparking squeal of a grindstone honing shears. She paused to twirl to a tarantella freshly cranked from an ancient barrel organ. That wooden clacking from behind the blue door—the only painted one—

was, she supposed, the ventriloquist's abandoned dummy silently singing.

Empty rooms? Once the creak of her footfalls was recognizable to whomever was listening, each afternoon seemed increasingly occupied. The puppy's whine became the whinny of a pony—a Shetland, like the pony she suddenly recalled having mounted to have her photo snapped at a carnival on a day she fell in love with horses. The whinny dissolved into the whistle of a kettle on a hot plate, or was it a violin reduced to a single string? The tapping of an old typewriter reminded her of Blind Pew's cane in *Treasure Island*, which in turn allowed her to remember that as a child she'd been read to at bedtime. Like every reminiscence here, it seemed less a memory than a déjà vu. She heard whispers, heavy breathing, sighs, doorknobs rattling, the thump of hooves, but the doors held fast, locked from without, and Auntie slept with the keys. The Girl heard the Old Spice jingle whistled to the scrape of a straight razor, and stooped to the keyhole to inhale a scent of aftershave. She remembered her father.

Auntie found her by the bay windows. On a pane fogged by the steam of her breath, the Girl had traced the face of the retreating moon. Two slick finger marks ran from its crater eyes.

"Oh, my, look at the moon," Auntie said. "But better to cry real tears, my dear. Let it out rather than this apathetic moping. Not that there's one way to grieve, any more than one way to love. They're shape-shifters, love and grief, aren't they, and they have many disguises. Yet one thing's sure, your mother wants you to be happy. How does Auntie know, you ask?"

The Girl had not asked.

"Because, my dear, if there's a bond even stronger than that between mother and daughter, it's the connection between identical twins. You've heard of twin telepathy? I assure you it crosses space, time, and the border of life itself. I sense your mother's presence as if it's my own, and she wants you to grow into a woman—beautiful, confident, and free. That's the shape my grief assumes—hope for your future."

The Girl did not remark that she had supposed the shape of Auntie's grief was that of a zombie topped by a cocktail umbrella—less a shape, actually, than the odor of 151-proof Demerara. She could smell its fermented cane in Auntie's air kisses, in the sweats from which Auntie woke moaning, in the wake of her vermilion kimono as she paced the house at night with a candle to the clink of ice cubes, bracelets, and skeleton keys. The odor mingled with the mildewed rot of the cavernous house. Trying to escape it, to draw a free breath, was the Girl's excuse for ascending the forbidden stairs.

Up those stairs, she could overhear Fine Feather perched on his swing, reciting poems as if foretelling the future between the pauses he took to strop his beak, and accosting his mirror in narcissistic bouts of lust or rage, when he became incomprehensible.

> Before the chapel of a beach umbrella, the mermaid
> bridesmaids frolic. Half bride, half horse,
> she gallops to the Waffle House
> overlooking waves
> of blood orange marmalade . . .

The poems were what raised in the Girl the suspicion that there was only a single roomer behind all the doors, a ventriloquist throwing his voice. He was the mewing kitten, whining pup, chattering monkey; the whinny, grindstone, and whistling violin; he cranked the hurdy-gurdy, put the kettle on, and typed with the tap of a blind pirate. Was he typing the oracular riddles that Fine Feather recited? If he could foretell the future, perhaps he could be trusted to recall her past.

The Girl stood poised to knock at the blue door, resolved to tell the ventriloquist that she was on to him and to implore his help, when Fine Feather began insistently repeating his own name, and at that moment, the Girl realized that from the very start she had misunderstood his simplest utterance. She remembered listening to an old rock song her father played that she'd thought went, *Hey hey you you get offa my clown.* What the parakeet had been saying all along was "Find feather." She looked down to see a neon-green feather slide from beneath the blue door. When she picked it up, a basso profundo voice commanded, "Fan feather." She fanned and, as if at the beck of a conductor's baton, the hurdy-gurdy, violin string, kettle, and grindstone played, while a whinnying, whining, caterwauling chorus rose to a crescendo. Above the din, from behind the blue door, in a fake German accent, a loosely clacking mouth shouted, "Fanfare! Fin Farther! Fain Führer! Fond Farter! Faun Fricker!" The shrill accompanying blasts of the lifeguard's whistle were sure to wake Auntie.

The Girl could see herself approaching a collision with herself as she raced down the corridor. By the time she reached the black-framed mirror, her pale, emaciated twin was waiting, holding her hands over her ears as she faded into the unreflecting dust.

"Don't go, please don't leave me here alone," the Girl said, releasing the feather as she reached to touch her twin, and as the feather floated to the floorboards the corridor went silent. The girl in the mirror, though she had no feather to drop, extended her hand, but it was to wave farewell. In a voice not unlike the parakeet's she said, "Find father."

The Girl heard jangling and footfalls slowly ascending the staircase, and she fled up the narrow, spiraling steps to the attic. She expected the attic door to be locked; when it opened, she expected to be swarmed by bats. Instead, she found herself beneath an unfinished cathedral ceiling, in a bare space shot through with sunlight from a triangular window and holes punched through the roof by a blue sky. She could see her breath and hear the creaking of the icy cove. She bolted the attic door.

A brass telescope stood before the triangular window. A battered steamer trunk decaled with Italian travel stamps occupied the center of the space. Beyond the trunk, a Chinese screen lacquered with emerald storks threw a shadow across the floor. She expected the trunk to be locked; when it opened, she expected to be swarmed by moths. It was stuffed with moth-eaten girls' clothing, two sets of everything, two Italian sailor hats, one of which she put on, two Communion dresses, two prom gowns still pinned with dried corsages, two pink bikinis, two scarves embroidered with anchors, two pairs of yellow boots. Two balding teddy bears. A hatbox of rusted white petals and loose photographs, each photo torn in half. Only the left halves remained. The same sullen girl glared from each torn print. At the very bottom of the box was a photo of that sullen girl as a young woman posing naked beside a striped beach umbrella, her lip derisively curled at the photographer. The Girl wondered if whoever was on the missing half of the print was naked, too. Another photo showed a woman in the rain, dressed for mourning, beside an open grave. A veil concealed her face, and one arm cradled a bouquet of white roses while the other held an open umbrella whose familiar gay stripe seemed out of place. Her black silk gloves set off her white, bandaged wrists. The Girl studied the photo; through the black veil she could see teeth flashing a smile. It was the only picture in the trunk not torn in two. The girl remembered her mother.

Wearing the sailor hat, an anchor scarf, and rubber boots, the Girl sat on the closed trunk, glancing from the window to the storks that flew across the Chinese screen. She remembered those birds from her parents' bedroom, remembered hiding behind such a screen from the somber guests gathered to say they were sorry her mother had gone away. None of them would say where her mother had gone or when she would return. Her father, wearing dark glasses even on such a thundery afternoon, whispered, "Don't worry, I won't tell where you're hiding."

The telescope looked out on real birds circling the cove. What had been a distant dot came into focus as a beach umbrella. The umbrella made it possible for her to imagine the ice as a strand of white sand exposed by an ebbing tide. The man out there looked to be ice fishing, with the umbrella for a shanty. Even through a lens that could bring the daylight moon close enough to count its pitted scars, she couldn't quite make out the man's face. He was wearing dark glasses— and why not, the day was dazzlingly bright. She could hear the random creak of ice, and another, metronomic creaking coming from behind the Chinese screen where a woman shawled in a vermilion afghan sat rocking.

"Do you remember me?"

"Do you think you are the right-handed twin?" the Girl asked.

"I am ambidextrous," the woman said, and smiled. "How could you forget?"

The Girl could hear someone trying to get into the attic, twisting the doorknob, jiggling keys in the lock, bumping a shoulder against the door.

"Would you like me to rock you?" the woman asked.

The Girl shook her head no.

"Too late for comfort? Then what would you like?"

"To walk out on the ice and watch the man fishing."

"Why?"

"To breathe in the sea air, to hear the gulls calling in voices I know are theirs."

"Ah, yes, to be alive and taste the salt on your lips, to sense the infinite ocean inside, to drown in—"

"I'd like to see what he'll pull up through the ice," the Girl said.

"And if it's some monster from below?"

"I'll say, Time to cut it loose."

"And if there's nothing at all to catch?"

"There's always the pull of the sea itself."

"And when the ice melts, my darling, what will you do?"

"Ride a horse along the dashing waves."

5

Mariel's beach umbrella was now all she and Bryan could still see of the place they'd staked out on the sand. From this distance one couldn't tell the umbrella was striped. The hoofprints they'd been following, without sight of horse or rider, were washing away in the encroaching tide.

"I wonder if we set our stuff high enough on the beach," Bryan said.

"You're limping," Mariel said. "Do you want to turn back?"

He'd sliced the ball of his foot on a jagged shell, but he knew, once she was on a quest, Mariel refused to give it up. "I'm not limping," he said.

"You're not? Then what do you call it?"

"Being Byronic."

"Look!" she exclaimed, shading her eyes and pointing ahead. "What is that?"

"A lifeguard chair?"

"The height of the Eiffel Tower?"

"We'll make it our boundary," he said. "We'll walk that far, climb up, and if we don't see a horse or a stable from there, we head back."

"Deal," Mariel said. "Why's a lifeguard tower still up? I thought once the beaches officially close they take those in with the rowboats and the volleyball nets. I still remember that feeling of summer vanishing overnight—everything gone including the lifeguards, all those hunky guys named Robbie and Tad my girlfriends and I had crushes on. We'd go to the beach in the bikinis we bought hoping they'd notice."

"You ever actually go out with one?" It would have been a routine question, except that Mariel so seldom mentioned men it seemed as if she were sharing a confidence. Bryan wanted her to keep talking.

"I had a serious love affair my sophomore year in high school, with Robbie—he didn't have a last name. None of us did. I'd spread my towel near his lifeguard chair, lie on my stomach, and untie my bikini straps. Our climactic moment came when I was eating a hot dog and Robbie said: 'You've got a dot of mustard on your face. Let me get that for you.' And he kissed my cheek and went, *yummm*. That was on the day before the beaches closed. 'See you next year, Pancake,' he said, and I ran into the water so he wouldn't see me burst into tears."

"Pancake?"

"As in flatter than."

"No way. So, did you see him the next year?"

"I dreamed of him all winter. I turned my pillow into Robbie, but by spring I'd sprouted breasts and was into tennis players. Our town hosted a qualifier for the Junior Nationals, and that next summer I had my first sexual experience, if you call giving a tennis brat a hand job . . . Oh, my God, that was Bummer Summer! The beach was off-limits. I'd completely forgotten that."

"Red tide? E. coli?"

"A girl drowned." Mariel pronounced it *drownded*. Maybe it was a local accent that he hadn't noticed before. Maybe he'd never heard her use the word until then.

"A close friend?"

"I didn't know her but to say hi. She was a loner, shy, withdrawn, one of those girls who makes you think anorexia might be a fatal self-absorption. I don't think she had any friends. Her drownding was a shock—like when any young person dies—but the reason kids stopped going to the beach was that these creepy stories started going around."

"Like what?"

"Look at the birds around the lifeguard chair—must be thousands!" Mariel said. "Maybe we're extras in a nature film on mass migration. What all are they?"

"Gulls, willets, sandpipers, cormorants, oystercatchers, curlews. What kind of stories did they tell about her?"

"That she had a thing for lifeguards—not just crushes, an obsession. She'd wear a skimpy hot-pink bikini, and swim out, ignoring the whistle, and pretend to be drownding. The lifeguard would have to pull her out of the water and she'd be like unconscious. Kids claimed she was doing that all up and down the beaches to get the lifeguards to give her mouth-to-mouth. It was awful how they talked about her. She died because one lifeguard thought she was crying wolf when she really was caught in an undertow. By the time he realized she was in trouble and rowed out, she'd gone under. The guy who didn't save her tried to take his own life by stepping on an electric rail. His legs were horribly burned, but he didn't die. They searched for a week but never found her body. Nobody wanted to go to the beach. They made up sick stories—as if being morbid disguised their fear—stories about a beach where kids went to get high at night and skinny-dip, where they heard a girl singing, before her body washed in, all luminescent and rotted and fish-eaten. I'm sorry I've remembered any of it. The hoofprints are gone."

The hoofprints weren't so much gone as lost among the encrusted tracks of countless birds, tracks that had accumulated over days, weeks—over summers, perhaps—and had assumed the shapes of fallen leaves, petals, fans, shells, butterflies, arrowheads, hieroglyphs. There was a nonstop throaty mutter, not merely audible but tactile, sonic gusts that stank of wet feathers and of the ocean floor distilled into fermenting fishy droppings. The beach was littered with guano and feathers.

"There's someone in that tower," Mariel said. She'd become quiet, morose, avoiding eye contact after telling the story.

"It looks abandoned."

"I can see his glasses flash," she insisted, as if Bryan were arguing.

"Where?"

"You don't hear his whistle?"

He stopped to listen. The birds moved off before them, increasingly agitated and noisy—they'd begun to honk and squawk and cry.

"My God, you don't hear that?" Mariel clapped her hands over her ears. "Someone's swum too far out," she said. "He's lowering himself down from the tower, but he'll have to drag himself to the water across the sand, across the feathers, across the shit." She turned to look at Bryan. Her face was lined with worry and streaked with tears. "Someone's drowning. Don't just stand there. We have to help." She whirled and raced toward the water, clods of sand flying from her white soles.

The birds exploded into flight.

Bryan started after her, but with his gashed foot he was

quickly outdistanced. "Was the lifeguard who didn't save the girl Robbie?" he shouted after her.

His voice was lost, like the sight of her in the whoosh of wings beating for uplift—drab shorebirds transformed into tumultuous white plumage. The beach itself seemed to rise. A million imprints—petals, butterflies, arrowheads, hieroglyphs—whirled into blinding spirals of sand. As he shielded his eyes, he glimpsed what had panicked the birds; it hadn't been her sprint for the water, but the riderless white horse galloping from the sea.

At the tower, he began to climb the peeling ladder. It was even higher than it had looked from the beach, high enough that one might peer over the horizon to determine if those far-off electric throbs were a brewing storm. The beach stretched below, unmarked now except for fresh hoofprints. And then he spotted the horse again, running along the surf with a woman riding bareback, naked, her pendulous breasts jouncing, her silvery hair streaming in the wind as they vanished into the distance. He continued his ascent. When he reached the top, he would sit and watch and wait for Mariel to return.

6

"And where you off to so fast?" asked the balloon man. He held a bouquet of colored balloons that threatened to lift him into the sky.

She'd been running lost through the bazaar that lined the puddled, cobbled streets along the pier where the sea whumped the seawall and pitched up spray.

"It's these lead boots keeps me feet on the ground," the balloon man said. "Got them from a deep-sea diver with the bends won't be needing them no more."

He held out a translucent white balloon as if offering a flower, but as she reached to take it, she noticed that all the other balloons were imprinted with the distorted faces of girls trapped inside and looking out.

"It's free for you, little doll face. Come back!"

His boots hammered the cobblestones as he chased her, seemingly unaware that as he labored to run the balloons were slipping from his hand and floating off.

She outdistanced him easily, her bare feet splashing through puddles, her hair flying. She passed a fire-eater who blew a flaming kiss in her direction, and a contortionist bent in a diving helmet that trailed cut lines, his voice echoing from inside: "You looks like a girlie needs a good hosing!"

The sea whumped the seawall with the reverberation of kettledrums.

She heard a tarantella before she saw the hurdy-gurdy man. His mascot—part monkey, part spider—danced, straining, at the end of a golden chain.

"Give a coin for Jocko's cup, jailbait, or else a kiss you must give up," the hurdy-gurdy man said. When she didn't stop, he released the golden chain. And though Jocko on his eight muscular legs accelerated as the balloon man could not, she was older now, and faster, and he couldn't run her down.

Waves whumped in from a horizon the gray of blue jays. A mica haze of atomized ocean hung above slick cobblestones. Rolling thunder roiled the whitecaps, the periscopes and shark fins and sounding flukes. When she came to a brimming horse trough, she stopped as if to drink, and doubled over, a stitch in her side.

A man with hound eyes, a hawk nose, a military mustache, tarnished hair, and a drooping gut smiled at her from the entrance to a shop whose doorposts were white plaster goddesses. He held a riding crop as one might a fly swatter. The goddesses were crisscrossed with bloody welts that presumably had been horseflies. Each time his hand rose to smooth his mustache, a goddess flinched.

"Do you train horses, sir?" she asked.

"Something better, young lady," he said. "I've a unicorn prances on your palm. A ballerina balances on his horn. Wind him and a tune makes her spin. Come inside before the storm and hear my whimsical collection from olden times the wide world over—ballerinas, gypsies, odalisques, nymphs. One has *your* name on it, perhaps."

"I'm afraid, sir, I don't have so much as a coin."

"Oh, it will be my gift to you."

"Don't go in," an old man in dark glasses and a crushed green hat whispered, as he pushed his piled dray past.

"But a storm is near and this kind sir has offered to show me his collection of music boxes."

"Years will pass and you won't come back out of his shop still yourself."

She glanced at the man in the doorway of his shop. He smiled and beckoned with his riding crop.

"Where did you get all those umbrellas?" she asked the man with the dray.

"I find them discarded, or maybe they find me—blown inside out, twisted, mildewed, lost, forgotten in pubs, left behind on beaches. Gamps, brollys, bumbershoots, parasols—some for rain, others for sun. I mend them."

The weight of the first *plip* of rain on the surface of the trough made it brim into a waterfall that rilled along the gutters. Rats chirped from the swirling sewers and scurried toward the white wooden belfry that overlooked the docks. Its carillon pealed helter-skelter in gusts off the sea.

"I'm afraid," she said, "a downpour is coming."

"Each is beautiful in its own way," the umbrella mender said. "Some are silk and some are canvas, but all are made of shadow. Don't be afraid. Sit and I'll push us along."

"Where are we going?" she asked.

"Why, on a day like this to the beach, of course."

Lightning unspooled along the ocean, the gutters, the lenses of the umbrella mender's glasses. A jagged bolt blistered the belfry. Bats sailed out, burning like heretics.

"This one's my favorite," he said, pausing to free a beach umbrella from the pile. "Found it washed ashore just yesterday. Who knows how long it's been at sea or from where it drifted. Its faded stripes are lovely still. And look at the lettering: *Ombra*. Italian, maybe? If it can support the golden weight of summer, don't worry about a thunderstorm. And when it opens, don't let the clowns surprise you."

"Clowns?" she asked.

"Or the jugglers or the acrobats. I think you'll like the beautiful bareback rider. That trough back there is for her horse."

"But how can all that be?"

"Why, my sweet girl, has no one ever told you, every umbrella is a big top?"

7

O look at the moon tonight. Look at the moon, Earth's O in the sky.

O all the spirits of love that wander by. O presences.

O silver face of night, you saw me standing alone. O soft embalmer of the still midnight, O somber soul unsleeping, without a dream in my heart, without a love of my own. O shades of night—vast, veiled, inexpressible. O orb that broods above the troubled sea of mind. O mysterious priest! O wondrous singer! O soft self-wounding pelican. O well for the fisherman's boy who rides the dolphin. O ethereal rhetoric, O hidden heart, O dark swells that rock a helpless soul. O wave god who broke through me. O I heard someone whisper please adore me. O Attic shape! O boat of stars, O black sail, O remember that my life is wind. This is thy hour O Soul, the free flight into the wordless . . .

Look at the moon tonight.

O look at the moon.

If I Vanished

"What if I were to vanish?"

"Vanish? Under what circumstances?"

"It doesn't matter."

"You mean, like—*poof!*—suddenly you're not there?"

"I'm not there."

"But there's always a reason, or at least a context. You suddenly moved away in the middle of the night? But why? Were you kidnapped? Abducted by aliens? An extraordinary rendition by the CIA? Did you fall down a rabbit hole? Was it amnesia? Vanishing cream? Did you meet someone else? Was there a note—maybe in invisible ink—an impersonal e-mail, a message on my answering machine saying, 'Goodbye's too good a word, babe, don't worry, *ciao*'? Should I show up at the Department of Missing Persons—is there really such a department? Or by 'vanish' do you mean that all trace of you would be wiped from my memory?"

"Say I met someone else."

"Well, see, that's a different question."

"You don't have to answer that one. I saw the answer in your eyes. They're more honest than you are."

"Where'd you come up with this?"

"I heard it in a movie."

"What movie? Certainly not *The Vanishing*."

"It was a western."

"Clint Eastwood? Duke Wayne? Roy Rogers?"

"Kevin Costner."

"Costner a cowboy? I hope it was better than *Dances with Wolves* when he went Native American. Pauline Kael said in her review that Kevin Costner had feathers not only in his hair but in his head."

"It wasn't Kevin Costner per se. It was Charley something, the character Kevin Costner plays, who gets asked the question—by Annette Bening."

"No, it wasn't Charley something. Characters in American movies are only poor excuses to watch movie stars. Can you remember the name of any of the characters Marilyn Monroe played? They're all Marilyn Monroe. Charlton Heston isn't Moses, Moses is Charlton Heston."

"Answer the question."

"First, you have to tell me if you want me to answer it as if we're in some movie. I don't know who's starring as us or what cynical hack wrote our dialogue, and that would be important because if Ceil and Ned are in an Ingmar Bergman Swedish cowboy film, then Ned's answer is going to be different than if, say, Quentin Tarantino is directing."

"You're stalling."

"Because a question about vanishing is easy to answer in a movie where the good guys always win. If we're in a western I reckon I'd say, 'If you vanished, ma'am, I'd mount my horse and ride after you to the ends of the earth. I'd ride to the silver mountains of the moon and back, gunning down Injuns and other swarthy Third World desperadoes until I found you again and we galloped off into a Technicolor sunset.'"

"In other words, you'd make fun of me."

"I'm making fun of cowboy kitsch, of the Big Tobacco Marlboro Man mythos, of the genocidal, racist, anti-environmental, *heil* Adolph Coors's right-wing all-American West."

"No, you're making fun of me. And you're wrong, by the

way. In the movie, he doesn't answer anything like that. He doesn't answer at all right away. He goes off to think about it, like you could have done, and he comes back with the answer."

"Okay, I give. Tell me the *right* answer."

"You want to know, go see the movie."

He doesn't see the movie until two years later, after she has vanished. Clearly, by "vanish" she hadn't meant that she'd be wiped from his memory.

Ned doesn't remember the title, if he ever knew it, but one night, unable to concentrate on any book in the house, he Googles *Western Costner Bening*, and finds fifty thousand five hundred entries for a film called *Open Range*. Kevin Costner not only stars in it; he also directed it.

According to the reviews that Ned skims, it's a movie about the war between free grazers and landowners: "A former gunslinger is forced to take up arms again when he and his cattle crew are threatened by a corrupt lawman." The free grazers—Costner as the gunslinger, Charley Waite, and Robert Duvall as Boss Spearman—are the good guys. The evil rancher who controls the law is played by Michael Gambon. Their economic clash is a moral contest: greedy corporate America versus the don't-fence-me-in values of the Old West. The conflict plays out against what many reviewers agree is a beautifully photographed "iconic vista"—Montana, 1882, a big-sky landscape that makes it look as if there were enough to go around for everyone, especially since the original free-grazing tribes have been eradicated. The film was actually shot in Alberta.

Reviews compare *Open Range* to classics like *High Noon*. Amateurs at Amazon rate it a four-star masterpiece. The Cleveland *Sun News,* where dollar signs rather than stars are awarded, agrees: 4½ $. It's a Hot Pick, "a paean to the Old West," for Boo Allen of the *Denton Record-Chronicle*, and an

A-minus for Roger Ebert, who praises its defense of the values of a vanishing lifestyle.

That mention of a "vanishing lifestyle" catches Ned's attention. He wonders if vanishing is a motif in the movie, a theme echoed in the love story between Costner and Bening, prompting her odd question: *What if I were to vanish?*

Other reviews are less enthusiastic. It's panned in *The New York Times*, the *Chicago Tribune*, and *The New Yorker*. *Rolling Stone* despises "its insufferable nobility," and *Newsday* complains of "the man's-gotta-do-what-a-man's-gotta-do excess" of the script. A couple reviewers find that it mirrors Bush's cowboy presidency, with his bring-it-on War on Terror and Wanted Dead or Alive rhetoric. It makes a Worst Movies of the Year list: "a Harlequin Romance with a gunfight at the O.K. Corral."

From the little that Ceil said, Ned had assumed that the movie was a love story, but the reviews mostly agree that Costner's relationship with Bening seems superfluous. Bening plays Sue Barlow, with what is described on Yahoo! UK as "the steely resolve" of "a spinster who has nearly given up on love." Iggy's Film Reviews cautions: "Even by Harlequin Romance standards, the ties that bind these two lonely folks are flimsy. Unless Sue placed a personal ad seeking a SWM, age 40–50, who loves dogs, cares about friends and has killed before and will kill again, the attraction between the two doesn't make a lot of sense."

Undeterred, Ned decides to see for himself. Whatever the answer to the question about vanishing, Ceil must have experienced a shock of recognition at something in the film. Tonight, his missing her has assumed the guise of curiosity, and curiosity is preferable to feeling her absence. It's late, already after eleven thirty, but he knows a Blockbuster that's open until midnight, and should be able to just make it.

———

The street has vanished, been whited out. He'd been so absorbed in cyberspace, he hadn't noticed. It seems to Ned that the snowfall should have a hiss of its own, something other than the swish of tires from the Dunkin' Donuts–lit cross street at the end of the block. If the legend that Eskimos have a hundred words for snow were true, there'd be an Inuit word meaning snow-that-makes-the-familiar-unrecognizable. Ned can't tell which of the plastered shapes lining the curb is his Volvo. He imagines having to go car by car, brushing off snow to find his, and when he realizes that he might not make Blockbuster in time, the intensity of his disappointment surprises him. Then he spots his car, dim under the only streetlight that's burned out. Rather than take the time to scrape the windows, he scoops snow from them with his bare hands. When the engine turns over, the radio plays. He flicks on the defroster, wipers, headlights. It takes only that time for him to recognize the piano version of Mussorgsky's *Pictures at an Exhibition,* the movement titled "Gnomus," which is meant to evoke the picture of a nutcracker in the shape of a gnome promenading on deformed legs. Ned practiced this piece for a whole semester in college when he still studied piano. He hasn't heard *Pictures* in years, and it occurs to him that sometimes one no longer listens to a beloved masterpiece in order to continue to love it. Even on the car radio, over the scrape of wipers, he can hear coughing from the audience. Perhaps the pianist is Sviatoslav Richter, at the legendary live recital in Bulgaria. Ned remembers reading that after Richter's possessed performance, the Steinway he used had to be junked. He doesn't wait for the engine to warm.

The snow-paved Blockbuster parking lot is empty and Ned leaves the car running, wipers swiping, radio broadcasting a movement titled "Catacombae," which echoes the spectral world beneath the streets of Paris. Ghosts seem to swirl across the deserted streets of Ned's city, as well. He rushes in and a white kid with rusty dreadlocks shoots him a dirty look from behind the counter, before directing him to the Action section. It only now occurs to Ned that the movie might be checked out and he scans the rack feeling ridiculously frantic. He's in luck, it's there between Steven Seagal's *On Deadly Ground* and *Once Upon a Time in Mexico*.

Open Range in hand, Ned opens the car door onto a blasting heater and the majesty of the last movement, "The Great Gate of Kiev." With no more reason to hurry, he silences the heater and sits in the idling car, staring out at a parking lot, watching as his tire tracks left minutes earlier are obliterated by snow gathering as it might in Kiev. The yellow Blockbuster sign subtracts itself from night. Beneath the blurred streetlights, ascending notes and falling flakes create the impression of a gossamer arch spanning Chicago Avenue. Ned slips the Volvo into gear and drives slowly toward the towering gate of snow that retreats before his headlights, impossible to enter, then topples disassembling before the whirling blue of an oncoming squad car. The vision is more imagined than hallucinated, and Ned wonders how long it's been since he was stoned for real. Not since a vacation when Ceil wanted to see what sex would be like on hashish. Instead of smoking it, they mixed it with honey and spices based on a recipe for a sweetmeat supposedly served by Alice B. Toklas at Gertrude Stein's soirees. That night ended in an emergency room, with Ceil faint, terrified, hallucinating. She later said she'd had an out-of-body experience and seen herself dead. "Keep talking to her," the doctor had told Ned. "Don't let her slip away." It's not a scene he wants to recall.

He thinks instead of the first time he heard *Pictures at an Exhibition*. His best friend in high school, Sal Rio, who played Fender bass in the band they'd started, had on an impulse stolen a Lincoln left idling in a valet parking lot. Their plan was to drive to Toronto, where Miles Davis was supposedly playing at a jazz festival. Neither Ned nor Sal had been to Canada. Instead, high, and joyriding after midnight, they cruised onto the Chicago Skyway, the city aglow beneath them. Ned punched on the stereo and when the orchestral version of *Pictures at an Exhibition* blared out they both began conducting wildly—not that either of them knew what was playing. When Sal dumped the car the next morning, he said, "Man, never made it to Miles, but all was not lost—we got to hear that Russian motherfucker." *All was not lost*, Ned thinks. After that night, it became their go-to phrase and still makes him smile.

Pictures over, Ned turns off the radio and makes a left into the Dunkin' Donuts that has lit the end of his block for the three years he's lived in the neighborhood. He's never had the urge to stop there before. Maybe it's where that cop car was racing from. Ceil claimed their coffee was good. If he's going to do something so peculiar as to stay up late watching a film that more than one critic complained was, at a hundred and thirty-five minutes, too long, a coffee is in order. He doesn't want to drowse off and miss the answer to Bening's question about vanishing.

A woman with lapis-lidded, sleepy eyes, a gold-studded nostril, and a caste mark that looks like misapplied nail polish glances up expectantly when he enters. Her face appears disfigured by a mole on her cheek, but as he approaches the counter, Ned realizes that the mole is the microphone of her headset. "The usual?" she asks.

He isn't sure whether the question is addressed to someone she's speaking with on the microphone or to him. She smiles, waiting for an answer.

"Depends on what's usual," Ned says.

In the hygienically bright lighting, the trays of frosted donuts look like replicas. He notices a surveillance camera and has a tactile sense of being filmed. It's as if he's stepped into a scene of infinitely repeated takes.

"Sorry, I thought you were someone else," she says. Her singsong accent would be perfectly in character if she were playing an Indian woman who works late nights at a Dunkin' Donuts. "He always has a small black coffee and a Bavarian Kreme."

"Good by me," Ned says. He's impatient to step back out into the hypnotic night, but the woman takes her time, selecting a donut, artfully creasing the bag, then fitting with inordinate care the lid on the coffee cup that reads *America Runs on Dunkin'*.

"Two eighty-two," she says, and, when Ned digs into his jeans pocket, she adds, "He always gives me a fiver. Tells me, 'Keep the change, donut girl.'"

"Maybe that handsome guy you thought was me will come by later," Ned says, handing her a five.

"No," she says, "no cabs tonight."

"He takes a cab here?"

"*Drives* a cab. He's never come in, just goes through drive-through. He always jokes I'm the most beautiful woman in the donut shop."

"Keep it," Ned says, and she stuffs the change into a Styrofoam tip cup on the counter. He doesn't call her donut girl. Their conversation feels scripted enough already. It was a mistake to stop here. Not only has the spell of what had come to seem like a quest been broken, but a night that seemed spontaneous now seems manufactured. *The snow is real*, Ned thinks, *and the music. All is not lost.*

"I told him it was my last night working here," she says. "I just wanted to say goodbye."

Ceil was right about the coffee—strong with a hint of licorice—but whoever his cab-driving doppelgänger is doesn't have the same taste in donuts. Ned crushes the bag with the half-eaten Bavarian Kreme inside and lobs it into a wastebasket.

He moves his laptop from the bedroom that serves as an office to an end table in the living room, inserts the DVD, and turns off the only lamp burning in his apartment. He tries to imagine Ceil alone in a dark movie theater years earlier, gazing at a panoramic screen that properly conveyed the big-sky landscape. Or maybe she saw it on a little seat-back screen, during a flight from London or Brussels. Back then, if she wasn't traveling for her work with a human rights organization, they'd spend every weekend together. It surprises him that he never asked her where she'd seen the movie. He's watching it now to see it through her eyes.

From its early scenes on, *Open Range* is a love story between cowboys, a *Brokeback Mountain* without kisses. Driving longhorns before him, a grizzled Robert Duvall gallops across the iconic landscape and one of the cowpokes remarks, "Old Boss sure can cowboy, can't he?" Costner answers, "Yeah, broke the mold after him."

Earlier, Ned had skimmed an interview online in which Costner said that "*Open Range* starts with language." The movie's dialogue is, as the reviews noted, a rehash of other westerns. Usually Ned avoids reading reviews beforehand, so as not to ruin any surprises, but there aren't any surprises in *Open Range*, unless its degree of sentimentality qualifies. Costner's Charley Waite has a cute mutt that follows him on the trail. Ned knows from the reviews that the dog is marked for death; he'd have guessed it anyway. It brings to mind *Hondo*, which Ned saw as a child, in which Apaches kill John Wayne's dog, Sam—Ned still remembers the name. Despite all the people slaughtered in *Hondo*, the only loss Ned really felt was the dog's. He wonders if a young Costner felt the same for Sam and never forgot the effect, both the loss and the justification of violence that went with it—clearly such savage dog-killers deserve extermination. Costner has already used the cruelty-to-canines ploy in *Dances with Wolves*. *Open*

Range ups the ante. As if one murdered dog isn't enough to establish that Charley Waite—no matter how many men he's gunned down—has a gentle heart, there's a scene where he risks his life to save a puppy from a flash flood.

Annette Bening doesn't appear until partway through. When she does, Ned is suddenly, nervously alert. He listens for the question about vanishing to be posed in Bening's voice rather than in Ceil's. It's not a question for the early stages of a relationship, but Ned knows that the film has reached the point when that question, and its answer, must be coming.

In the online interview, Costner said he thought Bening was "very heroic" for playing a woman her own age without wearing makeup. It gives her a mature, sympathetic look that's fitting for the nurse she plays. Ned imagines that it's a look Ceil could identify with, as she, too, was heroic about makeup. But then Ceil's face was still unlined, except for a worry wrinkle across her forehead, visible when she wore her amber hair tied back. The corners of her eyes crinkled as if she were squinting against the wind when she smiled. Ned can visualize her pale blue, windblown eyes, but not her face. Ceil traveled regularly for work, and early in their relationship, when they didn't see each other for a couple of weeks, he'd tell her that he was in danger of forgetting what she looked like. She'd pretend to be exasperated that he could forget so easily. He was kidding but only in part; after each absence the beauty of her face struck him anew. That was true of her nakedness as well. To remove her clothes was to release light. He'd watch her dressing or undressing in the mirror as if not daring to look directly into brightness. He wonders now what else he didn't look at, what else he didn't see.

Ned doesn't have a photo of her. On the few occasions when they took pictures, it was Ceil who snapped them. He recalls her fiddling with a new digital camera as they walked out onto a wave-sloshed pier under a bleaching summer sky.

Ceil stopped before a small fish that looked as if a wave had flipped it onto a pier. Ned thought she was going to photograph it, but she gently slipped the fish back into the water. They'd gone only a step when an Asian man fishing from the pier turned and yelped, "Miss, you throw away my bait!" Ceil was annoyed when Ned laughed, but by the time they reached the end of the pier, where gulls swirled around a man cleaning salmon, they were both laughing. Ceil asked the man's daughter to take a picture of them. They didn't know then, smiling for the camera, that later that night, stoned on hashish, they'd end up in the emergency room. Ned asked for a copy of the picture taken on the pier, as he'd also asked for a picture of her for his birthday present. Ceil gave him instead an antique letter opener that she said would accrue in value. Ceil collected letter openers, pens, and paperweights, which she traded on eBay.

It was that night, after Ned had talked Ceil through her near-death experience in the ER, that she told him about a long-distance affair she'd had before they met, with a man named Dom, who until then she'd only vaguely mentioned. He was a paleontologist who lived in Princeton and ran an online business selling fossils to museums and gift shops. She told Ned the story of how she regarded love at first sight as a cheesy cliché until it happened to her. Their affair had lasted for years and Ceil had subsequently sold or given away the fossils, geodes, gemstones, and meteorites he'd given her. She'd kept only a single rare fossil from the Cretaceous age, of mating dragonflies trapped in amber. Dom had photographed her naked so that during phone sex he could summon what she called "nonvanilla" poses—Dom had a thing for women and bottles. Ceil said posing for him was one of the most erotic experiences of her life. She described their nearly immediate rapport as "speaking the same language"; it was as if she'd met a male twin to a secret self she'd always felt was dirty. Dom, she said, had made it clean. Their sexual likeness had overridden their difference, including his right-wing politics. After she and Dom broke up, Ceil had asked more than once if she could come for a last visit, to watch while he deleted the intimate show he had directed, but he refused, claiming that it would be too painful for him to see her again. He promised to erase the photos. Still, Ceil worried that they were somewhere in cyberspace, posted on one or another of the websites Dom frequented.

Listening to her, Ned understood how profoundly in love she'd been with the paleontologist and the authority the relationship still had in her life. It brought to mind an earlier night with Ceil, in bed, when she'd called him what he thought was "mister" in a little girl's voice he hadn't heard before and then apologized. Had she said "master"? Ned wishes he'd thought then to ask: That "same language" that you spoke, what language was it? He'd wondered, but didn't ask, what it had taken for her to break that long relationship off.

Tonight, he wonders if perhaps Ceil had been sleeping with them both. It would have been easy, given her frequent travel. He wonders if she could have been that devious, if in fact he'd been the catalyst she needed to end things with Dom, if he'd been a player in a love-triangle drama she was directing, a love triangle he hadn't known he had a part in. He had felt uncomfortable having to press her for what was, in her word—or was it Dom's?—a simple "vanilla" photo.

It's nearly three a.m. Costner and Bening have grown closer despite the lack of chemistry between them. As one reviewer remarked, "If the two of them were any more upstanding, they'd be trees." Though Bening still hasn't asked the question, she has revealed to Costner that she "always hoped somebody gentle and caring might come along." The nurse she plays has up to this point abhorred violence, but when Costner replies, "Men are gonna get killed here today, Sue, and

I'm gonna kill them, you understand that?" she submissively answers, "Yes." After the climactic shoot-'em-up, modeled on the gunfight at the O.K. Corral in which the bad guys are wasted, Costner asks her again, "Those killings, they don't give you pause?"

"I'm not afraid of you, Charley," she answers. It's the moment in the film that reviews found least credible, given Bening's character. But Ned thinks that the film has finally got something right. Afraid? No, she's turned on, thrilled, ready to brag about her gunslinger. Peace be damned, she just wants to get laid.

Ned wonders what Ceil, who regarded George Bush as a war criminal, would have said about Bening's response. Often the best part of going to a movie together was the time afterward, when they'd stop for a drink and talk about what they had just seen. Tonight, Ned has carried on a one-way conversation with Ceil, as if she were watching it beside him. He's had many others with her since she vanished. He wishes he could make them stop, but they're growing more frequent, as if the lengthening of her absence is making their phantom dialogue more compulsive.

Costner shyly asks Bening for a kiss. Killing is easy for cowboys; it's smooching that takes nerve. The film is winding down, the time for asking is running out. But she doesn't ask. Ned watches as they ride out of town together—Duvall, Costner, Bening—under the big sky. Ned listens for her question. She doesn't ask it. After all that killing in support of a man's right to the open range, Duvall says that he's tired of the open range. He'd like to run a saloon in town, and maybe Costner could be his partner. Costner tells Bening he'll be back. They exchange happily-ever-after smiles. She turns back toward town, and Costner and Duvall ride off toward the dogies they've left on the open range.

Ned watches the credits roll.

He feels confused, then tricked. He has an impulse to replay the whole dull film. Could he have somehow missed the line? He vividly remembers that conversation with Ceil being predicated on the question about vanishing. He knows he didn't make that up. He can't understand why Ceil would have invented it, ascribing it and the answer to lines from a second-rate movie. There has to have been a mistake. Could she have conflated *Open Range* with some other film? He remembers her having complained that she wasn't sleeping well; she used to wake beside him in the middle of the night from dreams that made her moan but dissolved before she could describe them. Maybe she had dreamed the question. It's another thing about her that he'll never understand. He ejects the DVD and logs off.

Are you sure you want to shut down your computer now?

The screen goes wordlessly blue, and then blinks off, leaving the apartment lit only by the reflection of the streetlights in the falling snow. The blank windowpanes are fogging from the bottom up. He isn't tired. Ceil was right about the coffee at Dunkin' Donuts. He tries again to summon her face. If the myth about a hundred words for snow were true, there'd be a word for snow-erasing-its-own-memory. He has an urge to open the window and let the wind and snow blow in. He tugs at the handles, hammers the sash, but the window won't budge. The cold pane mists with his breath and body heat, and, when he wipes away the steam, his reflection peeps in darkly. He wonders if a person can forget his own face. He wonders if his cabbie double ever showed up for "the usual." All the windows but one are dark in the apartment building across the way. Lines he hasn't thought about for years, from a poem in *Doctor Zhivago*, come to mind:

> *It snowed and snowed, the whole world over . . .*
> *A candle burned on the table;*
> *A candle burned.*

It doesn't seem incongruous that the window across the way is lit not by the halo of a candle but by a bluish glow—someone watching television in the middle of the night or working at a computer, perhaps surfing websites. What if, in the vastness of cyberspace, whoever is up across the street should encounter an image of Ceil? Is it snowing the whole world over, even in Princeton, where the paleontologist may still be at his computer, filing through a gallery of pictures of ex-girlfriends, like a museum curator checking the inventory of his fossils and specimens preserved in amber, assessing the value they've accrued, before settling on a photo of Ceil?

Dom was burned out by too many field trips, Ceil told Ned, and he refused to travel unless it couldn't be avoided—travel was one of their many differences. So every few weeks she'd made the trip to Princeton. She marveled about the thousands of miles she had logged over the years to be with him. Between visits, they'd talked on the phone at least once a day. They had broken up over the phone, and she said she'd thought that going to see Dom one last time in person would be the "classy" thing to do. Dom offered to meet her at a hotel in New York but refused to have her stay at his house, and Ceil said she'd already spent too much time with him in hotel rooms.

Suppose Dom had allowed that journey back to Princeton, Ned wonders.

He sees her traveling to her old lover one last time along a track she knows by heart, the one she's ridden from Penn Station, or from the Newark airport, sometimes from Philadelphia. Wherever she begins, she disembarks at Princeton Junction and takes the shuttle called the Dinky. This time he isn't there waiting at the station to pick her up. She takes a cab along a familiar cobbled street, past the fudge shop and their breakfast café and the antique shop where she's foraged for letter openers, to a Victorian house where a wardrobe of hers still hangs in the closet of the master bedroom, and where on a velvet window seat shaded by filmy curtains the photographs were taken. She expects him to simply delete the file, but he opens it, and there the two of them are, preserved in digital light: Dom—though he isn't visible in the photo, she can see him—and herself, more real on the screen than she feels at this moment, younger, naked, spreading her legs at his command. Remember that afternoon, Ceil, he asks, how intense we were? What's happened to *us*? Remember the story you loved telling about how embarrassed you were when we first met because you could hardly talk for how I'd impressed you? What did you really come back here for today?

I need to be sure you've erased them.

But surely you know I could have hidden files and copies on disks and travel drives.

You wouldn't lie to my face.

Would you lie to mine? Is there someone else? Do you think I can't sense it? You couldn't leave me on your own. This horseshit about differences between us—as if they ever mattered to you with your clothes off. You're most devious to yourself. Do you think you'll find our kind of intimacy again? We'll be for each other an absence, like a phantom limb. You'll look for me in others, and they'll feel the overlap.

Erase them.

Do you love me?

Please, you know this has nothing to do with my loving you.

Please who?

Please, master.

So, *poof*! One gone. You think erasing a replica erases us? This one's always been my favorite. I've studied that little death on your pretty face a thousand times. I'm going to close my eyes and press delete. Tell me when you've disappeared. Gone?

Yes. Thank you. Now please erase them from Trash.

◆

"What would you do if I vanished?"

"You mean like—*poof!*—suddenly you're not there? So where are you? Lost in the ether? Traveling through time? In cyberspace?"

"It doesn't matter. Answer the question."

"Okay, I'll play. I'd ride to the ends of the earth, to the silver mountains of the moon. Or maybe they're borax."

"You think you'd find me there?"

"I'd follow your footprints across borax craters, ford molten rivers that parted like mercury, a starry sky guiding the way. On a summer day I'd walk out on a pier that juts out to infinity, and when I reached the end, if you weren't there, over the laughter of gulls I'd call your name, and if you didn't answer I'd follow the little fish you saved and he'd lead me to you."

"He'd lead you to nowhere."

"Then, one night in winter, I'd pass through the arch of a Great Gate of Snow and on the other side I'd be back in time in the city when it was ours. When all could never be lost. I'd hail the only cab out late. The cabbie would study me in the rearview, and in the mirror I'd see that his eyes were mine. I wouldn't have to tell him where to go. We'd drive from lighted corner to lighted corner for nights until I found the most beautiful woman in all of Dunkin' Donuts. The coffee's good here, you'd tell me."

"They do have good coffee, but I wouldn't be there."

"I'd hire a hypnotist who specialized in negotiating the release of alien abductees. I'd search the hidden records for all the secret prisons of the CIA. I'd wait in long lines at the Department of Missing Persons . . ."

"That's not the answer."

"After a while, I'd do nothing but go day by day without you. Sometimes I'd remember something you said, and have another one-way conversation. I'd walk around secretly talking to you, wondering where you were and what you were doing. I'd tell myself that wherever you'd gone I wanted you to be happy."

"You need to work on a better answer."

"What was the question again?"

"What would you do if I vanished?"

"But life is never that simple. One doesn't just vanish. There's always a why, or at least a context. You suddenly moved away in the middle of the night. Changed your unlisted phone number. Left no forwarding address so that mail was returned and e-mails disappeared into whatever graveyard file they go to. Was it amnesia? An overdose of vanishing cream? Did you meet someone else? Another catalyst? You're not the suicidal type, thank God, but still . . . or by 'vanish' could you really have thought that you'd be erased from my memory?"

"Say I met someone else."

"Well, see, that's a different question."

Paper Lantern

We were working late on the time machine in the little make-shift lab upstairs. The moon was stuck like the whorl of a frozen fingerprint to the skylight. In the back alley, the breaths left behind by yowling toms converged into a fog slinking out along the streets. Try as we might, our measurements were repeatedly off. In one direction, we'd reached the border at which clairvoyants stand gazing into the future, and in the other we'd gone backward to the zone where the present turns ghostly with memory and yet resists quite becoming the past. We'd been advancing and retreating by smaller and smaller degrees until it had come to seem as if we were measuring the immeasurable. Of course, what we really needed was some new vocabulary of measurement. It was time for a break.

Down the broken escalator, out the blue-lit lobby past the shuttered newsstand, through the frosty fog, hungry as strays we walk, still wearing our lab coats, to the Chinese restaurant around the corner.

It's a restaurant that used to be a Chinese laundry. When customers would come for their freshly laundered bundles, the cooking—wafting from the owner's back kitchen through the warm haze of laundry steam—smelled so good that the customers began asking if they could buy something to eat as well. And so the restaurant was born. It was a carryout place at first, but they've since wedged in a few tables. None of us can read Chinese, so we can't be sure, but since the proprietors never bothered to change the sign, presumably the Chinese characters still say it's a Chinese laundry. Anyway, that's how the people in the neighborhood refer to it—the Chinese Laundry, as in, "Man, I had a sublime meal at the Chinese Laundry last night." Although they haven't changed the sign, the proprietors have added a large red-ribbed paper lantern—their only nod to decor—that spreads its opaque glow across the steamy window.

We sit at one of the five Formica tables—our favorite, beside the window—and the waitress immediately brings the menu and tea. Really, in a way, this is the best part: the ruddy glow of the paper lantern like heat on our faces, the tiny enameled teacups warming our hands, the hot tea scalding our hunger, and the surprising, welcoming heft of the menu, hand-printed in Chinese characters, with what must be very approximate explanations in English of some of the dishes, also hand-printed, in the black ink of calligraphers. Each time we come here the menu has grown longer. Once a dish has been offered, it is never deleted, and now the menu is pages and pages long, so long that we'll never read through it all, never live long enough, perhaps, to sample all the food in just this one tucked-away neighborhood Chinese restaurant. The pages are unnumbered, and we can never remember where we left off reading the last time we were here. Was it the chrysanthemum pot, served traditionally in autumn when the flowers are in full bloom, or the almond jelly with lichees and loquats?

"A poet wrote this menu," Tinker says between sips of tea.

"Yes, but if there's a poet in the house, then why doesn't this place have a real name—something like the Red Lantern— instead of merely being called the Chinese Laundry by default?" the Professor replies, wiping the steam from his glasses with a paper napkin from the dispenser on the table.

"I sort of like the Chinese Laundry, myself. It's got a solid, working-class ring. Red Lantern is a cliché—precious chinoiserie," Tinker argues.

They never agree.

"Say, you two, I thought we were here to devour aesthetics, not debate them."

Here, there's nothing of heaven or earth that can't be consumed, nothing they haven't found a way to turn into a delicacy: pine-nut porridge, cassia-blossom buns, fish-fragrance-sauced pigeon, swallow's-nest soup (a soup indigenous to the shore of the South China Sea; nests of predigested seaweed from the beaks of swifts, the gelatinous material hardened to form a small, translucent cup). Sea-urchin roe, pickled jellyfish, tripe with ginger and peppercorns, five-fragrance grouper cheeks, cloud ears, spun-sugar apple, ginkgo nuts and golden needles (which are the buds of lilies), purple seaweed, bitter melon . . .

Nothing of heaven and earth that cannot be combined, transmuted; no borders, in a wok, that can't be crossed. It's instructive. One can't help nourishing the imagination as well as the body.

We order, knowing we won't finish all they'll bring, and that no matter how carefully we ponder our choices we'll be served instead whatever the cook has made today.

After supper, sharing segments of a blood orange and sipping tea, we ceremoniously crack open our fortune cookies and read aloud our fortunes as if consulting the *I Ching*.

"*Sorrow is born of excessive joy.*"

"Try another."

"*Poverty is the common fate of scholars.*"

"Does that sound like a fortune to you?" Tinker asks.

"I certainly hope not," the Professor says.

"*When a finger points to the moon, the imbecile looks at the finger.*"

"What kind of fortunes are these? These aren't fortune cookies, these are proverb cookies," Tinker says.

"*In the Year of the Rat you will be lucky in love.*"

"Now, that's more like it."

"What year is this?"

"The Year of the Dragon, according to the place mat."

"*Fuel alone will not light a fire.*"

"Say, did anyone turn off the Bunsen burner when we left?" The mention of the lab makes us signal for the check. It's time we headed back. A new theory was brewing there when we left, and now, our enthusiasm rekindled, we return in the snow—it has begun to snow—through thick, crumbling flakes mixed with wafting cinders that would pass for snowflakes except for the way the wind is fanning their edges to sparks. A night of white flakes and streaming orange cinders, strange and beautiful, until we turn the corner and stare up at our laboratory.

Flames occupy the top floor of the building. Smoke billows out of the skylight, from which the sooty moon has retreated. On the floor below, through radiant, buckling windows, we can see the mannequins from the dressmaker's showroom. Naked, wigs on fire, they appear to gyrate lewdly before they topple. On the next floor down, in the instrument-repair shop, accordions wheeze in the smoke, violins seethe like green kindling, and the saxophones dissolve into a lava of molten brass cascading over a window ledge. While on the ground floor, in the display window, the animals in the taxidermist's shop have begun to hiss and snap as if fire had returned them to life in the wild.

We stare helplessly, still clutching the carryout containers of the food we were unable to finish from the blissfully innocent meal we sat sharing while our apparatus, our theories, our formulas, and years of research—all that people refer to as their "work"—were bursting into flame. Along empty, echoing streets, sirens are screaming like victims.

Already a crowd has gathered.

"Look at that seedy old mother go up," a white kid in dreadlocks says to his girlfriend, who looks like a runaway waif. She answers, "Cool!"

And I remember how, in what now seems another life, I watched fires as a kid—sometimes fires that a gang of us, calling ourselves the Matchheads, had set.

I remember how, later, in another time, if not another life, I once snapped a photograph of a woman I was with as she watched a fire blaze out of control along a river in Chicago. She was still married then. Her husband, whom I'd never met, was in a veterans' hospital—clinically depressed after the war in Vietnam. At least, that's what she told me about him. Thinking back, I sometimes wonder if she even had a husband. She had come to Chicago with me for a fling—her word. I thought at the time that we were just "fooling around"—also her words, words we both used in place of others like "fucking" or "making love" or "adultery." It was more comfortable, and safer, for me to think of things between us as fooling around, but when I offhandedly mentioned that to her she became furious, and instead of fooling around we spent our weekend in Chicago arguing, and ended up having a terrible time. It was a Sunday afternoon in early autumn, probably in the Year of the Rat, and we were sullenly driving out of the city. Along the north branch of the river, a factory was burning. I pulled over and parked, dug a camera out of my duffel, and we walked to a bridge to watch the fire.

But it's not the fire itself that I remember, even though the blaze ultimately spread across the city sky like a dusk that rose from the earth rather than descended. The fire, as I recall it, is merely a backdrop compressed within the boundaries of the photograph I took of her. She has just looked away from the blaze, toward the camera. Her elbows lean against the peeling gray railing of the bridge. She's wearing the black silk blouse that she bought at a secondhand shop on Clark Street the day before. Looking for clothes from the past in second-hand stores was an obsession of hers—"going junking," she called it. A silver Navajo bracelet has slid up her arm over a black silk sleeve. How thin her wrists appear. There's a ring whose gem I know is a moonstone on the index finger of her left hand, and a tarnished silver band around her thumb. She was left-handed, and it pleased her that I was, too, as if we both belonged to the same minority group. Her long hair is a shade of auburn all the more intense for the angle of late afternoon sunlight. She doesn't look sullen or angry so much as fierce. Although later, studying her face in the photo, I'll come to see that beneath her expression there's a look less recognizable and more desperate: not loneliness, exactly, but *aloneness*—a look I'd seen cross her face more than once but wouldn't have thought to identify if the photo hadn't caught it. Behind her, ominous gray smoke plumes out of a sprawling old brick factory with the soon-to-be-scorched white lettering of GUTTMAN & CO. TANNERS visible along the side of the building.

Driving back to Iowa in the dark, I'll think that she's asleep, as exhausted as I am from our strained weekend; then she'll break the miles of silence between us to tell me that, disappointing though it was, the trip was worth it if only for the two of us on the bridge, watching the fire together. She loved being part of the excitement, she'll say, loved the spontaneous way we swerved over and parked in order to take advantage of the spectacle—a conflagration the length of a city block, reflected over the greasy water, and a red fireboat, neat as a toy, sirening up the river, spouting white geysers while the flames roared back.

Interstate 80 shoots before us in the length of our racing headlight beams. We're on a stretch between towns, surrounded by flat black fields, and the candlepower of the occasional distant farmhouse is insufficient to illuminate the enormous horizon lurking in the dark like the drop-off at the edge of the planet. In the speeding car, her voice sounds disembodied, the voice of a shadow, barely above a whisper, yet it's clear, as if the cover of night and the hypnotic momentum of the road have freed her to reveal secrets. There seemed to be so many secrets about her.

She tells me that as the number of strangers attracted by the fire swelled into a crowd she could feel a secret current connecting the two of us, like the current that passed between us in bed the first time we made love, when we came at the same moment as if taken by surprise. It happened only that once.

"Do you remember how, after that, I cried?" she asks.

"Yes."

"You were trying to console me. I know you thought I was feeling terribly guilty, but I was crying because the way we fit together seemed suddenly so familiar, as if there were some old bond between us. I felt flooded with relief, as if I'd been missing you for a long time without quite realizing it, as if you'd returned to me after I thought I'd never see you again. I didn't say any of that, because it sounds like some kind of channeling crap. Anyway, today the same feeling came over me on the bridge, and I was afraid I might start crying again, except this time what would be making me cry was the thought that if we *were* lovers from past lives who had waited lifetimes for the present to bring us back together, then how sad it was to waste the present the way we did this weekend."

I keep my eyes on the road, not daring to glance at her, or

even to answer, for fear of interrupting the intimate, almost compulsive way she seems to be speaking.

"I had this sudden awareness," she continues, "of how the moments of our lives go out of existence before we're conscious of having lived them. It's only a relatively few moments that we get to keep and carry with us for the rest of our lives. Those moments *are* our lives. Or maybe it's more like those moments are the dots and what we call our lives are the lines we draw between them, connecting them into imaginary pictures of ourselves. You know? Like those mythical pictures of constellations traced between stars. I remember how, as a kid, I actually expected to be able to look up and see Pegasus spread out against the night, and when I couldn't it seemed like a trick had been played on me, like a fraud. I thought, *Hey, if this is all there is to it, then I could reconnect the stars in any shape I wanted. I could create the Ken and Barbie constellations* . . . I'm rambling . . ."

"I'm following you, go on."

She moves closer to me.

"I realized we can never predict when those few, special moments will occur," she says. "How, if we hadn't met, I wouldn't be standing on a bridge watching a fire, and how there are certain people, not that many, who enter one's life with the power to make those moments happen. Maybe that's what falling in love means—the power to create for each other the moments by which we define ourselves. And there you were, right on cue, taking my picture. I had an impulse to open my blouse, to take off my clothes and pose naked for you. I wanted you. I wanted—not to 'fool around.' I wanted to fuck you like there's no tomorrow against the railing of the bridge. I've been thinking about that ever since, this whole drive back."

I turn to look at her, but she says, "No . . . don't look . . . Keep driving . . . Shhh, don't talk . . . I'm sealing your lips."

I can hear the rustle beside me as she raises her skirt, and a faint smack of moistness, and then, kneeling on the seat, she extends her hand and outlines my lips with her slick fingertips.

I can smell her scent; the car seems filled with it. I can feel the heat of her body radiating beside me, before she slides back along the seat until she's braced against the car door. I can hear each slight adjustment of her body, the rustle of fabric against her skin, the elastic sound of her panties rolled past her hips, the faintly wet, possibly imaginary tick her fingertips are making. "Oh, baby," she sighs. I've slowed down to fifty-five, and as semis pull into the passing lane and rumble by us, their headlights sweep through the car and I catch glimpses of her as if she'd been imprinted by lightning on my peripheral vision—disheveled, her skirt hiked over her slender legs, the fingers of her left hand disappearing into the V of her rolled-down underpants.

"You can watch, if you promise to keep one eye on the road," she says, and turns on the radio as if flicking on a nightlight that coats her bare legs with its viridescence.

What was playing? The volume was so low I barely heard. A violin from some improperly tuned-in university station, fading in and out until it disappeared into static—banished, perhaps, to those phantom frequencies where Bix Beiderbecke still blew on his cornet. We were almost to Davenport, on the river, the town where Beiderbecke was born, and one station or another there always seemed to be playing his music, as if the syncopated licks of Roaring Twenties jazz, which had burned Bix up so quickly, still resonated over the prairie like his ghost.

"You can't cross I-80 between Iowa and Illinois without going through the Beiderbecke Belt," I had told her when we picked up a station broadcasting a Bix tribute on our way into Chicago. She had never heard of Bix until then and wasn't paying him much attention until the DJ quoted a remark by Eddie Condon, an old Chicago guitarist, that "Bix's sound came out like a girl saying yes." That was only three days ago, and now we are returning, somehow changed from that couple who set out for a fling.

We cross the Beiderbecke Belt back into Iowa, and as we drive past the Davenport exits the nearly deserted highway is illuminated like an empty ballpark by the bluish overhead lights. Her eyes closed with concentration, she hardly notices as a semi, outlined in red clearance lights, almost sideswipes us. The car shudders in the backdraft as the truck pulls away, its horn bellowing.

"One eye on the road," she cautions.

"That wasn't my fault."

We watch its taillights disappear, and then we're alone in the highway dark again, traveling along my favorite stretch, where, in the summer, the fields are planted with sunflowers as well as corn, and you have to be on the alert for pheasants bolting across the road.

"Baby, take it out," she whispers.

The desire to touch her is growing unbearable, and yet I don't want to stop—don't want the drive to end.

"I'm waiting for you," she says. "I'm right on the edge just waiting for you."

We're barely doing forty when we pass what looks like the same semi, trimmed in red clearance lights, parked along the shoulder. I'm watching her while trying to keep an eye on the road, so I don't notice the truck pulling back onto the highway behind us or its headlights in the rearview mirror, gaining on us fast, until its high beams flash on, streaming through the car with a near-blinding intensity. I steady the wheel, waiting for the whump of the trailer's vacuum as it hurtles by, but the truck stays right on our rear bumper, its enormous radiator grille looming through the rear window, and its headlights reflecting off our mirrors and windshield with a glare that makes us squint. Caught in the high beams, her hair flares like a halo about to burst into flame. She's brushed her skirt down over her legs and looks a little wild.

"What's his problem? Is he stoned on uppers or something?" she shouts over the rumble of his engine, and then he hits his horn, obliterating her voice with a diesel blast.

I stomp on the gas. We're in the right lane, and, since he refuses to pass, I signal and pull into the outside lane to let him go by, but he merely switches lanes, too, hanging on our tail the entire time. The speedometer jitters over ninety, but he stays right behind us, his high beams pinning us like spotlights, his horn bellowing.

"Is he crazy?" she shouts.

I know what's happening. After he came close to sideswiping us outside Davenport, he must have gone on driving down the empty highway with the image of her illuminated by those bluish lights preying on his mind. Maybe he's divorced and lonely, maybe his wife is cheating on him—something's gone terribly wrong for him, and, whatever it is, seeing her exposed like that has revealed his own life as a sorry thing, and that realization has turned to meanness and anger.

There's an exit a mile off, and he sees it, too, and swings his rig back to the inside lane to try and cut me off, but with the pedal to the floor I beat him to the right-hand lane, and I keep it floored, although I know I can't manage a turnoff at this speed. He knows that, too, and stays close behind, ignoring my right-turn signal, laying on his horn as if to warn me not to try slowing down for this exit, that there's no way of stopping sixty thousand pounds of tractor-trailer doing over ninety.

But just before we hit the exit I swerve back into the outside lane, and for a moment he pulls even with us, staying on the inside as we race past the exit so as to keep it blocked.

That's when I yell to her, "Hang on!" and pump the brakes, and we screech along the outside lane, fishtailing and burning rubber, while the truck goes barreling by, its air brakes whooshing. The car skids onto the gravel shoulder, kicking up a cloud of dust, smoky in the headlights, but it's never really out of control, and by the time the semi lurches to a stop, I have the car in reverse, veering back to the exit, hoping no one else is speeding toward us down I-80.

It's the Plainview exit, and I gun into a turn, north onto an empty two-lane, racing toward someplace named Long Grove. I keep checking the mirror for his headlights, but the highway behind us stays dark, and finally she says, "Baby, slow down."

The radio is still playing static, and I turn it off.

"Christ!" she says. "At first I thought he was just your everyday flaming asshole, but he was a genuine psychopath."

"A real lunatic, all right," I agree.

"You think he was just waiting there for us in his truck?" she asks. "That's so spooky, especially when you think he's still out there driving west. It makes you wonder how many other guys are out there, driving with their heads full of craziness and rage."

It's a vision of the road at night that I can almost see: men, not necessarily vicious—some just numb or desperately lonely—driving to the whining companionship of country music, their headlights too scattered and isolated for anyone to realize that they're all part of a convoy. We're a part of it, too.

"I was thinking, *Oh, no, I can't die now, like this*," she says. "It would be too sexually frustrating—like death was the ultimate tease."

"You know what I was afraid of," I tell her. "Dying with my trousers open."

She laughs and continues laughing until there's a hysterical edge to it.

"I think that truck driver was jealous of you. He knows you're a lucky guy tonight," she gasps, winded, and kicks off her sandal in order to slide a bare foot along my leg. "Here we are together, still alive."

I bring her foot to my mouth and kiss it, clasping her leg where it's thinnest, as if my hand were an ankle bracelet, then slide my hand beneath her skirt, along her thigh to the edge of her panties, a crease of surprising heat, from which my finger comes away slick.

"I told you," she moans. "A lucky guy."

I turn onto the next country road. It's unmarked, not that it matters. I know that out here, sooner or later, it will cross a gravel road, and when it does I turn onto the gravel, and after a while turn again at the intersection of a dirt road that winds into fields of an increasingly deeper darkness, fragrant with the rich Iowa earth and resonating with insect choirs amassed for one last Sanctus. I'm not even sure what direction we're traveling in any longer, let alone where we're going, but when my high beams catch a big turtle crossing the road I feel we've arrived. The car rolls to a stop on a narrow plank bridge spanning a culvert. The bridge—not much longer than our car—is veiled on either side by overhanging trees, cotton-woods, probably, and flanked by cattails as high as the drying stalks of corn in the acres we've been passing. The turtle, his snapper's jaw unmistakable in the lights, looks mossy and an-cient, and we watch him complete his trek across the road and disappear into the reeds before I flick off the headlights. Sit-ting silently in the dark, we listen to the crinkle of the cooling engine, and to the peepers we've disturbed starting up again from beneath the bridge. When we quietly step out of the car, we can hear frogs plopping into the water. "Look at the stars," she whispers.

"If Pegasus was up there," I say, "you'd see him from here."

"Do you have any idea where we are?" she asks.

"Nope. Totally lost. We can find our way back when it's light."

"The backseat of a car at night, on a country road—adultery has a disconcerting way of turning adults back into teenagers."

We make love, then manage to doze off for a while in the backseat, wrapped together in a checkered tablecloth we'd used once on a picnic, which I still had folded in the trunk.

In the pale early light I shoot the rest of the film on the roll: a close-up of her, framed in part by the line of the checkered tablecloth, which she's wearing like a shawl around her bare shoulders, and another, closer still, of her face framed by her tangled auburn hair, and out the open window behind her, velvety cattails blurred in the shallow depth of field. A picture of her posing naked outside the car in sunlight that streams through countless rents in the veil of the cottonwoods. A picture of her kneeling on the muddy planks of the little bridge, her hazel eyes glancing up at the camera, her mouth, still a yard from my body, already shaped as if I've stepped to her across that distance.

What's missing is the shot I never snapped—the one the trucker tried to steal, which drove him over whatever edge he was balanced on, and which, perhaps, still has him riding highways, searching each passing car from the perch of his cab for that glimpse he won't get again—her hair disheveled, her body braced against the car door, eyes squeezed closed, lips twisted, skirt hiked up, pelvis rising to her hand.

Years after, she called me out of nowhere. "Do you still have those photos of me?" she asked.

"No," I told her, "I burned them."

"Good," she said, sounding pleased—not relieved so much as flattered—"I just suddenly wondered." Then she hung up.

But I lied. I'd kept them all these years, along with a few letters—part of a bundle of personal papers in a manila envelope that I moved with me from place to place. I had them hidden away in the back of a file cabinet in the laboratory, although certainly they had no business being there. Now what I'd told her was true: they were fueling the flames.

Outlined in firelight, the kid in dreadlocks kisses the waif. His hand glides over the back of her fringed jacket of dirty white buckskin and settles on the torn seat of her faded jeans. She stands on tiptoe on the tops of his gym shoes and hooks her fingers through the empty belt loops of his jeans so that their crotches are aligned. When he boosts her closer and grinds against her she says, "Wow!" and giggles. "I felt it move."

"Fires get me horny," he says.

The roof around the skylight implodes, sending a funnel of sparks into the whirl of snow, and the crowd *ahs* collectively as the beakers in the laboratory pop and flare.

Gapers have continued to arrive down side streets, appearing out of the snowfall as if drawn by a great bonfire signaling some secret rite: gangbangers in their jackets engraved with symbols, gorgeous transvestites from Wharf Street, stevedores, and young sailors, their fresh tattoos contracting in the cold. The homeless, layered in overcoats, burlap tied around their feet, have abandoned their burning ash cans in order to gather here, just as the shivering, scantily clad hookers have abandoned their neon corners; as the Guatemalan dishwashers have abandoned their scalding suds; as a baker, his face and hair the ghostly white of flour, has abandoned his oven.

Open hydrants gush into the gutters; the street is seamed with deflated hoses, but the firemen stand as if paired off with the hookers—as if for a moment they've become voyeurs like everyone else, transfixed as the brick walls of our lab blaze suddenly lucent, suspended on a cushion of smoke, and the red-hot skeleton of the time machine begins to radiate from the inside out. A rosy light plays off the upturned faces of the crowd like the glow of an enormous red lantern—a paper lantern that once seemed fragile, almost delicate, but now obliterates the very time and space it once illuminated. A paper lantern raging out of control with nothing but itself left to consume.

"*Brrrr.*" The Professor shivers, wiping his fogged glasses as if to clear away the opaque gleam reflecting off their lenses.

"Goddamn cold, all right," Tinker mutters, stamping his feet.

For once they agree.

The wind gusts, fanning the bitter chill of night even as it fans the flames, and instinctively we all edge closer to the fire.

Acknowledgments

My thanks to the editors of the magazines that first accepted these stories.

And a thank-you that spans years to Elisabeth Sifton and Amanda Urban.

Also, I wish to express my gratitude to the MacArthur Foundation for a fellowship that provided the time to write this book.

Printed in the USA
CPSIA information can be obtained
at www.ICGtesting.com
LVHW041655160724
785511LV00007B/501